Clara Awake

Copyright © 2017 Melinda Vandenbeld Giles

Except for the use of short passages for review purposes, no part of this book may be reproduced, in part or in whole, or transmitted in any form or by any means, electronically or mechanically, including photocopying, recording, or any information or storage retrieval system, without prior permission in writing from the publisher or a licence from the Canadian Copyright Collective Agency (Access Copyright).

We gratefully acknowledge the support of the Canada Council for the Arts and the Ontario Arts Council for our publishing program. We also acknowledge the financial support of the Government of Canada through the Canada Book Fund.

Cover design: Val Fullard

Clara Awake is a work of fiction. All the characters portrayed in this book are fictitious and any resemblance to persons living or dead, is purely coincidental.

Library and Archives Canada Cataloguing in Publication

Vandenbeld Giles, Melinda, 1973-, author
 Clara awake / a novel by Melinda Vandenbeld Giles.

(Inanna poetry & fiction series)
Issued in print and electronic formats.
ISBN 978-1-77133-369-6 (softcover).-- ISBN 978-1-77133-370-2 (epub).--
ISBN 978-1-77133-371-9 (Kindle).-- ISBN 978-1-77133-372-6 (pdf)

 I. Title. II. Series: Inanna poetry and fiction series

PS8643.A6876C53 2017   C813'.6   C2017-900307-0
                                               C2017-900308-9

Printed and bound in Canada

Inanna Publications and Education Inc.
210 Founders College, York University
4700 Keele Street, Toronto, Ontario, Canada M3J 1P3
Telephone: (416) 736-5356 Fax: (416) 736-5765
Email: inanna.publications@inanna.ca Website: www.inanna.ca

Clara Awake

a novel by
Melinda Vandenbeld Giles

Inanna poetry & fiction series

**INANNA PUBLICATIONS AND EDUCATION INC.
TORONTO, CANADA**

*To my mom Maria, my sister Anita,
and my daughter Maya.
You are my trinity of love.*

1

I DREAMED OF BRAZIL AGAIN. Ever since I first heard the sound of the drums and saw the swirling figures dressed in white, ever since I first felt the damp heat of the forest and the oppressive weight of the humidity, the dreams have followed me, waking me in the night. I would dream of dancing to the insistent beat of the Odún drums, my body moving in sensuous rhythm, my bare feet slapping the ground, my hands swaying in the air. I would spin until the world disappeared and all I could feel was the sensation of liquid heat pulsing through my veins and the power of the goddess descending into my skull. Often, the goddess would call to me, demanding that I answer to her.

Sometimes, I would hear another voice calling. A voice that was dark. I would wake from the dream, my heart racing, reassured to find myself back in my grad residence room, the familiar blue glow of the streetlight shining through the window. And then, as I started to feel safe again, I would see him, his yellow eyes gleaming at me out of the darkness. The banality of my studio room would suddenly become frightening and suffocating. I would grasp my throat, hear the coarseness of my own strangled breathing. And then he would be gone. I would find myself sitting upright in my bed, my body twisted in tangled, sweat-drenched sheets, my hair plastered against my cheeks. My eyes would run over all the books in my bookcase, the table with the red Guatemalan tablecloth from my travels that I loved so much, my white albino guinea pig making rustling sounds in the corner, and I would tell myself that everything was okay. Everything was normal. But I would know, deep down, that nothing had been normal since the day I first started studying the Odún.

And now, at last, I was back. After eight years of research, I was finally returning to the land of inspiration. I yawned and leaned over to open the airplane's window shade and look outside. Brazil—a vast expanse of green stretching out toward the horizon, tinged with the vibrant hues of sunrise.

As we descended into Rio de Janeiro, I wondered what it would be like this time. When I'd been in Brazil in August 1984, the country was still under military dictatorship. But things had started to fall apart and the following year the country had finally returned to civilian rule. I wondered what democracy would feel like on the streets. I squinted my eyes, trying to make out the distant curve of the Pão de Açúcar, Rio's famous Sugarloaf mountain, rising out of the misty haze of early morning. The view was breathtaking, the sun glinting off the Christ the Redeemer statue, atop the Corcovado, his arms reaching out to meet his glory. The plane's wings nearly touched the stretch of white sand below as we entered the Baía de Guanabara.

I had a list of names and numbers of people to contact. I didn't know any of them. Other than a few brief telephone conversations with an Associate Professor of Anthropology at the Universidade Federal do Rio de Janeiro, I had little to go on. Despite years of meticulous theoretical doctoral research, the reality of doing anthropological fieldwork in Brazil was daunting. It had been difficult to make any connections from afar, and I had finally decided that the only way to move forward with my research was to get on a plane and come to Brazil. I could have tried to plan everything out perfectly in advance, but until I actually got to my field location, I really couldn't know what to expect. Five years into my Anthropology PhD at the University of Toronto and I felt as confused as ever about what I was actually doing. I scanned through my papers to find the name of my contact.

"Dr. Eduardo Soares," I whispered, letting the sound roll off my tongue. What would Dr. Soares be like? Our conversations had been brief. As Soares had stated over the phone more than once, he didn't have a lot of time to spare for a graduate student. I was lucky that my advisor had worked with him during a conference at the University of Toronto a couple of years ago. Otherwise, I probably wouldn't have had *any* connections. The idea of a young white woman coming to their country to study an Afro-Brazilian religion for the purposes of her Canadian doctoral thesis was not well received. The worshippers of Odún were protective of their beliefs and secretive towards outsiders. They struggled to prevent international exposure of their religion. I was prepared for animosity, but hopefully not dismissal.

As the plane landed, I forced myself to focus on the task at hand. Otherwise, the jittery sensation in my stomach threatened to take over. Stuffing my notes back into my travel bag, I joined the throng of people departing the aircraft. As I entered the modern air-conditioned Rio International airport, I felt the familiar thrill of being in another country. Simply hearing the language and seeing the Portuguese signs were enough to get me excited. I was back. But I was a very different person from the carefree twenty-one-year-old I'd been eight years before. The girl who believed she owned the world, who wasn't afraid of taking a bus alone across the drug-smuggling Bolivian/Brazilian border and then from Corumbá through the Pantanal to São Paulo. I liked to think I had a little more sense now.

I knew that the moment I left the relative familiarity of the international airport zone and stepped outside, I would be entering a different world. And I could hardly wait. I made my way through the crowds to retrieve my luggage and take out a sufficient amount of money. What was the currency these days in Brazil? Luckily for me, they'd gone back to the *cruzeiro*. And then, finally, I exited the airport doors and truly entered Brazil.

Just as anticipated, the moment I stepped outside, I was enveloped by the intense humidity. This heat was what I remembered. I felt the perspiration collect on my forehead as I put down my heavy bags, and I revelled in it. I loved the feeling of the blazing sun beating down on my head. There was a sultry, alluring quality to the heat in Brazil, so different from hot summer days in Toronto. It was as though the heat and humidity itself could provoke languidness and sensuality, while the heat in Toronto aroused nothing more than irritation.

I barely had time to look around before a dozen waiting taxi drivers accosted me with offers of transportation. I shook my head, glancing around at the sea of faces. It wasn't as if I would recognize Eduardo Soares. And, we had not discussed the possibility of someone greeting me at the airport, so I didn't expect anything. But I decided to wait for a few minutes anyway, just in case. If no one showed up, I would get into a cab and head to the hotel my advisor had recommended. It was somewhere to stay until I could figure out a more long-term solution.

I was about to make my way to the taxi stand when a young boy ran up to me, and breathless, called out, "Miss Clara Lemont! Miss Lemont?" I nodded, assuring the boy that I was, indeed, the person he was looking for. Obviously relieved, he presented me with a wide toothy grin and immediately took my bags. "I pleased to meet you. I take you now to Professor Soares."

I found myself running to keep up with my bags, hardly able to navigate through the throng of people. The boy waved his arm around, indicating the chaos. "Carnival." Yes, I knew all about Rio Carnival. I had planned my trip specifically to be here in February so I could be part of it. A perfect, if somewhat chaotic, way to begin my fieldwork!

As I followed the boy, who was apparently looking for a specific taxi rather than the dozens waiting out front, I was almost run over by a group of excited school children. People were everywhere. The smell of hot sweat and cheap cologne filled the thick air. The boy suddenly tugged on my arm. "Stay with me or you get lost." I nodded. I had no intention of losing him.

The boy finally found the cab he'd been looking for. He ushered me, along with all my bags, into the back seat, and somehow squeezed himself inside as well. I felt only minor relief as the cab rushed off. The open windows provided a bit of a breeze across my hot forehead. For a moment, I closed my eyes. I just needed to catch my breath. But I couldn't keep my eyes closed for long. There was too much to see. I turned towards the boy, looking at him for the first time. He seemed more like a young man than a boy in the way he held himself, and in the look in his eyes, though he couldn't have been more than twelve.

"What is your name?" I asked in my limited Portuguese.

Relieved that I spoke Portuguese, he responded enthusiastically. "Francisco. But everybody calls me Chico. You are from Canada. That's what the professor told me. He told me to make sure I found you because it's Carnival time and you might get lost. He wants to see you right away." I smiled at the boy's rushed words, happy to hear that the professor did, in fact, have some interest in me.

"Are we going to the Universidade then?" I asked. Chico nodded. I felt a little strange meeting the professor right away. I was exhausted, hot, and hungry. I would have preferred to have gone to the hotel first. I tried to straighten my travel-wrinkled skirt. My hair, now frizzy from humidity, was a mess. I was relieved to find an elastic in my purse. There was little I could do to erase the effects of ten hours of flying, but at least pulling my hair back and tying it into a ponytail helped a bit. I needed to make a good first impression on Professor Soares. I wanted to appear professional and completely in control. I knew I had to be strong from the start. The academic world in this country was still predominately male-dominated and exclusionary.

As the taxi made its way through the various Rio neighbourhoods, I caught glimpses of the ocean only a few blocks away. I was happy that it took some time to get from the airport to downtown Rio. It gave me a chance to compose myself. My excitement started to outweigh my fear as we entered the *centro*. After working for so many years doing research in dark and musty libraries, it felt good to finally be back in Brazil. With the windows open, I could smell the hot air, taste the salt from the ocean, and hear the clamour of people shouting, car horns, and drumbeats. As we passed by one of the main squares, I craned my head out the window to catch a glimpse of the throngs of dancing people, still partying from the night before. I spied a large bandstand, samba music blaring from the speakers. The taxi continued to curve its way through the busy, narrow downtown streets and finally stopped in front of a nineteenth-century Victorian building. The aura of Carnival seemed to disappear in the vicinity of such an imposing structure, and the apprehension I felt increased.

"I'll bring you to the professor now." After paying the cab driver what was clearly a set amount Chico must have negotiated beforehand, I followed the boy up the stone staircase to the front entrance of the Universidade. It was a frightening building, evoking images of a nineteenth-century mental institution with its grey walls and dark, cold interior. The dampness inside those walls, in contrast to the heat outside, made me feel slightly off. I could swear my suitcase got heavier with every step I took. We passed through a series of dark hallways with tiny windows at the very top that allowed only a glimpse of sunlight to enter, despite the brightness of the day outside.

Exhausted and slightly out of breath, I finally caught up to Chico. So much for being composed. By the time I got there,

Chico had already knocked on the professor's office door. And there stood Dr. Eduardo Soares. I reached out to shake his hand and introduce myself, but something was wrong. As I lifted my eyes to meet his gaze directly, I felt myself being drawn in by his dark stare, as though I was slowly being immersed in deep, mud-brown water. I was mesmerized. I couldn't tear my eyes away. It was as though I was entering some other realm. I knew my eyes were still open, but in the dizzying universe I'd suddenly entered, all I could see was a plethora of colours and shapes and swirling, dancing figures dressed in white. It was happening again—the strange dreams and visions, the waking hallucinations. It was happening again, only this time it was much more powerful, and there was nothing I could do to stop it. And then, as suddenly as it had started, it was over. The swirling figures, the distant drumbeats, and the repetitive chanting that seemed to come from deep within my mind ... all disappeared.

I was staring into the professor's eyes once again. I must have fallen during my dizzy spell, since I was lying in his arms, cocooned in his embrace. I was keenly aware of the strength of his biceps and solid chest. He looked at me with concern and something else. Familiarity? The entire episode must have lasted only seconds, but the look in the professor's eyes was haunting.

"Some water for you, miss," said Chico, handing me a glass, which I accepted thankfully. I quickly extricated myself from the professor's secure hold and stood up, still feeling a little shaky. I couldn't bring myself to look at Soares directly again. I was embarrassed, cursing myself and whatever seemed to be possessing me. Why now? Why destroy such a crucial moment? What on earth would the professor think of me?

I realized then I couldn't push the dreams, the images that troubled me those lonely nights in Toronto, away anymore. Maybe I'd been reading so much about possession and Afro-Brazilian rituals that I'd somehow made them my own reality. I had felt so alone in Toronto. I'd moved there from Calgary to pursue graduate work without knowing a single person. And I'd been so immersed in my work that I hadn't made much effort to socialize. Maybe it was the isolation that had prompted the dreams. I'd hoped that by coming to Brazil, by starting my fieldwork and moving forward with my thesis, I could put an end to it. Whatever *it* was. But now, I understood that I was simply running away. Only you can't run away from your own mind. Was I going crazy?

"A little too much for a Canadian girl? Well, you better get used to the ways of Brazil if you want to work here." The professor's words were not said with sympathy. I lifted my head to look at him, and I saw only a man. Had that look of concern and familiarity been my imagination? Soares was nothing short of cold and distant now. But he *was* handsome. I had to give him that. Although it was cut short, the humidity made his coarse black hair curl slightly off his forehead, lending his austere appearance a softer edge. He was standing, casually leaning his angular frame against the doorjamb. His suit was pressed and his tie perfectly knotted. I couldn't help but notice the way his chest muscles flexed beneath his shirt, and how his wide shoulders filled out the suit. I wanted to touch the side of his face, to run my fingers over the slight stubble and firm jaw line, and then lightly trace his full lips. His dark skin glistened in the heat. I shuddered involuntarily and immediately stopped these thoughts before they could continue further. I handed back the glass of water. I had no intention of becoming this man's latest amusement.

"Thanks, but I'm all right now. It's a pleasure to meet you, Dr. Soares. I've heard a lot about your work, and I'm really looking forward to learning from you." I gave the professor a practiced smile. He took my hand politely and held on to it just a fraction longer than was necessary. I felt the warmth of our contact, and it made my stomach jolt unexpectedly.

"My pleasure, indeed. It's not every day a woman falls into

my arms so graciously." I pulled my hand back. Oh, he was going to be trouble.

"Well…" I began, laughing slightly, unable to stop myself, "I did just get off a ten-hour overnight flight." For a moment Dr. Soares said nothing. This was not turning out the way I'd imagined it would. A wry smile appeared on his face when he understood that I wasn't going to participate in his light flirtation.

"Point taken, Miss Lemont. Have you made arrangements for your accommodation yet?"

"Yes." I couldn't imagine coming to Brazil during Carnival not having made previous arrangements. I would never have been able to find anything if I hadn't arranged it beforehand. "But I would welcome some suggestions for more long-term accommodation."

Soares shook his head. "Just so we're clear, Miss Lemont, you are responsible for your own arrangements."

I was taken aback. Well, why did he ask about this then? And, couldn't he at least make the effort to be civil in the interest of academia? He looked to be in his late thirties, probably no more than ten years older than me. Of course, he was right. The Universidade was not sponsoring me; they were only, at their own prerogative, providing a base for me to begin my research. They were under no obligation whatsoever to house me, or to support my research. I had decided to come to Brazil to study the Afro-Brazilian religion of Odún, and, as researchers had done in the past, I had to find my own way. Although a few suggestions about accommodation shouldn't have been too much to ask, I thought, suddenly irritable.

"Of course," I said, through pursed lips. "In that case I'll take a cab to my hotel for tonight and meet with you tomorrow when I'm more settled." I leaned down to pick up my bags, but his hand reached out to stop me. I couldn't deny the warm pressure of his hand touching my skin once again. Now what?

"Please, I want you to stay in a place that is safe. For now, stay at the Belo Horizonté. I have made a reservation. Chico will take you there."

I shook my head. He was confusing me. Hadn't he just insisted I was on my own in this respect? "As I said, I've already made arrangements," I responded.

He wouldn't budge. "We have an agreement with the Belo Horizonté. They will give you a good rate." Chico was already picking up my bags. I felt resentful of the way Dr. Soares seemed to enjoy taking over. I didn't trust his motives. But I decided to go along with him for now. As I turned to follow Chico, Soares called out, "Tomorrow morning, eight o'clock sharp. And bring your thesis so I can review it again." Almost as an afterthought, he added, "Bring all your notes, too."

Reluctantly, I nodded and wondered why I felt so apprehensive. I wanted Soares' help, but why did he need all my notes as well as my thesis on the first day I arrived? Well, there was no point worrying about it. I gratefully sank back into the taxi while it raced down a few narrow side streets, arriving in front of a slightly worn-looking hotel. I would have to remember to cancel the hotel reservations I'd made before leaving. Annoyed, I wondered if I should have allowed myself to have been talked into this other arrangement. The hotel must have been beautiful once, with its ornate architecture and balustrades, but now the walls were crumbling, the white stone had dulled to an uneven grey, and the paint was chipping in places. I paid the taxi driver and thanked Chico for his help. Soares had assumed correctly that my cash flow was limited, and one night at the hotel I had arranged on my own would have used up a good chunk.

"If you ever need anything, *senhora,* you call Chico." I acknowledged his bright smile, but his eyes were murky pools of stale water. The effect was disconcerting. I felt a pang of sympathy. Did he come from one of Rio's many *favelas?* Did he return home each day with a few *cruzeiros* to give his mother for dinner that night? I'd read about the many children who lived on the streets of Rio in extreme poverty and were subject to violence and abuse. I'd lived a privileged white, upper middle-class existence my entire life, and I couldn't even begin to comprehend what it would be like to live like that. But maybe I was wrong. Maybe Chico wasn't one of the lost children of Rio. I reached into my purse and gave him some crumpled-up bills, significantly more than I had intended. He took the money in his fist and quickly ran away, as if afraid I might ask for it back if he lingered too long.

The air inside the hotel was slightly cooler, although the musty smell made it far from refreshing. The entrance hall was relatively grand, with a winding staircase leading up to the next level. I let the receptionist know I wanted to stay a few nights, and then lugged my suitcase up the stairs and into my room. As soon as I opened the door, I dropped my luggage on the floor. I gratefully kicked off my shoes and sank onto the bed, ignoring the groan of the bedsprings and the coffee stain on the cover. Sleep at last.

THE OCEAN BREEZE, carried into the room through the open balcony doors, felt refreshing on my hot skin when I woke later that night. I breathed in the slightly floral and musky scent, once again revelling in all that was Brazil to me. I stood up groggily and moved outside to stand on the balcony, gazing up into the bright night sky. The glow of homemade firecrackers lit the sky more than stars ever could. I listened to the sounds of Carnival, the constant samba rhythm that I could feel reverberating through the night air like the heartbeat of a living creature. It was an insistent rhythm that spoke of life and passion, and abandonment of all social norms and regulations. This was what Carnival was all about. I never could resist that music. I felt myself moving to the rhythm of the samba and knew that I had to be part of it.

I threw my skirt and blouse onto the bed and jumped into the shower, enjoying the sensation of cool water hitting my skin.

With my hair still dripping wet, I looked through my suitcase for something appropriate to wear. I had left the balcony doors open, allowing the sights, smells, and sounds to drift into the musty darkness of the small room. I decided on a dark, silky, flaring skirt and a tight red top. I looked at myself in the mirror. My eyes were glowing, my face was flushed, and my damp hair clung to the sides of my cheekbones. I was coming back into myself. I had led a rigidly organized life in Canada and I'd spent so many years studying inside closed rooms that I'd forgotten what it meant to be part of the outside world. But there was something about being in Brazil that released an energy inside of me that was primal.

I couldn't help thinking about the last time I'd visited Brazil. I was twenty-one and full of life and love. Everyone would ask, "Where is your Brazilian boyfriend?" and I'd nonchalantly reply that I had many. And it had been true at the time. Life had been a game for me back then. I'd been so busy partying that I hadn't even noticed the tense political situation around me. Although I was only twenty-nine now, I felt so much older, so much more responsible and serious. But every so often I longed to return to that stage in my life when I'd felt no fear, when I'd been completely free, done exactly as I pleased and to hell with the consequences.

Consequences were so much a part of my life now. I pushed aside images of my father and the expression on his face the day I left my hometown of Calgary to pursue graduate studies in Toronto. Graduate work in *Anthropology*. An MBA, now that would have been just fine. But a degree in anthropology? According to my father, it was bad enough I'd already wasted four years completing an undergrad degree in the social sciences. He would have preferred that I had started learning about the oil business, and following in his footsteps. But I'd never been interested in the commuting-cubicle lifestyle. I'd always wanted something different. And, I was still paying for it. Two years of a Master's degree and five years so far into my PhD and I was still racking up student loans. Thank goodness I'd managed to get enough scholarships to pay off my undergraduate tuition fees or I would have been in even more trouble. After coming back from Brazil the last time, I spent the last year of undergrad writing an honours graduate thesis about Odún before applying to research the same topic for my graduate degree. My father was not happy about this, and as a result, I'd barely spoken to my parents in years. I needed to shake this off, and decided that at least, for this one night of Carnival, I wanted to feel that freedom again.

I smiled at my reflection in the old mirror above the dresser. There was a purple mask on top, obviously discarded by the previous hotel guest. It was perfect. Taking a deep breath, I covered my face with it and wrapped a bright yellow scarf around my throat, allowing it to trail after me as I grabbed my purse and headed out the door.

The moment I stepped outside, I was swept up by the energy of the people around me. Many had already been dancing for hours, their sweat-stained bodies blending together and their eyes bright with an exhaustion-driven ecstasy. The insistent and erratic rhythms of the drums that caused possession in Odún were the same throbbing rhythms that drove people into their own forms of trance while dancing on the streets of Rio during Carnival. This was the appeal and the danger of Carnival. It was possible to dance oneself to complete exhaustion and even to a symbolic, if not real, death.

The crowd pushed me along. I was surrounded by a thousand kinds of faces, and, rather than fearing the crowd, I became a part of it. The different rhythms of the music were colliding together and creating a complete chaos of sound. I was propelled towards a main square where the party appeared to be in full swing. I could barely see the stage above the movement of bodies. I knew I couldn't make it to the *Sambódromo*, the enclosed parade street where the famous Rio Carnival floats were displayed. I would have had to buy tickets in advance.

But that was okay. I was still in Rio de Janeiro during Carnival, and I could enjoy all the block parties for free.

I wove my way through the crowd to get closer to the stage. The drummers were beating out the rhythm while the dancers, wearing barely more than their elaborate headdresses, gyrated to the beat. I watched in fascination as the people moved in unison, their bodies melding into one, their hips undulating, their breasts and torsos swaying to the insistent rhythm of the drums. I watched the sweat drip down naked skin and felt my body respond. It had been so long since I'd allowed myself to feel passion. I'd buried that part of myself. I had been so determined to move forward, to finish my PhD and make something of my life, to prove that I could do it. And I hadn't let anything get in my way. But, in order to do that, I'd had to shut off my emotions.

The last time I'd been in Brazil, the country had taken me out of my comfort zone, out of the carefully constructed and ordered world of academia. Brazil had showed me another way to live. And now that I was back, those old desires were resurfacing. I understood now why I'd chosen to focus my research on Odún.

The dancers moved off the stage in a flurry of colour as the next local group, a samba school offering their gifts to the Odún goddess, Yemanja, took their place. The dancers were all wearing white flowing dresses, their heads were wrapped with filmy, white scarves, heavy blue and white beaded necklaces around their throats. It was as if I'd stepped into my dreams. The images, the sensations ... they were real now. I was finally in the middle of it all. The images, sounds, and colours of Carnival weren't that different from the magical colours of the Odún ceremonies that had been haunting my dreams. And now that I was here in Brazil, feeling it again, being part of it, I knew I was in the right place. But I also knew that there was something more to it. There was something sinister in my dreams—something beyond the music and flashes of colour.

The music and colour only masked the darkness. I shook my head. I was here to complete my research. It was the only way to make sense of things. But for now, for tonight, I was just going to enjoy myself.

I tried to move closer to get a better look, and suddenly became aware of a man slowly gyrating behind me. Although with so many people it was impossible not to feel the strain and pull of other bodies, it was obvious this man was pressing himself against me intentionally. I tried to move away, but he only pressed closer. I felt myself responding, moving slowly to the rhythm he had created. We were doing our own dance, oblivious to the variety of sounds around us. The feeling of our two bodies so closely in tune filled me with a heady desire I'd never experienced before. All around me men and women were moving their bodies in unison, creating an orgy of sight, sound, and scent. The feel of this man's hardened body pressed against my backside, his hands firmly holding my thighs and pulling me closer, drew me into his rhythm so that we moved as one person, the heat, the drumbeats, the noise of firecrackers coursing through our limbs. I'd entered my dream and it was time to let go.

But no, not like this. What was I doing? This wasn't a dream. This was real. And it *would* have real consequences. I broke free from the man and escaped towards a side street where the crowd was thinner. I rested against the cool cement wall, taking deep breaths. The whirling sounds, the people, the heat, it all made me feel a little dizzy. I spied a shadow out of the corner of my eye. A man was approaching. I moved away from the wall and tried to slink back into the crowd, but he caught my arm. I turned quickly, trying to break his grip on me. His face was covered by a silver mask. It was the same man. I was afraid. But even with my heart pounding, I couldn't deny that I was excited as well. What was wrong with me? This was way too dangerous. When he realized my fear, he let me go.

He gave me a courtly bow, and, in a deep voice, he said, "*Desculpe*," by way of apology. I felt the rhythms of the drums in the heat of the air around me. I stared at him, wishing I could see his eyes or something more of his face. I didn't want him to go. Now that he no longer posed a threat, I wanted him to stay. I felt the wetness between my thighs and realized I'd wanted him from the moment he pressed himself against me. I tried to deny it in the same way I always tried to deny my desire. I tried to rationalize everything away. But this time, I didn't want to be rational. I just wanted to feel. There was something mesmerizing about this man, something I couldn't let go of. And it was obvious he felt the same way. He continued to watch me in silence beneath his silver mask, waiting to see what I would do. Would I tell him to go? I knew instinctively that if I did, he would leave. He would not force me into his dance; I had to go willingly. I fought with myself in that moment. Terrified and exhilarated by my own thoughts.

He started to dance slowly, seductively, in front of me. I watched his body sway, his hand reach out to touch my cheek ever so gently and trail along my hair. My body betrayed my mind by responding to his dance, my hips swaying almost involuntarily. The drumbeats in the distance grew louder and more intense, the beat unrelenting, matching the gradual intensity of our movements until the sound of our quick breathing filled the air. He moved closer to me, his hips moving faster and faster, and I found myself moving towards him as well. Soon we were locked together, our bodies moving in rhythm. I felt the muscles of his back tighten beneath my grip while his strong hands explored my body, cupping my breasts, my nipples hardening beneath the thin red material of my top. I could feel his cock pressed against my thigh and I wanted to feel it throbbing in my hand. I heard his groan as I stroked him gently at first through his shorts, my strokes becoming bolder as the rhythm of our dance intensified. I needed to feel him inside me.

He kissed my lips, the sweetness of his tongue dancing with mine. As his kiss deepened, he reached down to lift up my skirt. I ran my fingers through his hair. I was no longer thinking. I was only feeling. The heat and the music and the blinding lights enveloped us as he trailed kisses along my neck, my ears, my face. He pinched my nipples through my top, then leaned down and kissed my breasts through the fabric. In the next moment, he lifted up my shirt and expertly released my breasts from my bra, his tongue darting around my erect nipples until I could hardly stand it.

We continued this dance against the cool surface of the wall. He lifted me up as I raised my legs and wrapped them around his torso. I felt the entire length of his body pressed against mine, the hardness of his penis against my clit, the pressure making me shake with need. I pulled him closer and ran my hands down his chest, leaning down to kiss his collarbone and then further down until I released his penis from his shorts.

My entire body felt alive. I couldn't remember the last time I'd felt this way, if ever. I was always so controlled. I hated to lose myself, even in sex. But this was different. I was lost the moment he'd started his dance. He licked two fingers and, pushing my panties aside, he felt me, knowing exactly where to touch me. His palm pushed with just the right pressure while his fingers circled my clit, making me so wet. I leaned my head back and heard my own moan as I climaxed. And then, in the next moment, before I even had time to come down, I felt his penis come into me hard and fast. I gasped as I felt him thrusting deep inside, my muscles contracting again.

We had done this so many times before. When our bodies melded together it was as if we belonged together. It was both natural and exhilaratingly perfect. I was shocked by the depth of feeling, the depth of emotion. My body and soul felt united. I closed my eyes and let myself feel every sensation without holding back. He pounded into me, holding up my leg and allowing me to sink against the strength of his chest as he filled me. He slowed down, and we moved in rhythm together until I felt my orgasm rising again, and I pushed against him, my head leaning against his shoulder, my hands grasping his arms to prevent myself from sinking to the ground. I felt the hard strength of his arm muscles and the way they were flexing with each thrust. I felt the waves of heat and the pulsing sensation course through me, and I heard my own moans of release. I looked into his eyes in that moment and saw a depth of need that shook me even further. He paused and waited, his penis still hard inside me while my body shuddered, and when I finished, he continued to move even faster until I was once again feeling my building climax. Finally, I heard his groan while he came, and I felt myself coming again, this time fiercer and stronger than the time before. We held onto each other almost in desperation, our breathing erratic and the sweat dripping down our skin.

For a moment afterward, as I rested my head on his shoulder and we gently sank to the ground in exhaustion, I felt nothing but peace. But the moment lasted only a few seconds. The pounding in my ears had faded away, and I was left with nothing but a terrified coldness. I was lying in the stranger's arms, and that was precisely what he was to me again. A stranger. A strange man with a silver mask, whose name and face I didn't even know. I pushed him off and stood up. I had to get away.

"*Como se chama*," he called after me. I ignored his plea for my name and ran down the street, trying to escape the throbbing crowd, trying to escape myself.

After a night of wandering, I finally reached the hotel. I opened the door to my room with shaky fingers. I couldn't turn on the light switch because I couldn't face seeing my own reflection in the mirror. I may have wanted to experience freedom, but not necessarily like that. It had felt amazing. And, yes, there'd been some sort of connection I'd never experienced before—an incredible, deep connection that I couldn't explain. But the enormity of my feelings scared me; I was afraid that I could be consumed by my own desire. And now all I was left with was a stale taste in my mouth and the familiar battle in my mind—the desire for freedom versus the desire for control. I'd felt possessed in that moment. Possessed by that inner part of myself that wanted to break free from the repression. I stumbled blindly into the washroom and collapsed on the toilet.

Possessed. Why did that word keep coming up in my life? Ever since I'd started researching Odún, I'd felt a presence. At first it was just a heightened awareness, a sensation of being watched. But now that I was in Brazil, the presence was overpowering. I couldn't ignore it anymore. Having grown up in a Catholic world of saints and sinners, I was familiar with tales of satanic possession, and I believed that a combination of my religious upbringing and current research was creating a dark imaginary cesspool.

I looked up. Was there something in the mirror? It looked like some sort of shape. Was this real? Or just something I imagined? I no longer knew what reality was. The whole night had held a dreamlike quality. I edged away from the mirror. My fingers shook as I tried to reach for the light switch. The dark shadow seemed to be moving towards me. I fell against the wall. Okay. Now I was starting to feel scared. Yes, there was something there. Something … evil. The air chilled. And then I saw it clearly. Yellow eyes. Glowing in the darkness. Eyes staring at me, willing me to look into them. This couldn't be my mind playing tricks again. I couldn't take it anymore. All the frustration, anger, and fear I'd been feeling for months came out. I didn't want to be afraid anymore. I wanted to stand up to this thing, whatever it was.

"It's you again," I screamed. "I won't let you possess me again. Do you hear me? I won't let you!" I grabbed the closest thing, which happened to be a soap dish, and threw it with all my strength at the figure in the mirror. I jumped back at the sound of shattering glass. Shards flew through the air. I reached over to turn on the light and see what damage I'd caused. Of course, all I saw was my own reflection and broken glass. What was happening to me? Too exhausted to do anything else, I stumbled to the bed and collapsed. I just wanted to sleep and make it all go away. But the nightmares would make sure it never would.

I HEARD THE ALARM go off the next morning, but it was a struggle to open my eyes. The meeting with Dr. Soares. Shit. I crawled out of bed and stumbled into the bathroom. I had to be careful to avoid the shards of broken glass. Numb, I stepped into the shower. But as the hot water streamed over my body, memories from the night before came unbidden into my mind. The feel of his warm skin against mine, the saltiness against my tongue as I'd licked his neck, his strong hands cupping my ass when he pulled me closer against him, the pressure of his hard cock against my vagina. I took in a sharp breath, my heart racing, my body wet and thrumming with desire. This was insanity. I felt like I had no grounding anymore, my entire life had taken on a hue of the magical and unreal, as if I'd stepped off the plane and entered a parallel universe. I felt the hot saltiness of tears. I hated myself for crying. I sank down onto the floor of the shower and allowed the water to spill over me until I felt I could finally stand up. Resolutely, I managed to turn off the water and get myself dressed and looking presentable. I couldn't look at my face in the bathroom mirror anymore.

"TOUGH NIGHT?" The professor indicated that I should take a seat. His dark eyes examined me with a mixture of curiosity and something else. I noticed the slight scent of his aftershave, feeling a shock of recognition. Of course it was just a coincidence, but my body responded immediately.

"No, just jet lag." Accepting my response, for a moment, Dr. Soares looked into my bloodshot eyes and then turned away. I couldn't help noticing that he appeared a little worse for wear himself, but I certainly was in no position to comment. So far, I never seemed to be in a good frame of mind when facing Eduardo Soares. I took a seat across from him. As instructed, I handed over my thesis along with some quickly organized notes. He flipped through them in silence. I sat at the edge of my chair, waiting for some signal. Finally, he looked at me with an expression I couldn't read.

"Very interesting. So what is your plan now?" I hesitated for only a moment. I knew my "plan" had to be approved by the university if I hoped to succeed. I better make this good. I began my well-rehearsed speech.

"I intend to visit various Odún *terreiros* and establish communication with a particular one, where hopefully I will be allowed to live temporarily. I must also research the archives and gather more firsthand documentation about the history of Odún as it relates to its Yoruba origins. I will need to study the ethnomusicology of Yoruba and Odún drum rhythms and attempt to monitor brain wave patterns in relation to trance-like states and possession." I was hoping my knowledge of the *terreiros*—the Odún places of worship—would show Soares that I had done my research. During my entire speech, Soares' expression didn't change. When I finished, he continued to look at me blankly.

"I see. Ambitious, are you? How do you plan to monitor these brain wave patterns? Will you hook up willing Odún initiates to your little wires?" He was watching my reaction. I intentionally kept my expression blank. I wouldn't let him get to me. He continued in that arrogant and calm voice. "Don't think you're the first to come here. Brazil is very protective of its national heritage and its national pride. And Odún is part of that, whether willingly or not. A white American woman in Brazil. Has a nice ring to it. I'm sure you'll sell lots of books. But don't for a moment think you're bringing anything new that Brazilian academics and Odún initiates haven't already written and published about in Portuguese." Oh, I understood.

I suddenly understood only too well where this conversation was going. For that matter, I also understood my role in this charade. He had placed me in a hotel because he didn't intend for me to stay very long in Brazil. He'd read my notes only to see my position, maybe driven by curiosity. He had nothing more to learn from me and had no intention of letting me learn anything of Odún. But he did strike a raw nerve. What he said was true. I didn't know enough Portuguese to read academic texts about Odún unless they were written or translated into English. This was definitely a gap in my research, and indicative of much academic research where English has become the dominating language and brilliant international work often does not receive the credit that it should.

I returned his stare. Well, I wasn't going to reveal my vulnerability. He couldn't get rid of me that easily. But as I continued to look at him, I felt the strangest sensation of familiarity, yet again. Even caught up in anger, I couldn't shake it. What was it about this man? His voice, so deep and musical. Even though his words were harsh, the voice in which he spoke them held me captive. What was wrong with me? Damn it. This was the last thing I needed. It was ridiculous to be obsessing like this.

"Nothing to say?"

Okay. I needed to start facing reality. The only way to deal with this was to approach the situation directly. "I may be a young *Canadian* woman," I stated, placing special emphasis on the word *Canadian,* "but, as you said, there've been others who've come to Brazil to study Odún. And they've been successful. And yes, there are many great works by Brazilian scholars and Odún initiates that I admire and recognize. But what I came here to do is something different. I'm doing an ethnomusicological and biological study of ritual and possession. Something never before explored. I believe my research can aid both academia here and abroad, and I may even return something of importance to the *terreiros* themselves. If you're not interested in working with me, then I'll work independently. Although I would like to work with the university, I don't need you. I'll continue my research with or without your endorsement."

I could feel my heart pounding faster with every word. I was all bravado. Could I really work without the university's support? The university and its professors were intricately linked with Odún, both financially and politically. The university had always given Odún protection through all the political upheavals and particularly during the military dictatorship. The allegiance had always been strong between academia and this famous Brazilian religion. Without the support of the university would the *terreiros* even accept me? Or would I be cast out like an intruder?

Professor Soares no longer made an attempt to remain cordial. "Your arrogance is to be admired." He paused, studying me more closely, as if he had made assumptions about who I was but no longer felt so certain. "I am the *ogun* for a majority of Rio's largest *terreiros*. I provide funding and support. Without my endorsement, you'll get nowhere."

Such cold words. He dismissed me from the room with a wave of his hand. I couldn't move. I was too filled with anger and fear. I couldn't let this happen. I couldn't let this one man ruin everything I'd worked so hard for. After spending eight years of my life studying Odún, I wasn't going to leave Brazil without a fight.

"You know, we could accomplish so much if we work together. If you're afraid of how I'll represent Odún, wouldn't it be better to work with, rather than against me? That way you'd know exactly what I was doing. And I would listen to your advice because I believe there's a lot you can teach me. But if you turn me away now, I'll find the answers on my own, and you may not like the results I publish in North America."

I left him with a rational argument. He wanted to protect Odún from prying academics, but what better way to protect something from the enemy than by joining their ranks? The professor smiled at me again, but this time his eyes casually moved downward. My stomach tightened. Against my will, I felt myself respond to his gaze. We were like two statues, fixated upon one another and yet at a standstill.

"Hmm, well I shall truly enjoy your presence then. Perhaps we should begin with a drink tonight?"

I couldn't respond. I couldn't deny the way I felt when his dark eyes assessed me. But I certainly wasn't going to show it. This was just another way for him to exert control and make me feel unsettled. I would not allow him to do that. "No thanks."

Without waiting to see if he had more to say, I reached out my hand for my papers. With only a second of hesitation, he returned them without a word. I opened the door and let myself out. For a moment I stood in the open courtyard, and took a few deep breaths. Eduardo Soares had gotten to me. But I would succeed without him.

2

THE TRAM CURVED UP the narrow roads while I hung on desperately. I was amazed by the young boys who clung effortlessly onto the edge of the *bonde*, and jumped off with just as much ease. I had left behind the beautiful and picturesque Baía de Guanabara to climb the hills into Santa Teresa. I'd read a lot about this quaint area of Rio. It was once the wealthy suburb of the elite, who rode the tram every day to work in the city and then escaped into the peace of their little community at night.

As I peered out the window, I could imagine the Santa Teresa of the nineteenth century, with its narrow cobblestone streets and old colonial mansions. But these once-beautiful mansions now stood in disrepair; many were divided up to house numerous families. And the old streets, though still picturesque and nestled in the lush hillsides, were also dangerous. The presence of the *favelas* covering the hillsides posed a constant threat to this small community. Although it would probably be more accurate to say that the increasing redevelopment and gentrification of Santa Teresa posed a greater threat to the *favelas*. I remembered the hotel clerk mentioning how Santa Teresa had become a refuge for artists in the 1960s and '70s, and, since its colonial, rustic charm had not faded over the years, I could see why.

I looked again at the address on the crumpled-up sheet of paper I dug out of my purse. In my limited Portuguese, I asked the tram driver to let me know when we approached the street I was searching for.

After leaving the university yesterday and realizing that I would be doing my research without institutional support, instead of packing my bags and giving up, I decided to forge ahead with my plans and not look back. It was obvious that the first thing I needed to do was find a place to live. There was something so inherently appealing about this area. I also liked the idea of living close to the *favelas*. Many *terreiros* were located within the heart of the *favelas*. If I wanted to do my fieldwork properly, I would need to immerse myself in the culture. But living in the *favela* itself was not something I felt prepared for. Something about the idea of "slumming it" in the name of research just didn't sit right with me. I would always be aware that at any moment I could leave, and my *favela* time would be an "experience" rather than my entire life—similar to the popular "*favela* tours" that always left a bad taste in my mouth. Besides, if I was perfectly honest with myself, I knew I couldn't do it. I didn't have any street smarts, and I was only too aware of my own naïveté.

The driver told me to get off at the next stop. Following the directions I had hurriedly scribbled, I walked down the street checking the number signs. I'd found this place in a local newspaper advertisement for long-term accommodation. I would be renting the top floor of a house, giving me access to a private bedroom and bathroom. It sounded like a perfect arrangement, and the rent seemed reasonable too.

The busy streets gave the area a real sense of community and I liked the neighbourhood immediately. Men were sitting on the benches, relaxing in the late afternoon sunlight and smoking their pipes; children were playing soccer up and down the narrow side alleyways; and women shouted from their balconies to one another in friendly conversation as they hung out brightly coloured laundry to dry. I passed by several bakeries and grocery shops and I smiled, thinking how nice it would be to wake up in the morning to the aroma of fresh bread in the air.

Number 42. I looked up at the quaint, historical home, similar to all the others on the street but for the fresh coat of yellow paint. Good. Whoever owned the house obviously took pleasure in keeping it in good condition. I noticed a small balcony on the upper level and hoped the white French doors leading towards it would be the doors of my bedroom. The floral scent of a bougainvillea tree hung in the air, the blooms trailing over the balcony and to the side of the house. The bright pink flowers were a stark contrast to the yellow hue of the home. I knocked on the front door. There was something about the house—the smell of the flowers, the bustle of activity. Ever since I'd seen the address in Santa Teresa, I'd been certain it would be perfect.

"*Olá?*" An older lady answered the door, her silky robe flowing in the soft breeze, her dark hair tucked behind a colourful, embroidered shawl. For just a moment, I stared at the woman, thinking how strangely beautiful she was. Her eyes were a soft hazel, and her smile was gentle and kind. As with all my experiences in Brazil thus far, my reaction to this stranger made no logical sense. I only knew that I felt a distinct sense of immediate kinship.

"Hello! I saw your advertisement for a room to rent, and I am very interested." I spoke falteringly in Portuguese and the woman shook her head.

"That's fine. I do speak English. Yes, the room is still available if you would like to see it. Please come in." She stepped aside to allow me into the entrance hall. And then it hit me. *I knew this home.* For a moment, all I could do was stand there, taking in my surroundings and trying to pull myself back to reality. But I didn't succeed.

I couldn't shake the feeling that I'd been here many times before. I knew the winding staircase that led to the upper level where the bedroom stood, with the French doors opening onto the balcony, the faint aroma of the bougainvillea drifting into the room on sultry summer nights. Lying in my bed at night, I could see the stars. I would watch those brilliant stars as I lay there waiting, waiting for my lover to come through the French doors, climbing up the balcony like Romeo meeting Juliet. The memories washed over me. I could smell his masculine scent and see his soulful eyes. Soulful dark eyes. Not the yellow eyes of my nightmares but the mesmerizing deep brown eyes of my mysterious lover. *They haunted me...*

I shook my head. I had to stop this. I was back in the little entranceway with the woman looking up at me curiously. She had said something. Her lips were moving, and she was waiting for a response. Embarrassed, I forced myself to act normally.

"I'm sorry. The coolness in here is so refreshing after the afternoon heat. I just needed a moment." I smiled, wondering what my expression had been just a few seconds earlier. My mind had taken me away to a world of memories.

Memories? How could a person have memories of a place they'd never been to? How could I know what that bedroom looked like before I'd even entered it? These were not memories. They were insane fantasies. Fantasies that included my secret Brazilian Carnival lover whom my conscious mind had determined to forget. It scared me that I couldn't keep my unconscious thoughts from emerging while standing in plain daylight in a stranger's home. My nightmares were becoming far more than illusions; they were starting to become my waking reality.

"Oh, the heat. It never goes away. Come here, dear, and I'll pour you a glass of lemonade." I nodded gratefully, moving in the direction of the kitchen.

"Well, it appears you know your way around already." The woman laughed as I turned around, realizing in shock that I'd gone ahead of her.

"I'm so sorry. That was terribly rude." I didn't know what

else to say. That I had been to her home before in some previous life? Sure. That would make a great first impression.

"Come along. You were headed straight for the kitchen, where I intended to go." Once seated at the kitchen table, I sipped the lemonade gratefully.

"This is so good!" I said, enjoying the sweet but limey flavour of the juice on my tongue.

She smiled in response. "Ah, yes. Brazilian lemonade. Lime juice and condensed milk. We do love sweet things here." She smiled and so did I. The kitchen was painted a bright orange with cheerful flowery curtains at the window. It was pleasant and homey. Immediately, I felt at peace.

"You have a lovely home," I commented.

"Yes, well I hope you like it. Of course, upstairs you will have your own private washroom, and there is a fridge and small hotplate so you can warm things up, but you are always welcome to use this kitchen for other things. I live here by myself, so I welcome the company." I looked at the woman more closely. There was something so wonderful about her. I couldn't describe it. I only knew that I'd felt somehow happy from the moment I'd entered the little home. Did she feel even a hint of the kinship I felt towards her? It seemed to be mutual. "Are you a student then? And you're from the States, I take it?"

"No, I'm from Canada. And yes, I am a student. I'm working on my thesis here."

The woman nodded with interest. "And what are you studying?"

I was hesitant to answer. I had no way of knowing how this woman might feel about Odún. "I'm studying the association between possession and religious ritual."

She gave me an amused smile. She knew I had tactfully evaded the question. "And which Brazilian religion are you studying for this purpose? Perhaps it is Odún, *não?*"

I smiled and nodded.

The woman looked thoughtful but didn't say any more. "Well, we have not even made introductions yet! Lisboa Durana."

I reached out my hand in greeting. "Clara Lemont." When we finished our lemonade, Lisboa stood up with a flourish and again motioned for me to follow.

"It's time we see the room, *sim?* I hope you will like it because I like you already." As we climbed the rickety staircase, I realized my earlier vision had been correct. I tried to conceal my amazement. The room was exactly as I'd imagined it, except for the rosy wallpaper and the décor. In my imagination, the bed had been covered with a white, lacy bedspread, the furniture a deep mahogany, and the walls painted a pale sea green. Looking at this room felt like when I returned home for Christmas that first year I'd been away at school, and discovered my parents had redecorated my room. It was the same room. But everything was decorated differently.

I sat on the bed. The frame was an antique polished brass, the bedspread a splash of coloured cotton. The furniture was sparse yet functional. A dresser with a mirror stood in the corner, and a small wooden desk stood against the other wall. The curtains, though ... they were the same. Long, lacy curtains gently swaying in the scented breeze. And the French doors, they were still white, slightly opened to reveal the early evening sky. The sun was just beginning to sink below the horizon.

I walked over to the balcony, opening the French doors wide to let myself out. I breathed in the scent of bougainvillea and allowed the blossoms to brush my cheek. But suddenly I was transported, a jumbled series of visions and sensations taking over. I heard voices and laughter, shouts of joy and anger, and a wash of emotion coursed through my body—heat and desire mixed with pain and confusion. I felt as if I'd entered a time warp, and I needed to escape. I moved off the balcony and turned to face Lisboa.

"You seem to like it very much," Lisboa commented, her expression questioning.

Impulsively, I closed the small space between us and took Lisboa's hands in my own. "It's perfect here. I think we're going to become very good friends."

THREE WEEKS PASSED. I was right. Lisboa and I did become good friends. But nothing could erase the fact that I had yet to attend a single Odún ceremony. I leaned my neck back, trying to stretch out the kinks. I felt thoroughly exhausted. I'd spent hours in the historical research library going through documents. The majority were written in Portuguese, so I was required to gather the information and then hire an interpreter to help me read the documents—a tiring and tedious process. While I could speak limited Portuguese, I wasn't fluent enough to read the academic material.

Eduardo Soares had certainly made good on his word. Any efforts I made to approach one of the known *terreiros* in Rio were quickly stopped. The minute I introduced myself, the reception was cold and distant. I decided to focus on the historical research first and try to make some contacts in the meantime. Hopefully I could attend a ceremony as a personal guest. Of course, there were the tourist Odúns. These were ceremonies that mimicked the initiation rites, designed to ignite tourist imagination. People paid good money for such an entertaining performance. But I would rather not attend a ceremony at all than be jaded by theatrics. I was here to study a religion, not an art form. Although, at times, the two intersected.

I'd found my interpreter by placing an ad in the student newspaper. She was a young anthropology student fluent in English and Portuguese and, therefore, invaluable to me. She was willing to work long hours, and in exchange I paid her well. The 1992 economy was so inflated that the Brazilians could hardly afford a loaf of bread. What was only a few *cruzeiros* to me would help support Catalina's entire family.

The dim lighting in the basement of the library cast a yellowish glow on both our faces, reflecting the exhaustion in our eyes.

"It's getting late. You should go home," I said, feeling guilty for having kept her in the library so long.

"What about you? You work so hard."

I smiled at the concern in the young woman's voice. "When you are committed to something as I am, you have to work hard."

I waved goodbye and listened to her retreating footsteps breaking the silence of the library. Sighing, I decided to organize my notes. As I bent my head, I felt another presence in the room. Without Catalina by my side, at this time of night, the library was a lonely place. I was in the basement and searching through old documents covered in dust, so I wasn't likely to encounter many people. But someone was definitely in the room.

I looked up, feeling a powerful presence. And then I saw him. He stared at me with those dark eyes, our gazes locking.

"Wha... what are you doing here?" I stammered, annoyed by the catch in my voice. I was all too aware that we were essentially alone in the basement. If I screamed, no one would hear. He stepped closer, until his hands were resting on my desk. I felt my body respond, and I cursed myself for my desire. I could smell the faint scent of his aftershave and couldn't help noticing the outline of his strong biceps beneath his light shirt. Inadvertently, my mind suddenly imagined myself slowly undoing each button of his shirt while my hands caressed his muscled chest, my fingers pressing against his dark skin. Whoa! I had better stop right there. This was the man who was preventing me from moving forward with my fieldwork—the very same man who might potentially ruin my chances of an academic future, especially if he wouldn't help me gain access to my field site. He was the gatekeeper. What was wrong with me? It was like that one night of sex during Carnival had created a demon in me, making me lust for more.

"I came here to find you." His voice, so musical. His eyes, the soulful eyes of my dreams.... *Who was this man?*

Oh, no. I couldn't break the stare. Why didn't it occur to me sooner? It was obvious. And there was no avoiding it now. I looked at his hands, his fingers, slender yet so full of strength. Those hands had traced my hair, my cheek, my breasts. Those same hands had circled my waist, pushing me against his cock, pressing me closer, bringing me to... Shit! I could hear my quick breathing in the silence. I felt it again. The inexplicable connection. But not *him*. Not Eduardo Soares. Was this some kind of cosmic joke?

He just watched me, not saying anything. Every thought was probably flashing across my face. Including my desire.

"So, you do remember." He spoke softly. The way he was looking at me. I couldn't speak. I couldn't even move. Those dark eyes stared into my own, as if he wanted to find something, to know something. What was this connection? I'd felt it the moment he first touched me. I wanted to deny it. But I couldn't anymore. Damn him. Suddenly, all I could feel was anger. No, this wasn't a cosmic joke. It was a set-up. Of course. It became blindingly clear. He had known what hotel I'd been at. Maybe he'd waited for me. He'd seen me leave and he'd followed me. What did he want from me?

"Oh, that's a good one. Well, I'll give you that much. You acted the part pretty well. So how many foreign graduate students do you fuck before sending them home? Must be fun." I stood up, spitting the words out even though I wasn't sure I actually believed them myself. I didn't believe in coincidence so there really was no other explanation. And so I lashed out with the only logical defense I had. But Eduardo's reaction wasn't what I had expected. He didn't look surprised by my anger or even defensive.

"No, that's not it at all. You have to believe me. Hell, I don't blame you for feeling that way. I guess I would have thought the same thing." He nervously ran a hand through his short, bristly hair. Nervous? This was not the Eduardo Soares I knew. But then he looked at me again. "There's something else going on here, Clara. I needed to find you. I didn't know it was you. I didn't know until last night."

"And what happened last night that made you remember?"

He shook his head. "Look, I don't even know why I'm here. I just needed to see you. I had a dream last night and you were in it. I looked into your eyes ... and then I realized it was you that night."

I couldn't understand what was happening. Who was this apologetic, confused man? And what did he want with me? I hated this man. He'd made my life in Brazil a living hell, and now he had come to implore me? "Look, I don't care what happened between us. It was a mistake and it will never happen again."

I knew this wasn't true even as I said it. The words came from my rational side. The part of me that demanded control. The part that couldn't accept something I couldn't understand. But the entire time, I couldn't take my eyes off his. And I couldn't stop the memory of his chest against mine, his breath in my ear, the sound of the drumbeats and the sticky, salty smell of a Rio summer night.

Eduardo shook his head. He knew I was lying. He closed the space between us, coming around the desk to take my arm. "You can't mean that. Clara, you've haunted my days, my nights. You don't know what you've done to me. You can't turn me away like this."

I was in shock. This man, so cold, so calculated, had suddenly become desperate. What was happening? Was I imagining this? Was I dreaming? I felt the warmth of his hand on my arm, and it was only too real. I didn't want to turn him away. I wanted to feel the way I'd felt that Carnival night. He was standing so close now, his lips just inches away. I could feel his breath on my face. If I looked up, I would drown in his eyes. All I needed to do was raise my head just a fraction. But as Eduardo took one step closer, the hardness of the desk pressing against me was enough to bring back reality. I didn't understand my own desire. I tried to push him away, but he wouldn't let go. His arms encircled my waist as he whispered something in Portuguese into my ear. He lifted me onto the desk, kissing my neck, and unfastening my blouse at the same time. And I didn't resist.

There was no point fighting it. I needed to make love to him again. I needed to feel that connection. Each morning I would wake, my body hot and sweaty from a night of phantom sex with my mysterious lover. The dreams had been so real, and the reality was so very dreamlike. At this point, I didn't care anymore. I just wanted to feel him inside me.

He was undoing the zipper of my jeans while I fumbled with his. I couldn't seem to get at him fast enough. I pushed all the papers aside and settled myself against the cool of the desk. He lifted his head and looked at me for a moment. I nodded, nearly holding my breath. He brought his lips against mine. I didn't want to make this personal. But when he looked at me like that I couldn't help it. I felt something. I couldn't deny it. There was something in his eyes that was so much deeper. When he kissed me, I wanted to feel all of him. I wanted to understand him, to know him. His tongue gently traced my bottom lip.

"Now," I whispered, pulling myself forward. He swiftly took off my panties and his fingers glided over me, caressing my stomach, my hips, and then entering me. He moved inside my wetness, stimulating my clit and then pressing his palm against my pelvis so that I pushed against him, desperately craving release. He continued to kiss me the whole while, his tongue encircling mine, his kiss firm and demanding. I reached down and released his penis, and, in the next moment, I felt him move on top of me. My heart pounded as his strong arms tightened around me, his body moving against mine. "Come to me now," I whispered.

He paused for a moment, looking into my eyes, and I nodded, letting him know that I was more than ready for him. I watched as he pulled out a condom and rolled it over his hard penis, my entire body tense and waiting. He looked up and met my gaze, and he smiled. I breathed in quickly as he entered me. I wanted him to go deep. And he did. Again and again. I felt myself pressing into him, my muscles contracting with each thrust. I leaned back on the desk, raising myself higher by placing my hands flat on the wood. And as I pressed against him, I let the orgasm take over. I allowed myself to feel that total abandon, that complete surrender. And I loved the look in his eyes that gave me this freedom.

He held me as he came. And I clung to him, wanting to feel all of him, never wanting to let him go. But then it was over. And the splinters in the desk and the dusty smell of old books returned. And suddenly, I didn't like being controlled by some other force, whether it was lust or love. I had no idea. But how could I possibly love a man I didn't even know? And yet I clung to him for just a moment, not wanting him to pull out, wanting to keep him inside me forever. My body was still pulsing from my climax. He kissed me gently, touching my face and stroking my hair. And he continued to hold me close, the feeling of his arms circling me making me feel so safe and secure. But we couldn't stay this way. As much as I loved the feel of him, the hard desk was pressing against my back. I pulled away, handing him a Kleenex for the condom. He stood back, giving me a half-smile while he cleaned himself.

"I guess, uh..." He didn't know what to say either. He quickly zipped up his pants. I got up off the desk. I felt shaky and nervous, my vagina still wet and throbbing, wanting him again. I put my clothes back on distractedly, refusing to meet his eyes. I couldn't even think of him as Eduardo yet. He was still Professor Soares. Whom I'd had amazing sex with. Twice. But it was so much more than that. I couldn't explain it. The strong connection I felt with him scared me. And my automatic reaction was to run.

He cupped my face gently in his hands. "Clara..."

I brushed his fingers away. "Look, I just need to find a bathroom, okay?" I started to walk away.

"Clara, what are you doing?" I heard the surprise in his voice. But what was I supposed to say?

I turned around, keeping a good distance between us. "Look, that was good. I'll admit it. But it sure as hell isn't happening again. At least not until you let me in to one of your *terreiros*."

"You had sex with me so I would accept your research?" He stared at me. And I could feel the anger. And the hurt.

"Yes, I did. How does it feel to be used?" I couldn't understand what I was doing. Why was I antagonizing him like this? What was wrong with me? We had an incredible connection. We both knew it wasn't just sex. There was some sort of amazing chemistry going on here. But I didn't like the loss of control. And I wasn't going to let it happen again.

He slammed his fist on the desk. "*Puta.*"

"What did you say?" I turned back.

"I called you a whore. That's what I did. What kind of woman are you, anyway?"

I couldn't seem to stop myself. There was something about this man that made me lose all rational thought. I walked straight back to where he stood at the desk and lifted my hand to slap him across the face. But he was too quick. He caught my wrist in a strong grip.

"Don't even think about it. I don't know who you really are. I only know that you have been my obsession since you came to Brazil. Obviously, the feeling is not mutual."

We stood there for a moment. I didn't attempt to break free from his grip, knowing that it was useless. Even in this moment of fury, the strength of his hold on my wrist ignited a certain excitement deep within me. I couldn't ignore or hide from his power. He was like a drug to me.

Abruptly, he let go. "You want more, don't you? Well, I have no intention of being used again."

I watched him leave the library, his back straight and his stance proud. But I felt his pain. How could two people who barely even knew each other ignite so much emotion? There were no explanations for anything in my life right now. But somehow, somewhere, I would find the answers.

3

I SAT AT THE KITCHEN TABLE sipping my morning tea and reading the paper as sunlight streamed through the window. I enjoyed these calm, cool mornings, before the heat of day could penetrate. I scanned the news sections, looking at the pictures and trying to decipher the headlines. Mayor Bento Velho was splashed all over the front page. Apparently, he was big news. Brazil had its first democratically elected president after over twenty years of military dictatorship. Fernando Collor de Mello had been elected in December 1989. It was February 1992, so he hadn't been president for all that long. The new mayor of Brazil, Bento Velho, was part of this new social order, this new Brazilian democracy. And he certainly managed to make an impression. Not all of it good—that was for sure. It looked like he worked really hard to create a dashing public image, despite rumours of scandal and corruption. What else was new in the political world? Still, there was something about the picture of Bento Velho that caught my eye. I couldn't describe it exactly. His chiselled features and dark hair gave him that international playboy look that probably didn't hurt his electoral results. But there was something about his eyes. He was smiling, but his eyes were blank. I shivered.

I pushed the paper aside and considered my plans for the day. I intended to return again to the library for more research. Yes, the library. My mind took me back to that evening... Eduardo, his dark eyes and hot touch, our bodies blending together. My body responded, getting wet just at the thought of him. Imagining him kissing my breasts, touching my face, while I held onto his arms, feeling the strength of his biceps flexing. The images and sensations followed me everywhere, even when I tried to focus on my work. It had been over a month since I'd seen him last. He hadn't approached me again. Nothing had changed. He remained vindictive in his condemnation of me to the various *terreiros*, and I still couldn't gain access to a single Odún ceremony. But I dreamed of him every night. Whatever force had brought us together that first Carnival night still kept us connected. Although we were apart physically, our minds were united. And it terrified me. Did Eduardo share the same dreams? If he felt the same intense connection, why didn't he approach me again? Why didn't he try to bring me closer into his world? The world of Odún. I'd pushed him away that evening in the library. There was nothing I could do to change that. And I wasn't even sure if I had actually wanted to. I was still so confused about my feelings for him. If I was his obsession, he, in turn, was my nemesis.

"You're looking thoughtful." Lisboa swept into the kitchen, her long skirt flowing behind her as she piled the bags of groceries on the counter. "Come, have some fresh mango." She gave me a bright smile, obviously hoping to pull me from my pensive mood. I'd been living in her home only a short while, but I felt like I'd known Lisboa forever. She welcomed my presence in the bright, cozy kitchen and often invited me down in the evenings to sit together on the front porch. It was great to have someone to talk to after another lonely day of research.

We sat across from each other at the table, eating the juicy mango. "Lisboa, can you tell me anything about Rio's mayor?" I pointed to the news section and the flashy pictures of Bento Velho. Lisboa seemed surprised by my question and hesitated to respond.

"Bento Velho." She said his name, rolling her tongue over it. "Yes, well..." she shrugged her shoulders. "What can one say? This city would look very different if Gonçalves had won. And he should have, you know." Lisboa said these last words almost fiercely. I could tell she was trying to mask the strength of her emotions on this topic.

"Francisco Armando Gonçalves from the Workers' party. He was the one who talked about left-wing reform and social change. Am I right?" I asked. "And Bento Velho just barely won, didn't he? By campaigning on the strength of President Fernando Collor de Mello's message about a new Brazil? He wanted to transform Rio de Janeiro into a world-class city."

Lisboa nodded. "A new Brazil indeed." She laughed. "You know your history, Clara. I guess all those days in the library have come to good use. Yes, well, the world *should* notice our beautiful city. Especially when the streets are lined with blood in the name of tourism." She was silent. I knew Lisboa had a lot more to say on the topic, and I hoped to coax it out of her. I couldn't explain why I was so interested in Rio's current mayor. I just knew that I needed to know more.

"Let us not waste our time with this. Clara, we have far more important things to discuss." Once again, Lisboa evaded my questions. But she got my attention. "I know why you look so pensive all the time."

Surprised, I looked up from the paper. "You do?" I forced myself to wait while Lisboa finished her mango, wiped her hands on a napkin, and sat back comfortably in her chair with a look of feigned resignation on her face.

"What can I do? I see you, day in, day out, always so frustrated. It's the Odún," she sighed, shaking her head. Puzzled, I waited for her to continue, because, I knew full well, Lisboa was working herself up to something. As we got to know each other better, I quickly realized Lisboa's love for grand theatrics.

"You do not know the simple secret, do you?" Her eyes held a hint of mischief.

"Secret?" What was this sweet lady up to now?

"You are in Brazil to study the Odún, no?" I nodded in agreement. "Then what are you doing? Every day I see you drowning in your papers. Papers you have plenty of in Canada. The Odún you do not. What can you even begin to learn without feeling the beat of the drums?"

I knew what point Lisboa attempted to make, but it was useless. "Lisboa, I'm not accepted by any of the *terreiros*. I have to work first to gain the knowledge and then, hopefully, their trust. It's going to take time."

Lisboa shook her head emphatically. "Dear child. I cannot take it any longer. You must face the Odún. Patience is not a virtue in this country of ours. You will never be respected or gain any trust through cowardice. The only way to acceptance is to become one with the community. You will never gain trust as an observer, because you will remain an observer forever."

What was Lisboa saying? How could I become one with Odún? I wasn't even Brazilian. "Are you suggesting I train to become a daughter of the gods?" It was a crazy suggestion. But I couldn't help noticing that Lisboa was now very calm.

"Do you think I speak from ignorance? Child, I hear the words. I am not deaf. Where do you think I go every Thursday night?" As comprehension dawned, I couldn't imagine why I hadn't seen it sooner. Lisboa herself was a daughter of the gods! And all this time I'd been living directly in her presence. But why had she kept it a secret and watched me suffer in silence for weeks?

Lisboa could see the questions in my eyes. She reached a hand out to me across the table. "It is not easy for me, either. Eduardo is a powerful *ogun*. There is a long-standing relationship there. One I am hesitant to break. But, dear girl, if I were to initiate you as one of the *terreiro*, how could he refuse? Odún will accept all of its followers with open arms. We deny no one."

I couldn't believe what I was hearing. My Lisboa, the kind, elderly woman whose room I rented; Lisboa was a *mãe de santo*, an Odún high priestess. I almost laughed at the irony.

And the incredible good fortune. But then again, I had been drawn to this house ever since I first read the newspaper ad for accommodation, so maybe it was time I started accepting forces in the universe beyond mere coincidence. I realized what it took for Lisboa to approach me like this, to reveal the authority of her position.

I also realized the enormity of what she offered. To accept and train an international student—a woman whose only objective was to study the religion and bring the knowledge home with her—to train her to be a daughter of the gods—it was almost an atrocity. Could she, a high priestess, allow one who did not have the calling to enter the confines of the Odún world? Only certain people could train to be daughters of the gods. The gods called to them in various ways, through dreams, through occurrences in their lives. Many of those called were believed by society to suffer from mental instabilities. They were not mentally unstable. They needed the power of the gods; they needed the unification with that other part of themselves to quiet the restlessness, the nightmares, and the callings from within the deep recesses of their minds. They were often people whose past lives still haunted them, ghosts of their former selves who refused to let go. Unfinished business in a past life or sudden, violent, or unjustified death—any one of these reasons could cause a person's inner soul to be restless and to require unification with her reigning Orixa.

And then it hit me. I *had* been called. I felt the tears come to my eyes as I continued to stare at Lisboa.

I could tell that Lisboa had waited for this moment. She had probably been watching and waiting since the day we met. She had probably felt the same connection I did, but she was waiting to see if her instincts proved correct. "Clara, I see your light on every night. I see the haunted look in your eyes. I felt the aura of your presence the moment our hands first touched. You must find your inner soul, that deeper part of yourself that only you can recognize. I do not understand how or why the gods have called upon a young, Canadian girl, but they have, and it is not up to me to question. You are here in Brazil for far more than you realize. You cannot fool yourself by believing that you are here to only study the Odún. It is your calling, child, and you must obey it, or it will drive you insane."

Her eyes held so much wisdom. I felt as though she could peer deep into my own soul and see all the fears I kept hidden so close. The fear of the demons within my mind. The silent fear of insanity I had so desperately held at bay until now. The fear of being possessed by some force that was not my own. It suddenly made sense. If I continued to fight it, there would be no release. Allowing the tears to fall, I nodded. It was okay to cry this time. I wasn't going to hate myself for it. I'd been struggling for so long. All those dreams, the nightmares—they were all part of it. And what about Eduardo? How did he fit into this? Could I do this? Did I really believe it? And did I even have the strength? Looking at Lisboa, I realized I had no other choice. Ever since I'd started studying the Odún, I'd been looking for answers. And, now, finally, here was someone who was willing to give them to me. "Yes, I would be honoured to train with you to become a daughter of the gods."

We looked at each other in silent understanding. I felt the first real peace I'd experienced in years. I was soon to be released from the captivity of my own mind.

I SMELLED THE INCENSE from far away, its cloying aroma filling the air and adding an edge of excitement. The stars glittered in the night sky, the glow of a nearly full moon lighting the way along the rocky path. I followed behind Lisboa, no longer my friend Lisboa, but the *mãe de santo* now. During the ceremony, I knew Lisboa would transform into another identity, possessed by the great goddess Yemanja. I could hardly wait to witness the transformation. I was a little scared, but the excitement was too overpowering for the fear to take control. At last, I was going to witness an Odún ceremony. Lisboa told me that before she could even begin her teachings, I had to know the world I was about to enter. I had to experience the drums and the dancing, the orgy of pleasure and pain, and the sacrifices to the gods. I had to witness it before I could make a coherent choice.

I saw the glow of the fires in the distance as we approached the ceremony site. Mãe Lisboa whispered in my ear that this was a special ceremony. They were welcoming new initiates into the Odún circle. They held the ceremony way up in the hills, within the protective covering of the lush forest, where the gods could hear them all the more clearly. The forest was the home of the gods, and it was there that their voices were the most powerful. Lisboa had established her *terreiro* in the secrecy of these hills. She'd explained to me how her one-room *terreiro* built of corrugated tin had turned into a small community over the years. As she welcomed increasing numbers into her *terreiro*, the need for space to house the initiates meant constantly adding rooms to the main hall and building a circle of small wooden homes around the initiation centre. They used whatever materials they could find. Eduardo had helped provide the funding. Many of the people who lived in the *terreiro* community had nowhere else to go. It wasn't much, but at least they had a roof over their heads. The initiation hall had an enormous kitchen where many of the women came to cook for their families. There was a garden out back and a pen for chickens and goats. They were a self-sufficient community, growing their own food. It was here that the daughters of the gods lived.

I could hear the drums. The drums, which I had always found so intoxicating. It had been the sound of the drums that had first brought me to Odún. I heard their exotic and compelling rhythm, and it drew me forward. I saw the shadowy figures moving against the firelight, and I felt a thrill of anticipation. Lisboa mistook the look in my eyes for fear, and she took my hand in support. In the glow of the flames, I could see the dark shapes of the surrounding huts and then the large clearing in front of the initiation hall where the bonfire blazed.

"Follow me and I will introduce you to my world." The shadowy figures moved aside to give us room to pass. I felt the warmth of perspiring bodies pressed close together, their heavy breathing sounding in my ear. I inhaled the scent of fresh pine mixed with the incense, sweat, and smoke fire. I looked into the whites of their eyes and realized that they were already in a different place—their vacant stares, their open mouths, their hands reaching out for me, touching my long dark hair and staring into my blue eyes. They spoke to me in a language I didn't understand. Nagô, I supposed, the ancient language of the Yoruba slaves from Africa who were torn from their homes and brought to Brazil in chains, only to express their defiance in the form of this religion. It had been a struggle of resistance, and their power washed over me, their strong voices calling and rising in unison, creating a haunting and mystical chant to match the insistent beat of the drums.

I shrank away from it all. I was overwhelmed, and my own fear came forth with shocking clarity. Was this too much for me? I'd been waiting so long to experience this. What, exactly, was I so afraid of? Lisboa pulled me forward, her tight grasp on my hand keeping me from caving in. I had to be strong. I hadn't come all this way to turn back now. I waited for the demons in my mind to take possession, but, for the moment at least, they allowed me to rest.

As the crowd parted, I found myself in the centre of the circle of faces, with the heat of the bonfire touching my skin. Lisboa let go of my hand and told me to wait by the side. In fascination, I watched as a tall, broad-shouldered man appeared out of the shadows. His dark skin was black with soot from the fire, and his hands were covered in blood, but there was no mistaking the intense glow of his dark eyes. I felt a shock of recognition, excitement, fear, happiness.... All of those emotions I'd managed to ignore came rushing back. I felt so much for this man. Just seeing him again filled me with longing. I didn't understand what I was feeling. I just knew that I needed to be here. To be with Eduardo. There he stood, one hand holding a live creature up to the heavens while the fire glinted off the shiny surface of the knife he held in his other hand. His eyes were riveted on the knife, just before he raised it and, in one swift motion, sliced the head off the chicken.

I heard my cry before I could stop it. I was standing so close. As the chicken's blood spurted everywhere, I felt a warm sensation drip down my cheek. I was transfixed by the scene, too shocked to even wipe the blood off my face. The chicken's head lay lifeless on the ground while its body writhed convulsively in Eduardo's grasp. His skin gleamed with the blood he smeared on his chest. He was wearing only black shorts, and I could see the strong muscles of his legs and the curve of his stomach meeting the chiselled muscles of his smooth chest. I remembered those strong muscles holding me tight while his lips trailed kisses over my body.

I willed him to look my way. As if he sensed my presence, those intense eyes of his finally met mine. Once again, our gazes were fixed. I expected to see surprise or anger that I was standing there witnessing an Odún ceremony, but what I saw held me transfixed. He stared at me with open desire. If he could, I thought, he would have taken me right then and there, and fucked me hard. The thought made me crazy. His eyes, just moments before ignited by the adrenaline rush of the sacrifice, were now lit with a deep need. It was as if we were the only two people in the world. I moistened my lips and began a slow, seductive dance to the drum rhythms. I was losing myself again—to the music, the drums, Eduardo's eyes watching my every move. It was sensuous and heady to feel my body move like that again. To feel alive, desirable. It felt good. I lost myself within his penetrating gaze. His eyes were undressing me slowly, moving languidly over my body until I felt completely naked. And I ran my eyes over his entire body too, down to his black shorts where his hard-on was visible. I felt my breath quicken as I imagined pulling his shorts down and putting his huge cock in my mouth, sucking and licking the entire length of him while his fingers gently stroked my clit, making me soaking wet with desire. I imagined him striding over, taking my hand, and pulling me into the forest, his grip firm and unrelenting. He would kiss my neck and put my arms against a tree, then lift my skirt and fuck me from behind. It would be fast and furious and merciless. I could feel him inside me, pushing his cock so deep with each thrust while I moaned in ecstasy. I would reach back and grab his hands while he pushed deeper. He would caress my ass, arched against him, and then he would give me a good hard spank while his cock pulsed inside me. The sting of his spanking would intensify my pleasure as a deep orgasm would take over my whole body, making me collapse into his arms as he came at the same time.

My vision was so real, it was almost as if he could read my mind. As if it had actually happened. I knew he felt the same. Whatever connection pulled us together, I knew in that moment that Eduardo felt it too. I knew by the way he looked at me. In just a few short moments we made love to each other across the firelight. The impact of our bond was so strong that we didn't even have to physically touch.

The moment was broken, though, as Mãe Lisboa calmly approached Eduardo, blessing the chicken and allowing drops of its blood to flow into a rusty container. Meanwhile, the drumbeats had never lost their rhythm. And the dancers, who had stopped to observe the sacrifice, continued their chaotic movements, rushing forward to smear themselves with the blood. Blood was life and power. Having studied the rituals of Odún for my thesis, I knew the sacrifice was meant for the new initiates. In a private pre-initiation ceremony, they needed to have their heads anointed with blood to allow their personal spirits to enter. Although I'd read all the literature on these initiation ceremonies, it was a very different thing to witness.

Eduardo Soares, as the *ogun,* was given the responsibility and honour of carrying out the sacrifice, while the *mãe de santo* collected the blessed blood to bring it to the initiates who waited inside. I stood on the edge of the circle now, the pushing of hot, sweaty bodies having moved me into the shadows. Lisboa turned around, her face, hands and white dress now streaked with the same blood that marked my cheek. She indicated for me to follow. I didn't want to tear my eyes away from Eduardo, but I had no choice. My body was still shaking from the force of my own desire.

Lisboa stopped in front of the entranceway to the hall where the initiation was to take place. The hall was a simple corrugated tin structure with no doors or windows. Two wooden posts were erected in order to create the illusion of a grand entranceway. Beyond the main hall, the building stretched out in a maze of inner rooms and corridors. I saw Lisboa lay dust on the four corners of the entrance and make the sign of the cross. "It is to bless Exu, the god of the crossroads. Without his blessing, we cannot begin. You know of Exu?"

I nodded. *Exu.* I'd read about Exu, the trickster god of the Odún pantheon. The missionaries had called the Yoruba god the devil. But I wanted Lisboa to continue. Hearing the words from a practitioner was very different from the textbook versions I'd read. "Please, tell me more."

"Then you know that if you are not careful to appease and offer the appropriate sacrifices to Exu, you could leave yourself defenseless against enemies who may use Exu's power for themselves. Many a life has been destroyed by this." Lisboa's eyes were dark as she gave me a direct look. Despite the heat, I shivered in response. "But Exu is not the devil, despite what you may have read." Lisboa's voice was caustic. "There is no true evil in the Odún pantheon. Evil comes from within, from a human source." Lisboa tapped her chest for emphasis. "But if a human with bad intentions gets Exu to do her bidding, well, then…" Lisboa's voice trailed off. I understood.

I knew that Odún was a blending of Yoruba, Fon and Bantu beliefs with Catholicism. During the time of slavery, the slaves were prohibited from practicing their own religious beliefs and adopted the saints of Catholicism as cover for the many goddesses and gods of the Yoruba pantheon. Over time, the gods and goddesses and the Catholic saints became identified with each other and equally incorporated into what is understood today as Odún. But Catholic ideas about heaven and hell, good and evil, cannot be so easily translated into the Yoruba belief system. Nothing can ever transpose so simply. The complexity of Odún could not be explained as a direct association between Exu and the devil, Olorum and God, or Oxala and Christ. I realized the layers of complexity, and I wanted to know more, to witness the intermingling of belief systems and rituals in practice. I observed the sacrifices placed in the entranceway, realizing the sacrifices were there to appease Exu so he wouldn't enter the hall to disrupt the ceremony and attempt to possess one of the initiates.

We stepped over one of the crosses lying at the four corners of the entranceway and entered the incense-filled hall. The smoke was so thick that I could barely see or breathe at first, intoxicated by the heady, sensual muskiness of sandalwood. Lisboa directed me to a simple wooden chair at the side of the hall and introduced me to an elderly woman. The woman's back was hunched over with pain, her face etched with the wrinkles of the years she had passed through.

"Mãe Aninha, may I introduce you to Clara. She is to become my initiate." The elderly woman slowly raised her eyes. I was surprised by the intensity of her gaze despite the frailty of her outer appearance. She didn't look upon me kindly.

"Who is she to be your initiate, Mãe Lisboa? You cannot initiate an Exu. It will bring the anger of the gods upon us all."

I was surprised and frightened by the woman's tenacity. Why had she referred to me as an Exu? Was it only to suggest that, as a foreigner, I represented evil and a threat to the security of the *terreiro?* She raised an accusing finger at me as she leaned her craggy face forward, staring directly into my eyes. And then she whispered something in Nagô. I felt my skin crawl.

"Mãe Aninha, although I respect your wisdom, you would be wise to remember that I am the *mãe de santo* of this *terreiro*, and, if you disapprove of my wishes, realize that you are only here at my invitation." Shaking her head with disapproval, Mãe Aninha dropped her gaze and returned to her defeated position, slumped in the chair.

"Mãe Aninha is an observer. The gods have allowed her to rest in her old age. She was once the great *mãe de santo* of her own *terreiro*. I let her come here so she can still remain connected with the Odún world. But she is very set in her ways and often more trouble than she is worth." Mãe Lisboa sent an affectionate but slightly exasperated look at her friend. "Still, I never underestimate her wisdom." She gestured toward a chair in the corner, and added, "You will sit here for tonight as an observer."

With these words, I was left to sit near the still grumbling Mãe Aninha. I watched Lisboa stride across the floor, calling out a variety of commands in Nagô to her fellow Odún members. They responded by reorganizing the wooden chairs, pushing them to the side of the hall, and gathering their things together. I wasn't sure what Lisboa meant when she said she never underestimated Mãe Aninha's wisdom. Was she hesitating about initiating me? I felt the tense anticipation in the air as everyone waited. The drumming outside had stopped, and the silence was suddenly deafening. I could hear only the loud, rasping sound of people breathing and the scraping of chairs across the hard surface of the floor.

In the next instant, I saw the drummers enter the hall, giving their blessing to Exu. "Only men can be drummers, and only women can be possessed by the gods." I turned at the sound of Lisboa's deep voice behind me. She'd circled the floor and returned to me. She gave me a small smile. "The teaching process must begin, no?" she said, waving her arm toward the large room before us. "This is your textbook now, Clara."

I smiled in response. Lisboa was absolutely correct. I may have spent years reading and researching Odún, but this was my first real experience of it. "Tell me everything, Mãe Lisboa," I said.

Lisboa grabbed a chair and sat beside me. "I have only a moment, but I will at least explain a little of what is happening here. You know, a lot of people, academics in particular—" she shot me a sideways glance "—might see this as a power play."

I tried to follow Lisboa's thought process. "The fact that only the men can drum, you mean?" I asked, remembering reading literature on the fact that, while Odún was a predominantly female-dominated religion, it was still the men who controlled the women's possession through the drum rhythms and therefore ultimately held the power. I was definitely interested in hearing Lisboa's perspective since that interpretation never felt accurate to me.

"Ah-ha. I see you have read the books, no? Well, has it not been all male academics that have studied the Odún? What do they know?" She threw her hands up in the air and sighed.

"Well, there have been a few female academics..." I offered, but Lisboa was on a roll.

"Now, anyone who really understands Odún knows that it is the religion of women. The men may pound the drums, but it is the women who hold their destinies in the palm of their hands. It is through them that the gods speak, and the gods do not come from the drums, but from the inner recesses of the women's minds. Odún has always given power to women, did you know?"

Mãe Lisboa turned to look directly at me. "It is very important you understand this, despite whatever you may have read. It is only women who can be trained to be *filhas*, daughters of the gods. Possession is not a sign of weakness, but a sign of strength. And it is only women who are strong enough to withstand possession and allow their minds to feel release."

I nodded in response. Lisboa's perspective was so unlike the academic studies I'd researched in which possession was seen as weakness because the person who was possessed was perceived as having lost control of their own mind. But in the Odún pantheon, this was considered a strength. I was fascinated. It completely made sense. I had researched possession for many years, but I was always unsatisfied with the answers I found. Here, finally, there was something I could grasp on to. The source of strength for the women of Odún existed in their ability to find release in a world where they were constantly monitored and under pressure. There was strength in being able to let go sometimes and trust in the energy of the universe.

Lisboa's voice rose above the increasing pounding of the drums. "Now, you know Odún comes from the African Yoruba religion, yes?" I nodded. "And in Africa it is the *babalao* who holds the power. A man." Again, I nodded. Lisboa smiled. "Well, here in Brazil, each house of worship, each *terreiro,* is led by a woman, a high priestess. The *mãe de santo.* In this case, me." Lisboa nodded her head in the affirmative.

"Of course," I said, noticing that Lisboa's attention had been diverted. She was now looking toward the entrance, and I followed her gaze. *Eduardo.* I watched as he walked proudly behind the drummers. I felt my stomach tighten.

Lisboa pointed toward Eduardo. "Now every *terreiro* has its patron, the *ogun.* The one who provides financial and political support," she sighed. "And that is always a man." Lisboa was silent for a moment as we both watched the drumming procession. "He likes to think he holds the power but he does not. Money, politics ... ha! We women, we are the ones with the power of the gods, and nothing can be stronger than that." She winked at me. "And we control the money and politics too. I have over one thousand members of my *terreiro.* That's over one thousand votes. And do you think at election time my members will listen to the *ogun*? No. They will listen to the *mãe de santo*. Well," she raised both hands into the air and stood up, "enough for now, no?" And, with that, she lifted her skirt and swiftly headed off.

I watched her walk away and then turned my eyes almost involuntarily back to Eduardo. I watched him as he took his place at the centre of the hall, surrounded by the drummers. I wanted him to look at me again. I needed to feel his presence. He did turn his head in my direction, but he didn't see me; or maybe he chose not to see me. His eyes were glazed over. Maybe when men were possessed they didn't dance or roll their eyes backwards only because they weren't trained to control the outward signs of possession. They were affected by the drums just as much as the women, but they were trapped by it.

I knew that beyond the ceremonial sacrifice, an *ogun*'s function at ceremonies was limited. Eduardo's main purpose tonight was to observe and allow his presumed authoritative presence to be noted. I realized that I resented him. And it surprised me. Despite whatever connection we had, he had refused to allow me entrance into the Odún world. If it hadn't been for Lisboa, I wouldn't be attending this ceremony. I resented the fact that despite the power of the *terreiro* falling within Mãe Lisboa's hands, the monetary power remained in the control of a man, namely Eduardo Soares. His power, rather than supernatural, was completely within the unfortunate realm of reality and political economics.

I was so at war with my unpredictable emotions that I wasn't as aware as I should have been of my surroundings. Trying to pull myself together and ignore Eduardo's presence, I tore my eyes away from him and focused on the side entrance off the main hall. I could see Mãe Lisboa with the new initiates. From all my reading, I knew that this was the moment when each initiate would go through the divination process and learn about her Orixa—her personal god, the one who possesses her. The tension and heat in the room was becoming almost unbearable. No one moved or spoke. The drummers sat in rigid silence. Nothing could begin until the initiates entered, ready to share the final stages of their long initiation process in a public ceremony. This ceremony, with the entire *terreiro* present, marked the public acceptance of the initiates into their new roles as daughters of the gods.

My body shook as the drummers suddenly began their slow drumbeats. I watched the new initiates enter the main hallway, their heads shaven and painted white, their eyes black pools of fear and uncertainty. They began with a practiced samba dance to fill the centre of the hall. They were dressed in a variety of colours to match the preferred style and colours of the Orixa with whom they were intimately connected. Although the drumbeats were measured at first, they gradually increased in tempo, allowing the initiates time to adapt. They had all been possessed before by their Orixa in various forms, but this was the first time they would actively call upon the gods to possess them. They were no longer vulnerable. They were in control now, dictating when and where the gods could emerge. They were no longer open vessels of reception that the gods could use and abuse at will. The intense initiation process would have taught them about the secret powers of Odún and the ways to control their possession.

I watched with concern as one girl fell to the ground, her body writhing as if in epileptic convulsion. It was too soon. The drums had not yet commanded the arrival of the gods. A group of women from the *terreiro* ran to the girl and monitored her seizure, making sure she didn't hit her head or injure herself in any other way. When the convulsive movements ceased, the poor girl lay on the floor motionless. I felt like screaming for them to stop. Couldn't anyone see that the girl needed medical attention? But the drums continued on, only becoming more varied and intense. The women picked the young girl off the floor and carried her out of the hall to the side room, where I saw them attempt to revive her with water.

Her eyes opened again as she sputtered the water from her mouth. I sighed with relief. The girl had not been ready for the initiation ceremony and would require further training. A mistake not often made.

My attention returned again to the dancers in the centre of the hall. Other members of the *terreiro* had gradually joined them; one by one they were moved by the gods to begin their swaying, beautiful motions. Although the young girls were radiant in their new outfits—their shaved heads now bound by colourful scarves, their bright skirts swishing with every movement—I was mesmerized by the lyrical dancing of the elderly *terreiro* members. Their bodies, which had appeared aged and weak just moments before, were now filled with energy and effortless grace. They moved with a dexterity that defied age. Even Mãe Aninha. Although her legs no longer allowed her to walk, her eyes and her body swayed with such passion that she was transformed into a young woman again, in spirit if not in form.

I had to prevent myself from getting too caught up in the dancing. I had to block out the drum rhythms and the mesmerizing pull of the dancing. If I didn't, I was afraid I would find myself thrown into convulsive fits as the young girl had been. I couldn't allow my spirit to emerge just yet, even though I knew it had been struggling for months to do just that. The presence in the mirror, the feeling of being watched in my Toronto apartment, the force, or whatever it was that had pulled me towards Eduardo—it was all connected to this, to the Odún, and to the Orixa that I now knew was lodged within the recesses of my mind. It seemed hard to believe. But I'd felt it since the day I first heard the drums of Odún. Was this the answer? I'd been fighting it for so long. Trying to gain control of my life and deny the intrusive force that had taken over. As I looked around, I realized I needed to find new answers. And I had to open my rational mind to the possibility of alternate explanations.

The dancing became increasingly more frenzied. I watched as the initiates moved from their graceful, elaborate samba rhythm to uncoordinated and frenetic movements. The alteration was clearly visible. Their arms flayed out and their bodies began to shake. Perspiration dripped from their faces as their eyes flew up to the heavens and were replaced by blank, white sockets. It was terrifying and mesmerizing at the same time.

I couldn't stop myself from looking at Eduardo once more, just to see his reaction. His eyes were no longer riveted on the convulsive movements of the dancers, but on me. I met his stare for one brief moment and quickly slid my eyes away. I couldn't stand it. I was having a hard enough time remaining in my seat with the drum rhythms pulsing through my veins, making my heart race erratically. I needed to release the energy within me. I shook my head and covered my ears with my hands. I could feel the vibration of the drums in the floorboards beneath my feet, the stomping of the dancers making the weak boards reverberate. I felt my body sway and my hands reach out to pick up the rhythm. My eyes closed, but I could still see the swirling colour. I needed to feel the dance. But before I could rise and join the group of bodies in the middle of the floor, I felt firm hands reach out to grab my outstretched ones. I opened my eyes and stared at Eduardo, not really surprised to see him.

"If you give in to the drums now, you will be lost forever." His deep voice, the words now spoken roughly, shook me back to reality. I felt such a struggle. I wanted to be one with the dancers. I wanted to allow myself the ecstasy of possession, to allow myself the freedom. But Eduardo wouldn't allow it. He grabbed my arm and dragged me forcibly out of the hall. We stood just beyond the entranceway, our breath coming in quick gasps, my eyes still hazy and Eduardo's dark with unconcealed anger. He shook me hard, and I felt defenseless in his grasp. I didn't even try to fight. I was completely drained. Whatever incredible burst of energy that had compelled me in the hall, with the drums and the heat and the incense, had evaporated in the rush of humid air that greeted us as we left the smoke-filled room. My lungs breathed in the fresh air, but my eyes could find no place to rest. Finally, inevitably, they rested upon Eduardo.

"You took me away from there. I was so close!" I screamed, pounding my fists against his chest. He allowed me my anger for a moment before clasping my hands and holding them behind my back while his body pressed me against the corrugated tin siding.

"Do you know what you came close to? Do you? You have no idea what the Odún is about, and yet you come here, hoping to be possessed by the gods. They are not your gods. Do you hear me? A person can be driven insane by those drums if they allow it and don't understand it. That's exactly what would have happened to you if I didn't stop it."

His words shocked me into silence. I knew he was right. Damn it, I wasn't going to cry now. I couldn't stop it. I felt hot tears stream down my face, mixing with the dried up blood. I didn't understand anything anymore.

"Eduardo, I don't know what's going on." I looked up at him. I must have been a mess. And I saw the anger drain out of his body in that instant. It was replaced with something else, a look of concern, of tenderness. I didn't think those dark eyes of his could ever express such an emotion. He took my hands and brought them to his lips, kissing them softly.

"Ah, Clara. Don't make this so difficult on yourself."

I held on to his hands. I needed his support. "Sit with me?" I asked. He nodded, and together we sank onto the soft earth, leaning our backs against the cool tin siding. He held me for a moment. I couldn't believe this was the same man whom I'd felt such anger towards. How was it possible? How could he be so gentle now? "You know, ever since I first heard those drums, they've called to me." Eduardo didn't say anything. I was looking into the forest now, my eyes searching the darkness for answers to the questions I didn't know how to ask.

"You know so much more about this than I do. How did you know? That first time?"

Eduardo touched my face softly. "You know, this is the first time we've ever really talked."

I laughed, the sound hollow and somehow misplaced. "It's crazy, isn't it? I mean, what are we doing? I don't even know you, but..." I turned just a fraction, and I could feel Eduardo's breath on my cheek. The way this man made me feel was incredible. I could make love to him again right here. The emotional part was all screwed up, but there could be no denying the physical chemistry and the inexplicable bond that went beyond all reason.

"I feel it, too, Clara." We sat listening to the sounds of the night for a moment. Beyond the tiny scope of light from the hall, darkness surrounded us. It was an inky kind of blackness. The kind of blackness in which shadows don't exist. But for some reason, I wasn't afraid.

Eduardo leaned his head back, relaxing against the tin siding of the initiation hall. He kept his arm firmly around my shoulders. "I think I always knew. I wanted to understand. That is why, of course, I went into academia. But ever since I was a young boy, I felt things differently." I wanted Eduardo to continue, but he didn't.

"I'd never felt anything like this until I started studying Odún." I looked at Eduardo. "I had a perfectly ordinary suburban Canadian childhood. I'd never heard of Afro-Brazilian gods. I only knew about Jesus and the Catholic saints, and between Communion and Confession, I didn't think there was anything else to believe in."

Eduardo laughed. "An ordinary suburban Canadian childhood. Hmm. And how would one define such a thing?"

"Oh, I don't know, minivan, stay-at-home mom, dad in the oil business, house with a big, green front lawn, perfect neighbours. I grew up in Calgary. That's how most people live there." I shrugged my shoulders. "Like I said, nothing remarkable. In fact, my life was pretty boring until I came here for the first time."

"You'd been to Brazil before?"

"Yes. When I was twenty-one. It was the first time I heard the drums. It's the reason I changed my major to Anthropology. So I could study Odún."

Eduardo nodded. "So our reasons for entering academia were not that different."

"No." I smiled. "In fact, it sounds like they were similar."

Eduardo took my hand and traced his finger gently along the lines. "Clara, I don't understand why you have come into my life. But I cannot deny what I am feeling." His eyes met mine. I felt the power between us. The surge of energy and magnetism. But then I saw something else. The fear. "Clara…" Eduardo hesitated and looked away. "I might start to really care for you."

I nodded, urging Eduardo to look at me again. "And what would be so wrong with that?" I whispered, touching his face and feeling the day-old stubble.

Eduardo shook his head and stood up. I felt the coldness the moment his hand left mine. "I better get back in. They're going to miss me. Clara, why don't you go out back and wait for Lisboa there. Don't come in to the ceremony anymore."

I nodded, standing up as well. He seemed distant suddenly. Almost perfunctory.

"Eduardo?" I wanted to reach out, to know what he was thinking.

But he didn't turn around. He just said in a quiet voice. "Clara, for your own good, you have to stay away from me. You have to stay away from Odún and return home where you belong."

I stood there in stunned silence. How could he say that now? After admitting what he felt for me? "What?" I couldn't think of a better response. "Eduardo, I thought…"

He turned around for one brief moment and met my eyes. I

was shocked by the pain I saw there. "Clara, there is so much you don't understand. I don't want you to get caught up in all of it. It's just too dangerous."

"All of what? What are you talking about?" I knew it was pointless. He was already striding away. I watched his retreating figure as he entered the hall and slammed the door. I felt as if he'd slammed it in my face. I didn't understand Eduardo. And I didn't understand myself. We'd had an incredible moment in which I'd felt closer to him than almost anyone in my entire life. And he'd taken that moment and thrown it back in my face. After the shock wore off, I started to feel angry. And the anger felt good. It sure as hell felt better than pathetic sadness. I would hold on to that anger, and it would carry me forward. Because damn it, this fight wasn't over yet.

4

AFTER THE FATEFUL NIGHT of the Odún initiation ceremony, I didn't see Eduardo for some time. My life had suddenly become consumed by the initiation process, leaving time for little else. At first I feared for the security of Lisboa's *terreiro*. I wasn't sure it could survive without Eduardo's financial and political leverage, but Lisboa only laughed at my concerns. "He will not dare to discontinue his support. That man. He is all talk and little action. Besides, we go way back." She winked at me.

I decided not to ask what Lisboa meant by that, although I couldn't help wondering what, exactly, the relationship was between Lisboa and Eduardo. She certainly wasn't afraid of him, but there was an aura of respect there. Even Lisboa couldn't deny his powerful influence. Occasionally, I caught her discussing the need for my initiation with her fellow colleagues in fervent tones, who were clearly not in favour of this. They didn't even attempt to hide their hostility for the *estrangeira*.

I tried not to think about Eduardo. If I allowed myself to remember the depth of emotion I'd seen in his eyes, I would lose myself. Why he continued to push me away was a mystery to me. It was obvious that I wasn't going to leave Brazil, despite his best efforts. Why couldn't he accept that? Why didn't he acknowledge the bond we shared? I couldn't control his actions. I could only continue to do what I'd come to Brazil for. And that was to understand the Odún.

A few days passed after the ceremony before Lisboa was willing to discuss it. I waited patiently for her to decide the moment. We were sitting at the kitchen table, with the heat of day just beginning to wane and the warm evening breeze drifting through the open windows. Lisboa and I shared our usual evening tea.

I'd spent the day searching music stores for Afro-Brazilian chants and samba music. In town, I'd managed to find a bunch of used records in all states of disrepair, yet priceless in their musical worth. Collections of Villa-Lobos, Antônio Carlos Jobim with his famous "The Girl from Ipanema," recordings from the legendary João Gilberto, carnival recordings, samba rhythms, and, best of all, an old academic recording of an Odún initiation ceremony.

I'd returned home and enthusiastically borrowed Lisboa's scratchy record player to listen to the records. Both Lisboa and I sat in amicable silence for the moment, enjoying the haunting, lilting strains that emerged from the straining megaphone in the living room. This music was more ethereal than demanding, unlike the Carnival music, which forced itself upon your soul like a raging siren. It was lyrical and magical, and it seemed to blend with the setting sun casting golden shadows on the fading floral curtains and the singsong of birds in the twilight.

"It's time," Lisboa said suddenly. Broken from my moment of peace, my heart started to pound erratically. Time for what? I sat while Lisboa went to fetch something. Having studied a bit more about the Odún initiation process, I couldn't help wondering what this meant. Time for Lisboa to determine my level of strength, level of suggestibility, level of endurance? I'd never been to an Odún consultation, although I knew this was Lisboa's main purpose in the *terreiro*. Mãe Lisboa was like a great mother to all the members of the *terreiro*, curing them of their woes and easing life's problems. In a world as transient and often cruel as Brazil, such a mediator was much needed, especially when many children were often separated from their birth mothers out of necessity. People would come to her and pay various sums for a consultation with the cowrie shells. A fee was required to be initiated into Odún. Lisboa told me she used a sliding scale. For those who couldn't afford it, she often didn't charge anything at all. Particularly for the poverty-stricken, abused women or homeless children she often took in. But for those who could afford it, she charged an exorbitant sum. It was a great source of pride for a family to say that one of their own was a *filha*, a "daughter of the gods." I knew Lisboa used the money to house the initiates. It wasn't cheap maintaining a small community, even with Eduardo's financial support.

I wasn't surprised when Lisboa returned with her head wrapped in a white kerchief, symbolizing the power of her Orixa, Yemanja. Her transformation from my friend Lisboa to the great and powerful *mãe de santo* guided by Yemanja was clearly visible. She sat at the table, her back erect, her face expressionless, her normally warm eyes glazed over. Her hands held the cowrie shells, which she threw with silent force onto the table. I shuddered slightly, frightened and exhilarated by the presence of this force, so much greater than myself, witnessed across an old, wooden kitchen table. The normality of my surroundings and the abnormality of my situation felt incongruous. At the Odún ceremony—where the drums beat fiercely and the wilderness enclosed us all in its tight, protective, and yet dangerous cocoon—I didn't feel as afraid as I did now. Now, witnessing the transformation of my friend in her very own kitchen terrified me.

The sixteen cowrie shells laid across the table formed a variety of patterns, which sent a message related to the Odún cosmology. I listened as Mãe Lisboa called in Nagô to the gods of the pantheon, beginning as always by requesting the permission of Exu. She spoke to them in prayer and seemed to wait for their response. I sat in stiff silence. When Mãe Lisboa finally addressed me directly in English, I realized that she was no longer Mãe Lisboa. I was now speaking with Yemanja, the great goddess of all the deities who was tied to the Catholic Mother Mary. Strong and yet variable like the ocean, she could heal or harm at her own whim.

A part of my consciousness couldn't accept that I was in the presence of a god. Although I had grown up Catholic, any vestiges of structured religious belief had evaporated over the past eight years. But I did believe in energy sources. And in the possibility of something spiritual existing beyond the capability of human comprehension. And the more I'd read about the Odún, the more this possibility had started to become plausible. I didn't doubt that Lisboa was possessed. But was it a possession that her mind created? Was it, perhaps, physiological? Psychological? Or was there really an external force? Considering the problems I'd experienced myself, I could only hope the answers existed within the strange and complex Odún belief system. I thought back to the initiation night. It had been far too real. Despite logic or reason, I knew that the only answer was to believe in the Odún gods. I had no other choice. The alternative was to accept my own madness.

"You are very troubled. You are trying too hard to rationalize." She smiled, but it wasn't Lisboa's open grin. It was a thin, watery smile, not reaching the eyes. I looked into those eyes. Stagnant pools of brown. Where had Lisboa gone? So vibrant and full of spontaneity, her eyes bright and curious and full of life's wonder. The woman who spoke to me now was ancient. Her eyes revealed no life, nor did they reveal death. They revealed absolutely nothing. How do the eyes of a god appear to humanity? Do the gods have eyes, or do they watch us with their minds, penetrating our consciousness yet acquiring no physical form themselves? It made sense that the gods should use human beings as receptacles for their messages to earth. As spiritual energy, how else could they speak but through a form we would recognize?

"Yes, I do try to rationalize," I said, my voice was somehow foreign to my ears. Compared to the dark and powerful strength of Yemanja's voice, mine sounded meek and frightened. Yemanja laughed, a whimsical sound, somehow discordant with her features. But according to the Odún books, Yemanja could change like the ocean breeze, and you had to be careful of her fierce mood swings.

"You are chosen by the gods for a reason. There is disharmony..." She paused in concentration. In surprise, I saw tears slide down her cheeks, and her hazy eyes cleared with the saltwater. Yemanja was gone. Lisboa looked at me, her expression cautious and even a little scared.

"There is a great power within you. Some kind of war waging inside the recesses of your subconscious, which must be allowed to reveal itself."

I nodded, hoping for understanding, solutions. Maybe my dilemma was my own agnostic attitude. Maybe all I needed to do was accept the existence of the gods in order to be unified with my inner self.

Lisboa shook her head and took my hands in her own. "My dear Clara. I have done many consultations for new initiates. You know that the purpose is to divine your reigning Orixa. The belief being that once you unify with your Orixa, you will feel peace. I feel the presence of your Orixa, but I feel something else as well. Something I have never felt before. It is an energy field within you, and it fights to escape. Yemanja, you know, helps me with my divinations. But she has abandoned me. She will not tell me what this energy is about." I shook my head. I didn't understand. What was Lisboa trying to tell me? Everything was suddenly too confusing.

"We will start tomorrow with the lessons. You need to learn the rituals and practices. You need to understand the Odún. But tonight we will begin by appeasing Exu. I pray Exu is not the force within you." Exu? What was she talking about? Lisboa led me towards the kitchen door, and I followed blindly. Once outside Lisboa rubbed a sticky, black paste over my face and in a circle around me, whispering Nagô incantations the entire time. She painted a cross on my forehead with the remaining herbal paste.

"This will protect you if the presence is evil. Every night, until we determine otherwise, you must return to this spot and rub this herbal mixture on your face and in this circle as I have done." She handed over the small bottle. I felt the coldness of the metal as I took it in my hands. I didn't know what to say, so I didn't say anything. As we returned inside, I felt strangely as if I'd just entered some voodoo horror flick, in which incantations and herbal remedies were used to ward off evil spirits and cast nasty spells on unsuspecting individuals. Although this was no laughing matter, I suddenly had the irresistible urge to laugh and cry until my stomach hurt from the effort. I stifled this urge and instead whispered goodnight to Lisboa. I needed to get away. Be on my own. I couldn't trust myself. I was beginning to question everything again. This world was so foreign. And even though Lisboa had become a good friend, I didn't recognize her tonight.

I sat on the bed in the darkness for a long time, listening to the night sounds. What world had I entered, and would I escape it as the same person? There seemed to be no turning back at this point. I suddenly felt disconnected and far from my family. Since I'd moved to Toronto, my father had barely spoken to me. My mom, though, tried her best to call and write. I flew home once a year at Christmas and somehow managed to survive the tense week, coming back to Toronto each time feeling more worthless than the year before. I had so much riding on this Anthropology degree. I was determined to show my father what a success I could be. But, so far, this hadn't happened.

After my first trip to Brazil, I'd returned to Calgary and switched my major from Business to Anthropology. In fourth year, I chose Odún as the topic for my honours thesis. The nightmares and hallucinations hadn't begun yet. At the time, Odún was simply something fascinating to study. But then I came to Toronto and started serious research for my master's thesis and now doctoral dissertation. I started waking up in the middle of the night, my sheets wet with sweat, my body aching. I moved five times that first year, each time believing the place I had rented was haunted. But I couldn't escape it—that feeling of being watched. No matter where I went. I started to isolate myself. I became obsessed with the research, spending all my hours in the library or in my grad residence. I distanced myself from everyone I knew, including my mom.

It went far beyond long solitary nights of studying and in-depth research. At that point, it had even become questionable whether or not I could continue to claim Odún as my field of academic study. We all become immersed in our research, and the idea of any form of research being unbiased and objective is impossible, but still. What is the line between academic study and complete immersion? Does it matter? If immersion enables the data, then maybe it remains valid or even more so. I started thinking about all those insider/outsider conversations, in terms of both research and life. Who belongs and who doesn't? How do we create those divisionary lines, and who gets to make those decisions? At the end of the day, aren't we all insiders and outsiders at some point? How can we even define anymore who is the foreigner or the *estrangeiro*? Although the evening was warm, I shivered, wondering what my future would hold.

THE DAY WAS BRIGHT as usual, sunlight pouring through the trees. We sat outside the ceremonial initiation house, our blankets spread on the grass and red sand. Today was the beginning of my lessons in Odún. I was amazed that Lisboa had time to give me such personal attention. Normally, the initiation process took place in small groups. But, as Lisboa explained, since I wasn't fluent in Portuguese, things were different. Not only did I have to learn more Portuguese, but Nagô as well. I'd been spending my days listening to Lisboa's teachings and my nights studying languages and ritual material. There was a lot to memorize. Lisboa seemed to feel great reverence for whatever power I supposedly had, and, after that day of divination, she treated me with an almost glorified respect. I finally asked Lisboa to just be my friend, and our relationship resumed its familiar character. But I knew she was fascinated by me, and this inspired her dedication to my spiritual awareness.

"There are a few basic things you must learn first. This may already help you to understand what is happening in your subconscious mind." Lisboa glanced up, a small smile on her lips. "I know about your nightmares. Dear child, I hear you pacing every night." I nodded, and Lisboa took my hand. As we looked at each other, I knew that Lisboa believed in the reality of my nightmares, maybe more so than I did. She also feared them.

Lisboa spread out a sheet of paper on the blanket and began to draw. I watched in fascination as she explained the Odún belief system. "Everything, *tudo*—" she spread her arms wide to indicate the universe "—all begins with *axe*. This is the energy. *Axe* brings all of this—the sun, the trees, the sky—all together.

"*Axe* collects in things—the cross, the statue of Jesus or Mother Mary, the gourd we use to grind the chicken bones. It collects in these objects, and the objects then become very, very powerful. But the *axe* will disappear if it is not constantly renewed. That is why we must have rituals, sacrifices, offerings. And, of course, possessions. Energy, *axe*, is power. The more *axe* we get, the greater the power of our *terreiro*. So you understand, yes?"

I nodded in response. The ritualistic sacrifice of the chicken, the initiates drinking the blood and becoming possessed—these were attempts to embrace the power of the gods. As long as it was not the power of Exu.

"Every person chosen by the gods has an Orixa. Remember, I tried to find yours with the cowrie shells. The time will be right during your initiation ceremony. I am sure your Orixa will be revealed then."

"I certainly hope so." I sighed, looking away.

"Clara, it is not easy, but believe me, your Orixa wants to be revealed. You just have to accept it." The sun beat on my head, and the blanket began to feel itchy under my skin. I couldn't explain my sudden feeling of irritation. I had to concentrate.

"You know that your Orixa is like your personality soul. You have your conscious identity—which is part of your family, your friends, your day-to-day life—and then there is your subconscious identity. This is your darker side. Most people never know this part of their minds. It is the identity of your dreams, your nightmares, your deep inner soul, your past selves. This is your Orixa. It is like tapping into the dark and powerful energy of a universal soul. But you must be careful. When you tap into this energy, you expose it." Lisboa paused for a moment, making sure she had my absolute attention. I forgot about the itchy blanket, the ants, and the sticky heat. "You do not want the power of Exu to take over your Orixa and dominate your soul."

Lisboa's last few words were spoken almost in a whisper. She no longer looked at me. She looked at her drawings, on which she had scribbled a picture of Exu. It was a dark shadow, and I watched as Lisboa used her crayons to pencil in the yellow eyes in the midst of the blackness. Despite the heat of the day, I felt a cold shiver run through me. I was transfixed by those eyes.

"How can you know this is Exu?" I asked, pointing at her picture. Lisboa shook her head.

"I do not know. But I do know what I have seen and it is these two yellow eyes, staring at me from out of the dark shadows." I felt my body stiffen, and Lisboa looked at me with concern. "You have seen the eyes of Exu?"

I felt confused and disoriented. What exactly had I seen that night in the hotel bathroom? I'd felt a presence. "The first night I arrived here. I was in the bathroom, and it was dark. I saw a shadow move across the mirror, and then..." I paused, not sure if I wanted to continue, not sure if I wanted to expose myself to the memory of that night again. That night ... and Eduardo.

"And you saw the eyes, in the mirror." Lisboa filled in the remainder. I stared at her. "Exu is following you, Clara. I was afraid of that." She paused, and the silence between us felt thick with unanswered questions. I wasn't even sure if Lisboa had the answers for me. After looking off into the distance for a moment, Lisboa stood abruptly, gathering up her drawings in a rush.

"Well, it is still early afternoon. You should take a bit of a break, hmm? Working so hard all the time. Look at your pale face." Lisboa's voice was falsely cheerful. She reached out and pinched some colour into my cheeks, but I felt the tension. I knew Lisboa had ended the conversation deliberately and was making an attempt to establish normalcy again.

"I need to take care of some business in the *terreiro*. I shouldn't be more than an hour. Why don't you relax, walk around. Should I meet you back here?" She threw the papers into her bag.

"Sure. I might just sit here and read for a bit."

"But not too much reading, hmm? Your eyes need a rest sometimes." Lisboa smiled and waved. "*Até logo.*"

I watched as Lisboa's swaying form disappeared from view. I tried not to bring up the image of the yellow eyes, but it was now impossible to ignore. Could it have been the power of Exu invading my dreams and making me insane? Was the power of Exu trying to possess me? With this kind of thinking, pretty soon I'd need to dig out my crucifix and ask for an exorcism. But Exu wasn't evil. I was so immersed in the Christian concept of the devil that it was hard to think past that. Exu wasn't the devil. The real evil existed in the human force that evoked Exu. So who could possibly be calling upon Exu's power to possess me?

I stood up, deciding I did need a bit of a break, after all. I started to walk along the dusty road toward the *terreiro*, planning to explore a bit more of the community. But a sleek black car drove past, out of place in the poor surroundings. With the *terreiro* located in the hills just outside Rio, a person would need a specific reason to go out of his or her way like that. Lisboa had told me that the location of her *terreiro* was intentional. She wanted space to house the initiates. But she also wanted secrecy. I watched as the car swerved to the right and headed in the direction of the *terreiro*. Why would someone who owned such a fancy car visit an Odún *terreiro*? Of course, it wasn't unknown for wealthy patrons to frequent the *terreiros* for consultations, but there was something about the dark windows...

Should I check it out? I wanted to understand the political workings of Lisboa's *terreiro* better. I had no doubt that Lisboa knew the majority of Brazil's best-kept secrets. I continued walking towards the *terreiro,* but I picked up my pace. Just as I was about to turn around the corner, I heard voices. Something about the tone made me hesitant to go any farther. I listened carefully, straining to understand the Portuguese.

"Now, surely that's not necessary." Lisboa's voice. Soft, cool, persuasive.

"Mãe Lisboa, how many times do I have to tell you? Time is running out. You're not listening."

I peeked around the corner and saw Lisboa standing at the entrance of the *terreiro,* firmly placing herself between the entrance posts. A position in which no harm could be done to her because this was the place of Exu, the four corners at every entrance, and she held his power in that moment. What would be so noxious to Lisboa that she would evoke Exu for protection? She didn't show her fear, but I could almost taste it from the look in her eyes. On her face she held a cool smile, her arm lazily reaching out to touch the man's face. This was a side of Lisboa I'd never seen before. Seductive, beguiling, dangerous.

"Come, come now, Duarte. We wouldn't want your wife to know about your little bits of fun, hmm?" She spoke as if in pleasant conversation, but the man jerked back.

"Lisboa, you can't taunt me anymore. There's something much bigger here than just you and me. Threaten me all you want. It's not going to work." I took a step back, hearing the sound of crunching dried grass beneath my feet. Duarte stood resolutely while Lisboa sighed dramatically.

"Really, darling, there is no need for this." She reached out her hand again, but this time the man clasped her wrist and held it firmly. I saw the smile disappear from Lisboa's face.

"Don't you dare touch me," she said in an even voice, pulling her wrist back and placing herself back in the entranceway.

"Is he going to protect you now?" The man laughed. A cruel laugh. I wanted to do something. To stop him. But I knew I could only watch.

"You will not tell me what to do." Lisboa's voice was strong now. She placed both her hands on either side of the wooden entrance and stared at the man. The wooden posts stood strong beside the corrugated tin of the initiation hall. It may not have been a grand entranceway, but it was the pride of the *terreiro*. He stepped back.

The fear had disappeared from Lisboa. Her body seemed to rise, and her eyes became black pools. "If you do not leave my *terreiro* immediately, I will curse you." Lisboa's voice had become thick and dark.

"There are other powers, Lisboa. Powers far greater than your Exu."

"I will do whatever it takes to save my *terreiro*."

"Then you know what to do." Duarte's voice was calm, frightening. They stood there, staring each other down for a moment. Finally, Duarte broke the silence. "I'm just a messenger,

Lisboa. The Macumba powers are far greater than you and I combined, and I can't stop them for you."

Lisboa scoffed and spit at his feet. "Take your dirty black magic rituals. I'm not afraid of them."

"No?" Duarte gave Lisboa a quiet stare. "You should be. If you care at all about your initiates."

I could see Lisboa fighting to maintain control of her emotions. She took a deep breath and said in a quiet voice, "Do not ever threaten me again. You will pay the price."

Duarte backed off without a word, shaking his head. I watched as he strode toward his car and drove away, leaving a trail of red dust in the air. As soon as his car disappeared from sight, Lisboa crumpled to the ground.

"Lisboa!" I cried, running to where she lay. I felt it again. That dark and heavy presence. The chill that seemed to enter my very bones. I held on to Lisboa's hand. It was ice cold. I dragged her out of the entranceway and into the main hall. I looked back to where Lisboa had lain, and there were ashes there, spread evenly, marking exactly where her body had fallen. Choking on my rising panic, I ran to the kitchen sink to get some water and sprinkled it on Lisboa's face, hoping to revive her. She coughed and sputtered and spat out a few Brazilian swear words.

"Clara." Lisboa stared up at me, her face registering shock.

"Please tell me, Lisboa. Tell me what's going on here."

Lisboa sat up, looking into my confused eyes, and just shook her head. "What were you doing here?"

"I saw the black car, and I was curious..."

"Curious. You were curious. Don't you think there is a reason I keep things secret from you?" She wiped her forehead with the end of her long sleeve, noticing the ash stains. I just watched as she examined the ashes on her white shirt and saw the trail from where she had lain. She closed her eyes for a moment, and, suddenly, she looked much older than her sixty-odd years.

When she opened her eyes again, she looked at me imploringly.

"Clara, listen to me now and listen well. When you came into my house, I had no idea how you would affect my life. But I know now that you were meant to find me. I don't understand exactly what is happening, but let me tell you this: I think you have been sent here for a reason. Someone is very, very afraid of you and wants you gone."

I shivered. Not dead. She just said gone. "Why on earth would anyone be afraid of me?"

Lisboa reached out and touched my hair. The gesture was almost motherly. "Child, you have great powers." She said the words as a statement, but it told me nothing.

"Come now, help me up." With Lisboa leaning on me, we managed to reach one of the side rooms where she could lie down on a cot. I handed her the glass of water to finish and sat down beside her. I could hear the faint noise of other initiates. But no one seemed to have noticed us. The room smelled musty. The candles were still smoking from the initiate training earlier, and the smoke rose in curls towards the ceiling where it formed strange patterns. I sat on the cot, leaning my head against the flimsy tin siding, while Lisboa closed her eyes and relaxed. I watched the smoke curl into shapes. The room was windowless and therefore airless as well. The heat fell in waves of perspiration on my forehead. I felt the grainy texture of the cot beneath me and thought of the young woman I'd seen at the initiation ceremony. The young woman who had become possessed too soon and was carried away to lie down on this cot. What was happening to me? Would I become like that young woman? Taken over by a force I couldn't control? I closed my eyes and decided that, whatever else might happen, I was still in control of my own mind. At least for now.

5

THE FRENCH DOORS WERE OPEN, and the intoxicating scent of the bougainvillea tree wafted into the living room with the warm, evening breeze. I was comfortably ensconced in the big corner armchair, trying to concentrate on a novel.

"A cup of tea?" Lisboa sailed into the room, and placed a warm cup of herbal tea into my outstretched hand.

I sighed. "Oh, yes. I think I'll need some strong herbal tea to sleep tonight. Or maybe something even stronger."

Lisboa took a seat across from me on the couch. She plumped up the cushions and settled herself in, breathing in the soothing aroma of the lemongrass tea.

"Yes, yes. Nothing like a cup of tea to soothe the nerves. And maybe with a shot of *cachaça*?" She winked, but I noticed again how weary Lisboa looked. Her hair, normally piled on top of her head, now hung loosely down her back, and her eyes were the colour of silt water. We sat in silence for a few minutes. I waited for Lisboa to talk. To explain what had happened that afternoon. "Clara." I put my book down and leaned forward, anxious to hear Lisboa's words. "The things you heard—don't let them fool you. You trust me, no?" I nodded. But a little nagging voice in the back of my mind questioned even this.

"Please. You must trust me. Whatever you saw or heard today…" Lisboa paused, taking a small sip of tea. I could tell she was planning her words carefully. Something she never normally did. "You know I must protect the *terreiro*. That man is a threat. You must be careful. Don't trust anyone else."

"Lisboa, you need to tell me everything." I was tired of the riddles. I didn't want to guess anymore.

She held on to my gaze. "If I knew the answers, believe me, I would tell you. Now, you remember what we discussed the other night. About Exu?"

"Of course I remember. Every night you want me to protect myself by rubbing the herbal paste on my face and in a circle around me."

Lisboa appeared to be concentrating. I wasn't even sure if she'd heard my response. "Yes, yes. I did say that. But I think I might have been wrong. It is not Exu we must fear. It is something else. Remember what I told you about Exu? He is not evil. In the Odún belief system there is no true evil. Exu is a trickster. You cannot trust him. It is only when his power falls into the wrong hands that it becomes evil."

The shadows across the floor seemed to lengthen. I felt myself shiver involuntarily. I could almost see those yellow eyes watching me beyond the cozy glow of the living room. I looked towards the open French doors, and felt a gust of wind rush through and brush my cheek coldly. The wind should be hot, not cold. I jumped up and ran to close the doors, having to forcefully push them shut. Once closed, the room seemed eerily silent. I turned around, and Lisboa stared at me.

"He calls to you, Clara."

"What are you saying? That I'm evil?" This was too much. I stormed out of the living room and ran up the winding staircase. I just wanted to close my eyes and escape from everything. But Lisboa followed me. I went into my room, slamming the door and feeling like a rebellious adolescent. I didn't want to push Lisboa away like that, but I was tired of her evasiveness. Exhausted, I collapsed on the bed, and closed my eyes. Lisboa must have gone back downstairs, because I didn't hear anything outside my door. As I lay there in the dark room, I noticed a strange odour. I leaned over and flicked on the light switch, wondering where the smell was coming from. Yes, there was definitely an odour in the room, like something rotting. It seemed to be coming from the balcony. Without thinking, I opened the balcony doors. Oh my God. I heard my scream as if it came from far away even as I felt the hoarseness in my throat.

There lay a dead chicken with its head sliced off, the dried up blood having oozed from its neck and onto the white tile, gleaming a wine red in the watery moonlight. The smell was overpowering. I ran back into the room, barely making it in time to retch violently into the toilet. I heard a loud banging on my door.

"Clara. Clara. *Filha*. Please open the door!" Lisboa was shouting. I barely had the energy to remove the lock and open the door. Lisboa rushed inside and hugged me tightly.

"*Ai, ai,*" she cried. With the French doors still open, she could immediately smell the rotting carcass. She let me go and hurried over to where the decapitated chicken lay. She kneeled down on the red encrusted balcony and reached her fingers deep into the chicken's throat, where the blood was still fresh. She tasted the blood with her fingers, the red ooze dripping down her chin, and rubbed the blood in a sign of the cross on her forehead. Had she gone mad?

"What are you doing?" I cried, backing away now, wondering if maybe Lisboa was the one to fear all along. I stared at Lisboa's body, silhouetted against the moonlight, the blood shining almost black and staining her white blouse. She smiled, and, when I looked into her eyes, I realized that she was still Lisboa.

"Clara, blood is life. It is power. It holds the greatest amount of *axe* you can imagine. You must come here. You must rub the blood on your skin. It will protect you." I continued to stare. Lisboa stood up and came towards me. I felt the panic rise in me like a tidal wave. What insane world had I become a part of? I knew blood was life. I knew sacrifices were made to the gods. But not on the balcony outside my bedroom. I was rooted to the spot. Lisboa draped an arm around my shoulders and held me, whispering words of comfort.

"I did not mean to frighten you. But whoever left you this—" she flung her hands out, the bloody stains still visible "—may be good or evil. I do not know. But either way, you must protect yourself with the offering." Feeling numb, I allowed myself to be led back through the French doors. I sat on the bed while Lisboa made the sign of the cross on my forehead with the blood.

"Do not wash it off until morning. You will sleep unharmed." I nodded, saying nothing, feeling nothing. Satisfied, Lisboa took the carcass and flung it over the side of the balcony. She helped me to bed and tucked me under the covers, all the while whispering Nagô incantations. As I lay in bed, I could hear Lisboa washing the blood off the floor of the balcony and then leaving the room. For once, I fell into a long, blissfully undisturbed sleep.

I STRETCHED OUT LAZILY the next morning, feeling the brisk coolness of the sheets against the sticky heat in the room. The moment my eyes opened and I became fully conscious, I remembered. My pillow was stained with the blood Lisboa had painted on my face. I reached up to touch my cheek and outlined the remnant of the cross. So, it had been real. Lisboa had closed the lace curtains, but I could see through them to the street below. It was bustling with activity. I could hear voices and people calling out to each other. Judging from the slant of the sun, it appeared to be well past mid-day. I must have slept over twelve hours! This had been my best sleep since arriving in Brazil over two months ago. I didn't want to get up. I didn't want to look at my face in the mirror and be forced to wipe off the blood. In a strange way, I felt that the blood really had protected me.

I heard a light tapping on the door. "Clara? Clara? Are you all right?" Lisboa's voice was full of concern. How could I have ever doubted her?

"Yes, I'm fine," I called out, dragging myself out of bed.

"I have made some breakfast, or lunch, I suppose."

"I'll be right down." I heard Lisboa's footsteps retreating as I went into the bathroom. I scrubbed my face with soap and water without looking in the mirror, and pulled my hair back with an elastic. When I finally dared to glance at my reflection, the blood stains freshly scrubbed off my face, I was surprised by what I saw. My face looked clean and shiny from the scrubbing, and my eyes were clear and bright. With all my nightmares, I'd grown accustomed to the dark circles under my eyes. I felt energetic and well rested.

"So you did sleep well as I said, hmm?" Lisboa glanced up from where she stood at the stove, frying eggs. I could see the platters of rice and beans waiting at the table, and I wondered if I would ever get used to the huge Brazilian breakfast. There was also a heaping plate of mangoes and papayas. And, of course, a welcoming cup of *café da manhã* with some toasted French rolls. Perfection. I sat down and gratefully took a sip of coffee.

"Lisboa, this is lovely. Thank you! And yes, strangely enough I slept very well." Lisboa smiled and did not seem surprised. She came to sit beside me at the table, her long gown swishing behind her. The sun was slanting lazily into the kitchen, and the scent of fried egg and fresh coffee filled the air. Despite the crazy night, I felt at peace.

"You know, I have been thinking about it, trying to understand why someone put the chicken there for you."

"You said last night you didn't know if it was good or bad."

Lisboa shook her head, her sigh that of impatience. She stood up again and returned to the stove. "We know the power of blood is good, but I cannot help thinking that whoever sent this to you wanted to frighten you, *querida*."

I watched as Lisboa turned the eggs over, listening to the hissing and popping of the frying pan. There was something so wonderfully normal about waking up after a marvellous night's sleep and sitting at the kitchen table waiting for breakfast. I wanted to hold on to the normalcy, because nothing else in my life seemed to fit into that category anymore.

"Have you told me everything, Lisboa?"

"I have told you everything I know. And that is not much."

I stood up to gather the plates, and Lisboa placed a fried egg on top of the rice and beans. We sat across from each other in amicable silence for a moment as we ate our food.

"This is delicious," I mumbled contentedly in between bites.

Lisboa nodded and reached over to grab the paper. She laid the paper open in front of me so I could practice a bit of Portuguese and look at the pictures. I had been reading bits of the paper every day. I flipped through the news sections while taking sips of my coffee. A particular photograph caught my eye. It was a grisly shot of a young man lying on the ground, his leg twisted at an odd angle, with a large gash on his forehead. There were ashes all around him, making a circle around his body, but his eyes haunted me the most. They were wide open. I caught my breath, and Lisboa quickly snatched the paper away.

"What was that?" I asked.

Lisboa looked at the picture, her face unreadable. "That is another Macumba murder," she said in a soft voice. I felt a chill pass through the air.

"What is Macumba?" I was almost afraid to ask, but I knew that I needed the answer. Lisboa put the paper aside and looked at me.

"Macumba is a black magic cult. Oh, it has been around as long as Odún. It takes all the evil and honours it. Exu is the god. These people, they are the worst creatures. They worship the dead. You might say they worship evil itself."

I wanted to back away. I felt my heart racing, but I couldn't stop the questions.

"Who are they, Lisboa?" My voice was almost a whisper. I remembered all too clearly the circle of ashes I'd seen surrounding Lisboa's body when she fell.

"They are everywhere. Lately, the last few years I mean, they have gained power, you see. It used to be Odún that held the political power, but now…" Lisboa glanced into the distance, pausing a moment in her speech. "Now, they are becoming more powerful." As usual, as soon as I felt like the answers were close, Lisboa stood abruptly, nearly knocking over her plate as she did so.

"Enough of that nonsense. What will you do today? Or what is left of it?" She carried her plate over to the sink and busied herself with washing the dishes. I knew she wouldn't tell me anything else about the "Macumba murders." There were so many things that I wanted to be explained, but, for whatever reason, Lisboa was not willing to do so. Maybe because she didn't know the answers herself. Or maybe because she knew all too well, and she was afraid. I finished my breakfast and tried to help Lisboa with the dishes, but she brushed me aside.

"Go on. Do whatever it is you planned on doing today."

I smiled. "I might just go for a walk."

Lisboa patted my arm and nodded her approval. "Yes, some fresh air. That is just what you need."

I'D BEEN IN BRAZIL for over two months, and my entire existence had been so circumscribed that I'd barely seen anything of Rio de Janeiro. I did want to go for a walk, but what I didn't tell Lisboa was that I intended to go to the library. I decided to try and contact Catalina. Catalina had helped me before with translations, and I was sure I would need her help today. My Portuguese had come a long way, but it still wasn't good enough. I left Catalina a quick message before walking out the door and stepping into the bright sunshine.

Just as I left the house, I saw the shadow of a small figure. I walked towards the bougainvillea tree where I'd seen the branches move slightly. I should have been more afraid, but, at that moment, in the bright sunlight of late afternoon, I was simply curious. I thought it might have been some sort of animal hiding in the bushes, but, as I came near, I heard a soft cry. With surprise, I found myself staring into Chico's brown eyes. He jumped out from his hiding spot behind the bush, his arms waving. "Missus. I do nothing. Nothing."

I could taste the fear on his breath. Before he could run away, I grabbed his skinny arm and tried to hold on, but his wiry strength overpowered me. "Chico. Don't look so scared. What are you doing here?" But his wide eyes would not settle, and, before I could say more, he released himself from my hold and ran out of the small garden. I thought of running after him, but then decided against it. Why was he here? Spying on me? He'd looked absolutely terrified. A cold sensation crept up my back, and I tried to remain calm. Had Chico left the little gift of the severed chicken? Would he do such a thing? Did Eduardo hate me so much that he would resort to this? The questions tumbled through my mind as I stood there by the bougainvillea tree.

Eduardo. I'd intentionally blocked him out of my mind. But I couldn't block out the memory of his eyes, dark and knowing as he looked at me. The connection we shared. The feel of his hands on my body and his lips on my skin. I closed my eyes, allowing the memory to take over for just a moment. What had Eduardo said at our last meeting? He'd told me to go home. Not to get involved in gods that weren't my own. And he'd made no effort to reach me. Just when I'd begun to feel something, to believe that maybe beneath his hard exterior lay ... what? I asked myself cynically. My prince charming? Hardly. Blocking all thoughts of Eduardo Soares from my mind, I resolutely left the garden and made my way down the crowded street.

I managed to jump on a tram just as it was about to leave. I remembered the first day I'd taken the tram up the curving roads of Santa Teresa. I'd been so excited and afraid at the same time. I'd squeezed into the closest seat I could find, determined not to be caught hanging on to the rails. I smiled now, enjoying the hot sea breeze lifting my hair as I clung to the edge of the tram, crowded beside the other passengers. The tram curved its way down the hill, revealing tantalizing bits of the Baía de Guanabara below. As usual, it was a beautiful, hot summer day. The perspiration was already beginning to bead along my hairline. I got off close to the library, enjoying the short midafternoon walk.

The frigid air conditioning accosted me the moment I entered the interior of the library. Far from refreshing, it felt cold and clammy after the heat outside. I felt myself shiver as I made my way to the front desk. In halting Portuguese, I asked the librarian if she could assist me in finding newspaper clippings from the past few years. After two months, it had become easier to speak in Portuguese, but I was still far from fluent. She nodded and directed me towards a microfiche. It had been years since I'd used one of those. I wanted any information I could find about the Macumba murders. I had to know more. If Lisboa couldn't give me answers, I would have to find them on my own. I refused to sit in ignorance any longer. I somehow knew these Macumba murders were the missing connection. As I was scrolling through the pages of newspaper print, Catalina appeared at my side.

"Catalina, I'm so happy you got my message."

Catalina smiled, her eyes bright. "You know I am always happy to translate things for you." She took a chair and swivelled it around so that she was sitting beside me, facing the microfiche. Her face registered mild surprise.

"Why are you looking at newspaper articles?" she asked. I hesitated, knowing that I needed Catalina's help to translate the articles but suddenly uncertain how much information I should reveal to her. I knew Catalina needed the money I gave her. She was a hardworking student at the Universidade Federal do Rio de Janeiro, but I knew she had several part-time jobs as well. It occurred to me that I knew very little about Catalina other than the basic information she'd provided to get the position. I'd put up notices in the Universidade, and she was one of the students who responded. There'd been something inherently honest about her, and that was why I'd chosen her. She was young. Probably no more than twenty. I noticed today that she wore a plain dress, the edges slightly frayed but immaculately clean. Her dark hair was braided in one long pleat hanging down her back.

"I'm looking up something. I need your help to translate the articles." My words were cautious. "I need to find anything related to the Macumba murders."

Catalina stared at me in silence for a moment before dropping her eyes. At first, I thought she was going to refuse. I watched as her hands fidgeted on her lap. Finally, the young woman glanced up. "Best to stay away from that," she said.

I sighed, wondering what I would do if Catalina walked away. My Portuguese wasn't good enough to read the articles in detail. I was sure I would find something.

"I understand, Catalina, if you don't want to help me with this." I had to say it. I would not pressure her into doing something she was terrified of. Her fingers were knotted together. I could see she was thinking about what she might do.

"You will pay me a thousand *cruzeiros* a page?"

I thought for a minute. Wow. A thousand *cruzeiros* a page could get a little expensive for me. But what choice did I have? Catalina was driving a hard bargain. "If I pay you a thousand *cruzeiros* a page, will you do it?" Catalina nodded. I felt the relief wash over me like a warm tide.

"So, if you find anything at all to do with the Macumba murders, print it out." Catalina began working, skimming far more rapidly through the articles than I had. I continued my slow search, trying to pick out words here and there in the articles that might provide a clue. I could hear the clock ticking in the empty silence of the library, and I felt the small hairs at the nape of my neck rise as if I were being watched. From the moment I'd woken up that morning, I'd had the sensation of being watched. Had that little rascal, Chico, followed me here as well? I turned around, my eyes scanning the library. Nothing but rows and rows of books. There was one window, and, although it was a bright day outside, it cast only a meagre slit of sunlight on the floor. I shook myself, mentally telling myself not to get caught up in my imagination. I turned my attention back to the microfiche and looked closer as something caught my eye: a photograph of a young woman, lain out as if on a sacrificial altar, the whites of her eyes rolled back, her body contorted at an unnatural angle. I saw the ring of ashes around her body and the caption below, where the word "Macumba" sprang out of the page in bold, black print. I looked at the date. September 17, 1980. That was over a decade ago. Brazil had still been under military dictatorship.

"Catalina, what does it say?" I turned towards her, trying to keep the edge out of my voice. Catalina looked at the screen.

"It is a Macumba murder. One of the first. I remember it well." Her voice grew quiet. I noticed that she, too, glanced around the library.

"What can you remember?"

"I was young. Just seven years old. But I remember waking up one morning. Papa was reading the paper. He always liked to get up before the rest of us and sit in his favourite chair and…" Catalina paused, a small smile on her lips. "Papa is gone now, so I like to remember those days."

I nodded, wanting to hear the whole story in whatever way Catalina chose to tell it. "I'm sorry to hear that." I reached over to take Catalina's hand.

"He died a few years after that. I was ten. But anyway, before I begin with a new story… I woke up a little early that morning. I think I had a stomach ache." Catalina waved her arms in the air. "I don't know. It doesn't matter. I went into the living room wanting to surprise Papa. But when I got close, I saw his expression. I'll never forget it. I snuck up behind Papa to see what he was looking at, and I saw that picture. It was that exact picture." She shuddered and crossed her arms over her chest protectively. "It is so silly. They want to put us in a freezer with this air-conditioning. Anyway, it was all over the news for days. The woman, well…" Catalina hesitated, avoiding my gaze.

"Who was she, Catalina?"

Finally, she met my eyes. "She was a foreigner."

I felt a sharp stab of fear. A foreigner. Well, what does that mean? Tourists are killed every year on the dangerous streets of Rio.

"She was a student, actually. A young American woman." Catalina bit her lip. I was tired of people being so evasive. I wanted to know.

"Okay, Catalina. What? Was she studying Odún as well?" I'd asked the question more out of exasperation than anything else, but when Catalina nodded, I felt the prickle of fear race down my neck and arms. I had to stop thinking like this.

"Fine. She was also studying Odún. Tell me the whole story and don't leave anything out, okay?" Catalina was trembling. "Look, let's get out of here. It's way too cold. We can come back another day. Let's go to a café or something where we can talk." I took Catalina's arm and stood up. Maybe if we got out of that damp and dismal library, Catalina would feel better talking to me. Catalina nodded gratefully, and together we left the library. The late afternoon sun was slowly beginning its descent, and the air enveloped us in its warmth. We walked down the street, the fading sun casting dancing shadows on the pavement.

"It's so beautiful, your city," I couldn't help but comment.

"Yes, beautiful, but ugly as well. There is so much ugliness here. Sometimes I find it hard to see any beauty at all." I was surprised by the bitterness in this young woman's voice. She was so young and yet so cynical about the world. I had been so sheltered in Calgary. It was different growing up in a city like Rio. I wondered where Catalina lived. I was sure she didn't come from the *favelas,* but maybe from a small apartment in one of the outlying barrios.

"Do you know of any cafés in the area?" I asked as we passed by several shops and little eateries.

"Yes. There is a wonderful kebab shop a few streets down." I knew it had been a good decision to leave the library. Already, I could feel the fear lifting off my shoulders. We turned the corner, and, sure enough, there was a little eatery with a few tables scattered over the sidewalk, creating a kind of makeshift terrace. We took our seats and were welcomed by a short, friendly man, his balding head glistening in the receding twilight.

"Boa noite. Dois cafezinhos?" We both nodded as the waiter left to get our coffee. The evening breeze felt warm on my skin and the salty smell of the sea had a calming effect on me. The streets were crowded with people going home in the busy rush hour traffic. But our curbside café was a pleasing haven from the bustle. When the waiter returned, we sat and slowly sipped the black coffee. I'd never been much of a coffee drinker, but, since coming to Brazil, I'd rapidly become addicted to the dark, syrupy *cafezinho* served in little cups. It was as much a part of the social culture as talking, and I could hardly refuse.

"I see you have come to love our strong Brazilian coffee."

I nodded with a small chuckle. "Yes, but it does keep me awake some nights."

The waiter returned, and we ordered shawarmas. "You know, it's amazing the different types of food you can get in Rio." I could tell Catalina was still a little tense, and I hoped to put her at ease with some light chitchat.

She smiled. "I suppose you like meat then? Have you been to a *churrascaria?*"

I nodded yes, to both questions. "I'm doing my grad work in Toronto, but I'm actually from Calgary. It's in western Canada near the Rocky Mountains. Our ranching culture isn't all that different from yours."

"Yes, I know. The 1988 Winter Olympics."

"That's right." I smiled. Thank goodness for the '88 Olympics. Otherwise nobody would know where Calgary was.

Catalina looked intrigued. "But I bet you don't eat the intestines and everything else." She made a face.

"No," I laughed. "Those bits are not so appealing to me."

"But you're not vegetarian. You just ordered a beef shawarma."

"Oh, no. I eat meat. But I like to eat other things too." I was happy to see Catalina relax with our conversation.

"Catalina, do you want to talk to me now about the things you know?"

She looked away for a moment. Her eyes scanned the dark streets beyond the warm glow of the café. I felt bad putting Catalina in such a position, but I needed to hear her stories. I wanted things to make sense. If I was in danger, I wanted to know why. And what to watch out for.

"As I was saying, that was really the first Macumba murder. At least, the first publicized one. The murders have been taking place for generations. Ritualistic murders, that kind of thing." She took another sip of coffee. "The woman, the anthropologist. She had come here to study occult magic. Not exactly like you. She was interested in Odún, of course, but she was even more interested in Macumba." Catalina hesitated. I nodded for her to continue. "She found out some things, I guess. Things she shouldn't have known. That's why they killed her. At least, that's what Papa said."

"What sort of things?"

"There are rumours, of course. There are always rumours with things like this. I mean, when something gets in the papers, you know how it is, people talk." Catalina's words became more rambling. "There had been talk of a cult. The members of that cult worship evil and get Exu to do their bidding. These cults have become more popular now, especially in the *favelas*. People used to go to Odún houses, but now they go to these places. So Macumba has become powerful. They go to the *favelas*, and they get all the votes. There is talk...." Again Catalina looked around, the fear returning.

"It has been said that the very leaders of this country are part of this cult. And that they kill their opponents in the name of Exu." The waiter appeared with our shawarmas, his smile incongruous with our conversation.

Catalina and I sat in stiff silence as he placed the food on the table. I managed to give him a weak smile of thanks, "*Obrigado.*"

"You can trust no one. No one, anymore. The entire country is afraid. It is unspoken."

I listened to what Catalina said. But it was hard to accept her words at face value. "So people are murdered and everyone accepts it? How can this be kept secret?"

"Anything can be kept secret if there is no one willing to reveal it. People are afraid. This is not something new. During the dictatorship, yes, it was easier to cover it up. But, of course, some people knew. If it was your Papa or brother who went missing. But you learned to keep your mouth shut. It is more public now. They kill their opponents, and then they say, oh, another Macumba murder. We must give more money to the police force and patrol the streets better. They get into positions of power ... police officers, politicians. The crimes keep happening. And the power of Macumba grows stronger."

I'd read about the years under military dictatorship. I knew about the list of missing persons. But Catalina was suggesting it hadn't ended—just changed form.

"Are you talking about Velho here?" I asked.

Catalina cast a wary look around. "I wouldn't talk too loud," she whispered.

"Catalina, this is Brazil." I indicated our surroundings—the lush apartments, the tall buildings, the busy commerce, the wealth.

"Exactly." Catalina was quiet for a moment. It made me realize how ridiculous my statement had been. Yes, this was Brazil. A country whose first democratically elected president after over twenty years of dictatorship had been in power for just over two years. This was a country in flux. Anything was possible. "What is happening here is not so different from what happened in Haiti. Do not forget. They had their first democratic election in 1990 and President Aristide only lasted eight months before being ousted by a military coup. The military are still trying to hold on to their power. The Duvaliers used voodoo as their political weapon. Here they use Macumba. When the people start to believe, that is when it becomes scary."

"Do you believe?"

"Yes." Catalina had finished her shawarma. She sat still, twisting her hands nervously on her lap.

"If you're so afraid, why are you telling me all this?" I looked into Catalina's eyes, and she stared back directly. She looked at me with absolute faith.

"Because you can stop it." I let the silence hang in the air. Thick, dark silence. Catalina continued to look at me calmly.

"Catalina, what can I do? I'm just one person."

She didn't respond. Instead, Catalina asked for the waiter, and I brushed away her attempts to pay the bill.

"Catalina, why would you think I could do anything?" I couldn't let it go. Lisboa had been suggesting the same thing, that I had some sort of special powers. But I didn't feel special. I probably had more issues and neuroses than anyone.

Catalina didn't say anything for a moment. Then her eyes met mine. "Clara, I knew there was something different about you. But I was not sure until just now. It is the prophecy…"

"Prophecy?" Now we were getting somewhere. I waited for Catalina to continue.

"About the one." Catalina normally liked to go off on tangents, but this time she was choosing her words with care. "The one who will save the Odún."

I waited for more, but Catalina seemed to lose her nerve. "I'm sorry, Clara. I do not know what I am saying. I just like to dream up great stories. I have always had a crazy imagination. My mom used to say that..." She stopped mid-sentence. "I need to go home."

I couldn't understand what she was suddenly trying to hide. "Thank you, Catalina," I said quietly as we stood up. "Don't worry. You've been a lot of help today. And it's late. You're right. You should get home."

She nodded. We smiled at each other. I felt affection for the young woman. It was strange how much older she appeared when talking about the Macumba murders. Fear is ageless. But now, Catalina looked young and extremely vulnerable again.

"Yes, Mama might be worried."

"Why don't we walk together? Are you heading towards the metro?" We began to walk along the street, the crowd now having thinned. The after-work rush was over and the streets were quiet. An odd couple here and there strolled beneath the watery lights, and a man was curled against the curb. I could hear the sound of children playing and the barking of stray dogs. I didn't want to leave Catalina alone as she'd been so frightened earlier. Especially since I still had that sensation of being watched. We walked together towards the metro, and, as I left Catalina at the station, I felt a bit better. I said, "Take care. I'll be calling you soon again." I gave her five thousand *cruzeiros* for having helped me that day. I was surprised to see Catalina hesitate in accepting the money. "Please," I said with a smile. I wanted to give Catalina whatever I could. I felt another small tug of fear as I watched Catalina get on the metro. There was so much I needed to learn. There was so much I still didn't understand. Had I put Catalina in danger just by asking those questions?

6

THE AIR WAS THICK AND HEAVY *with humidity, the dark green trees dripping moss and hiding the sun. I could hardly breathe. I pushed through the bush, struggling to claw my way through the undergrowth. The howler monkeys rang out their mating cries, unearthly and eerie. The birds were shrill, their cawing filling the laden air. The ground moved with an army of ants, and the branches reached out with their choking embrace to claim me as part of the forest. I fought against their pull, hacking and slicing my way through with the tiny machete. Blood dripped down my leg, my heart pounded in my ears, and my throat clogged with the moist density. But I knew I was close. And he would be waiting for me.*

My breath a ragged pull, I cut my way through the last of the undergrowth and came into the clearing. I stood there a moment, my heart hammering in my chest, my lungs screaming for air. I was there at last. I had made it back once again. I turned around, motioning to the half-dozen emaciated individuals fighting through the forest behind me. They shuffled forward, their breathing heavy, their cries mingling with those of the howler monkeys. They circled around me in the clearing.

"We have arrived!" I exclaimed in Nagô, allowing my torn and blistered lips to split open into a triumphant smile. "You are now free!" I watched as I always did, finding renewal in the capacity of the human soul. Here we were—beaten and starved slaves transported from our African homes to a new

world across the ocean, dancing and jumping and hollering our freedom. We were slaves no more. Tears fell from many eyes as my followers danced around me. This is what it was all about. All the suffering, all the pain, all the heartache. It was all for moments like this. Moments when I could witness pure and unadulterated joy on the faces of people who'd had their souls stolen. I was giving them back their identity. And, for that, I would do anything.

But now, now all I wanted was to feel his embrace. The embrace of my King. He came out of the shadows, his dark eyes hidden from view. He walked toward us, majestic, regal, in command. He wore the traditional headdress and the red robe of his ancestors. He nodded to the people, who were awed and overwhelmed. "Welcome," he announced with triumph, his eyes coming to rest on mine. He raised his chin just a hint, acknowledging my presence. He was angry with me, I knew. He had wanted me to stop the missions. To remain by his side in Palmares as rightful Queen. There were other trackers, other good people who could have lead the rescue missions for the lost slaves. But not me. I was his Queen. And yet, I had gone anyway. I could no more resist the pull of the forest and the need to free my people any more than he could resist his need to rule as King. His eyes, so deep and magnetic, would not pull away from mine. I saw and felt his anger, but there was much more there, as well. Relief to see that I had returned safely. Deep love. Anticipation of our reunion that evening.

He walked toward me, taking my hand in his grip almost fiercely. "My Queen," he whispered, his voice smooth and caressing. He rubbed my bloodstained and callused hands gently, removing the machete. "You will have no more need of this." I tried to grasp on to my machete, but he took it from my hands. I felt my power evaporating within his gentle but firm grip. My knees weakened, and my lips moistened. The chemistry between us had always been strong. But I needed to stand my ground. I would not cower. Suddenly the heat, the rotting scent of dead leaves, the cawing of the birds, and the cry of the monkeys all intensified. The trees dripping moss reached their feathery arms toward me, encircling me in their grasp, choking me, blocking out the light and turning everything into darkness. I reached out for him, clinging to his gaze yet not able to hold on. I felt myself swirling and falling, deep, deep into an endless cavern of blackness....

I landed in a dark alleyway. The stench of rotting garbage filled the air. I looked around, desperately trying to understand where I was and what was happening. Flashing lights, a black rat, grainy rocks that chafed my skin, causing a tiny rivulet of blood to form along my leg. Amidst the stench of rot, I caught a hint of the ocean. I felt the moist breeze as it hit my cheek, stifling if only for a moment the heavy humidity. I was near the water; I knew that much. And judging from the swirling lights in the distance, creating dancing patterns in the dark alleyway, I was not far from the main drag. The traffic and noise of Avenida Atlantica was only half a block away. I could see it from where I stood. But this little alleyway was tucked secretly into a corner, indistinguishable from the busy avenue just metres away. I could even glimpse the whitewashed walls of the Copacabana Palace.

The white glow of a streetlight illuminated the dingy back alley. And beneath the lamp, shining like a deathly spotlight, lay the prone figure of a young woman. She lay there, her feet tied into an unnatural position, her face a horrified grimace. But her eyes were vivid, stark, and dark with terror. She was still alive, barely. They circled around her, their faces hidden behind masks, colourful and sinister in their festivity, the ghoulish smiling faces of the masked tormentors inhuman and terrifying. They were whispering incantations in a hushed and repetitive chant that gradually seemed to rise to a crescendo. I saw the ashes next. The ritualistic sprinkling of ashes at the four corners of the street, slowly moving inward until the ashes started to form a ring that began at the woman's forehead and circled *around to her feet. She was too afraid to even cry. And then I saw the axe, shiny and metallic, glinting off the streetlamp's glare. I saw one of the masked tormentors raise the axe high into the air, the light blinding my vision as he began to swing it downward ... and just at that moment the young woman's eyes turned toward me, and there was recognition there. The blackness in the girl's eyes deepened with agony and a silent plea. I felt the cry rise in my throat as I saw. They were the deep and innocent brown eyes of Catalina.*

"NO!" I CRIED, hearing the ring of my scream echo into the silence of an empty room and a bed sticky with sweat. I yanked myself free from the covers, my heart hammering in my chest. I stumbled out of bed, my eyes wild. This dream ... it was different from anything I'd ever experienced before. This time it was real— incredibly vivid and clear. I had *been* there. Both in the forest and in the dark alleyway. It hadn't simply been a dream. I looked down at my leg, the stinging pain stopping me short as I stumbled toward the washroom. A thin trickle of blood dripped down the side of my thigh, pooling on the carpet. I felt the terror rise in my throat as I pulled my nightgown tighter around my chest. I could only stare at the blood in dumbfounded silence and fear. Another scream lodged silently in my throat, caught and suspended. It *had* been real. Which meant it *was* real. Which meant Catalina could at that very moment be in danger.

"*Querida,* please open the door. Are you okay?" I could hear Lisboa's anxious voice as she banged on the door.

"*Sim,* Lisboa. I'm all right," I called out, making my way across the room. Lisboa flung herself into my arms the moment I opened the door.

"Clara, Clara, these nightmares. They have to stop." She embraced me. "If not for your sake, then for mine. My poor heart can't take it anymore." She moved away, fanning her hand against her chest dramatically. "*Ai,* Clara!" she exclaimed, catching sight of the bloody gash soaking the edge of my nightgown. "What have you been doing, child?" She moved closer, pushing up the nightgown to reveal the wound and muttering all the while. "Nightmares, strange visions, bloody chickens, and now this. Clara, Clara..." Shaking her head, Lisboa turned around and started to go back down the stairs. "Now you stay right here, and I will return with a poultice, *sim*?"

I rushed to grab Lisboa's arm before she could leave. "No," I said. "Please, Lisboa. You have to help me."

"But I am. You can hardly stand there bleeding on my nice rug." Shaking her head again, Lisboa attempted to break free, but I wouldn't let go.

"Lisboa, you have to listen to me. We can fix my leg later. Right now, we have to go to Copacabana."

"Copacabana?" Lisboa cried, shaking her head and laughing. "*Minha querida,* you're still asleep. Why would we go to Copacabana in the middle of the night?"

I felt another scream rising in my throat. "Lisboa, please," I said, trying to catch her eye. The older woman finally stopped fussing and looked directly at me.

"What is it? Tell me. You saw something in your dream, didn't you?" she said in a sombre voice.

I took both of Lisboa's hands into my own. "Lisboa, I dreamt about another Macumba murder. I think it's happening right now. I think if we can get there on time, we can stop it." I heard Lisboa's sharp intake of breath. She turned her eyes away from mine and fell silent. "Lisboa," I repeated, trying to will her to look at me. But Lisboa was no longer listening. Even while our hands were clasped in a tight embrace, Lisboa had disappeared.

"I cannot," she said so softly that I barely heard her words. Her eyes returned to meet my gaze, and the strong, determined woman I had come to know so well seemed to have vanished. Her eyes were empty, revealing no emotion. "Clara, you know not what you are dealing with. You must stay away." Her words were soft but fierce.

"It's okay, Lisboa. I shouldn't have asked. I should never have expected you to come with me. I'm sorry." I let go of Lisboa's hands and brushed past her, going to my closet. I told myself to breathe steadily and calmly, not to panic. I would go alone. I had no choice. Lisboa was right. It wasn't fair to expect Lisboa to risk her life for something that had nothing to do with her, something I didn't even understand. But I knew I had been given that dream for a reason. And I was going to stop this murder from happening. I hastily pulled clothes off their hangers. A loose T-shirt, a pair of jeans. I brushed past Lisboa and went to the washroom, quickly cleaning the cut, pulling my hair back into a ponytail, and changing from my nightgown into my clothes. By the time I came out of the washroom, Lisboa had left. I grabbed my purse, making sure I had some money for a cab, and ran down the stairs.

As I reached the bottom of the stairs and was about to go out, I saw Lisboa. My friend was dressed, her long hair pulled into a kerchief. "I will not let you go alone," she said simply, pressing some ashes and the statue of Exu into my hands. "For protection," she whispered. And then I caught the glint of the kitchen knife Lisboa held in her other hand along with a small, velvet pouch. "We are not crazy, *não*? Here." She handed me a pocketknife. "You must have something." I started to shake. I didn't understand what this was about and I was too terrified to refuse Lisboa's offer. I'd never physically fought anyone in my life. But Lisboa's calm confidence was reassuring and it gave me the strength to head out into the darkness of the night. I nodded briefly, thanking her with my eyes.

As we made our way down the hill from Santa Teresa into Copacabana in Lisboa's rattletrap of a car, I told Lisboa about my dream.

"So you say you could see the Copacabana Palace and Avenida Atlantica a half block away?" I nodded. Lisboa continued to drive, her eyes focused on the road. "Very good. It can only be in one spot then." We veered wildly into the darkness, the heat of a summer evening pressing upon us, the sparkling lights of Rio below. I could smell the ocean from the open window of the car. "We are close," Lisboa said. She parked the car on a vacant side street. I could see the lights of the Avenida a short distance away, exactly as I had dreamed. My heart started to race in fear. Was this a crazy, delusional goose chase? The moment Lisboa cut the engine, I could feel the danger in the strange stillness of the air. Lisboa turned to me, her face a mask. "We will walk from here."

I nodded, swallowing the lump in my throat. The moment we got out of the car, I was overwhelmed by the stench of rotting garbage and the isolation of the street. The distant sound of revellers was too far away to reach this small, dark spot of isolation. We crept silently, hugging the walls as we made our way down the street. I saw everything exactly as it had appeared only moments before in my sleep. The stench, the distant swirling lights, the black rats running away.... I sucked in my breath, afraid of what I might see. But I couldn't hear anything. No noise at all except the far-off rumble of traffic and the ocean waves. We fell against the coolness of the wall, the plaster crumbling, and I held my pocketknife fiercely in my hand. And then we rounded the corner.

I clamped my mouth to stifle the cry. There, beneath the white glow of the streetlight, lay Catalina. Her body was prone—her legs tied at an odd angle, just like in the dream—with a dark circle of ashes surrounding her. A thin trickle of blood dripped over the ashes, marking the spot where she lay comatose. Her arms were extended and I could see the gashes on her wrists where the blood was beginning to congeal. I felt lightheaded. This couldn't be real. I must still be dreaming. All of this was one dreadful long extension of my nightmare. It had to be.

Meanwhile, Lisboa rushed forward, untying the young woman. "Clara," she whispered. "There's very little time."

I watched as Lisboa checked for a pulse. "She is alive," she said, untying her kerchief and handing it to me. "Here, use this to staunch the flow of blood." I nodded, quickly ripping the kerchief in half and pressing it against Catalina's wrists. There were tiny gashes all over her body, but most of the blood was spilling from the young woman's wrists onto the gravel.

"Catalina," I choked, hoping to reach her. I couldn't think. I could hardly breathe. I was so grateful that Lisboa had come. She seemed to know exactly what to do. I looked around, only to see that the area was completely deserted. The perpetrators had left, assuming in the darkness of night that it wouldn't take long for Catalina's life to slip away in the rivulets of red. They hadn't anticipated a rescue mission. Catalina was meant to be found, but not until morning, when any hope of survival would have long vanished. But now, now she still stood a chance. I watched as Lisboa untied her velvet pouch, removing a thick poultice. She instructed me to move the kerchief for a moment while she applied the poultice and then tied the material tightly around Catalina's wrists. She then applied the poultice wherever there was a gash. "It will stop the blood from flowing. One thing about a *mãe de santo*. She knows about blood."

I continued to undo the bindings on Catalina's legs and tried to lift her head gently. "Catalina, we've come. You're going to be okay," I whispered, hearing the empty sound of regret in my voice, thinking even as I said the false words of reassurance that nothing would ever be okay again.

THE BRIGHT FLORESCENT LIGHTS of the hospital burned into my eyes as I sat and waited on the hard vinyl seat. Lisboa sat silently beside me. An antiseptic smell filled the air, along with the faint sounds of beeping, the murmuring of voices, and the white drone of the computer from the nurses' station. I took another half-hearted sip of my now cold coffee, allowing the harsh, bitter liquid to slide down my throat. I needed the caffeine. We'd been waiting for hours. We had brought Catalina to the closest hospital, and they'd immediately wheeled her in to the emergency department. There was nothing we could do now but wait.

I'd already called Catalina's mother. The poor woman had been lying awake wondering why her daughter hadn't come home. She'd rushed to the hospital, not questioning how or why I'd found Catalina, only praying to God that her daughter would be okay. She sat with Catalina's younger sister, huddled in the corner, their faces clouded over with worry and fear. They didn't blame me for anything. They thanked me profusely. They didn't know the whole story. Seeing their agony nearly tore me apart. Catalina *had* to be okay. The gravity of the situation was starting to hit me, now that the immediate adrenaline was beginning to fade.

"Clara." Lisboa turned to me, her eyes filled with pain. "You saw this in your dream. I hope and pray to Yemanja that young woman will survive. But next time..." She held my gaze, her words unspoken. "I fear for you, Clara. This was a warning directed to you."

I shook my head, not allowing my frightened thoughts to consume me. "I know, Lisboa. But you have to tell me everything. I have to understand what's going on here. I'm in too deep now to be ignorant." I clasped her hands.

Lisboa sighed, staring vacantly down the long, empty hallway—the hallway where they'd wheeled Catalina away only hours before. "I couldn't bear it if that had been you." She wouldn't meet my eyes. Instead, she removed her hands from my grip and smoothed down her skirt. "We will talk. But not now. Not here." Lisboa glanced in my direction, giving me a short nod. "Let's continue our silent prayers and wait for news."

I left it at that. I was too exhausted to argue. We looked up and saw the doctor approach. We both stood immediately, along with Catalina's mother and sister. I listened to the Portuguese words, understanding enough to follow the conversation.

"That young woman has lost a whole lot of blood. She's a lucky thing to even be alive, I tell you. But she's going to be just fine, just fine." He gave us all a brief smile.

"Can we see her?" Catalina's mother asked, and the doctor nodded, directing them to Catalina's room down the hall. Once they had left, he turned to Lisboa and me.

"Now, I'm thinking someone had better go ahead and tell me what happened here."

I hadn't anticipated this. Of course the doctor was going to be suspicious. He saw the wounds. He had read the papers and knew the tell-tale signs of a ritualistic murder. Only this would be the first time a Macumba victim had been saved. The last thing we needed right now was media. Catalina was clearly no longer safe. If we could keep things quiet, maybe we could get Catalina out to the countryside, have her go away for a while. Having her miraculous survival advertised would not do anyone any good.

I looked the doctor directly in the eye and responded in my best Portuguese. "She's my friend. We'd gone out for dinner and she didn't seem well. When I left her at the subway, I was already worried she might hurt herself. She'd mentioned this isolated corner where she planned to go. She's depressive, you see." I glanced at Lisboa, and she nodded. "I worried about her. Finally, I woke up my friend here, Lisboa, and begged her to come with me just to make sure Catalina was okay. I guess it's a good thing I trusted my instincts." I bit my lip, looking down briefly.

The doctor continued to stare at us blankly. "So, what you're saying is that your friend did this to herself?"

I looked up and met his eyes. "Yes, that is exactly it." Our eyes locked, and I felt a strange understanding pass between us. He knew about the Macumba murders as much as anyone. I was also pretty sure he could tell by the cuts that they had not been self-inflicted. But I was banking on his fear, on his reluctance to ask too many questions. And I'd guessed correctly.

The doctor nodded. "Then I think you better get that girl some help. Like I said, she's lucky to be alive." It wasn't until he turned and left that I finally inhaled a full breath of air. I was shaking.

"Clara, let's go." Lisboa steered me toward the exit, and together we made our way into the early morning light.

I gazed out the window as we sped down Avenida Atlantica. The glow of dawn cast pink hues over the ocean waves. The white, sandy beach stretched on for miles and miles, and early morning joggers were already busy along the boardwalk. The famous Copacabana beach. I noticed that Lisboa continued to drive along the Avenida instead of turning to take us back up into the hills of Santa Teresa.

"Lisboa, where are we going?"

Lisboa didn't respond for a moment. "Clara, I think it's best if you remain hidden for a while."

I felt the bile rise in my throat. "Are there things I should know, Lisboa?" I asked, my voice as calm as possible.

Lisboa nodded, her gaze fixed forward on the road. "From the moment I first saw you, I could feel your energy, your *axe*. It is strong, Clara, very strong." She allowed her words a moment for impact. "What I didn't know was why, or how. A foreigner, like yourself ... a student still. Why would the gods have given you this powerful gift? You radiate *axe*, Clara, and yet you are not even aware of it. Do you know how many *mãe de santos* would do anything to gain your kind of power? How many years, how many sacrifices, how much pain they go through all for...."

I watched as Lisboa seemed to choke on her own words. Lisboa was acting so differently suddenly, almost angry. Angry with me. Did I really know Lisboa? Could I trust Lisboa as fully as I believed? Almost since the day of my arrival in Brazil I'd placed all my trust, everything, into Lisboa's hands. Lisboa seemed so knowledgeable, and there I was, an ignorant foreigner carried into the midst of something only Lisboa could help me make sense of. But what if all along Lisboa was the one who couldn't be trusted? I stopped my thought right there. In this crazy world, and in this place where nothing ever seemed to make sense and my own idea of logic was useless, if I didn't trust Lisboa, I couldn't trust anyone. And then I truly would be alone.

"I am going to take you to a safe place. A place where we can talk properly. And I am going to introduce you to someone. Someone you already know, but not as he truly is. Not as I know him. You're right, Clara. You are in too deep. I've been fighting it from the start, but I can no longer ignore it. You are meant to be here. For whatever reason, the gods have chosen you, and who am I to deny their power?"

I felt like a weed being plucked and pulled in every direction with no control over myself or my destiny. Was I just a vessel of the gods? That's what Odún was all about, right? Allowing yourself to be a vessel, to be receptive to the gods, to enable them to access your soul and possess you, briefly merging the destinies of humans and the eternal, and allowing the cycle of life and death to continue.

"What about Catalina? When they find out she's alive, won't they look for her again?" I hated to voice the words, but I couldn't just leave Catalina behind with a mother and sister who had no understanding of what had happened and no way to protect her.

Lisboa nodded. "Yes, I will go back and speak with them. For now she is okay in the hospital. I will tell them that she has been chosen by the gods. I will tell them that I would like to take her on as a daughter of the gods and that I will pay for her expenses."

"But that's crazy," I couldn't stop myself from blurting out.

Lisboa laughed darkly. "We need to remove Catalina from society. And there is no other or better way. Her family is poor. They will be honoured. They will be pleased. They won't ask any questions. If her mother believes her daughter has been chosen, she will let her go freely. She will stay in the *terreiro*."

"But she can't stay there forever," I said, my mind reeling. "She's a young woman with a life, her studies, things going on ... she can't just disappear."

Lisboa glanced at me, her eyes sad and wise. "Ah, but she can, Clara. People disappear every day in Brazil. It's only when their bodies turn up again that it makes the news."

I choked on my own saliva. "Lisboa," I whispered.

Lisboa patted my hand briefly. "Don't worry about Catalina. I will keep her safe. She will be trained as a daughter of the gods, and she will live in the *terreiro* with the other *filhas*. It will give us time, Clara."

I nodded mutely. I was a fish out of water, floundering and still breathing, but gasping desperately all the while. I could just leave. It would be so easy. Take a bus to the airport. Jump on the next flight heading straight back to Toronto. I could be home in ten hours. But I knew it wasn't that simple. The dreams, the visions ... they weren't going to disappear. For some reason I had been called to this country, and, destiny or not, there was no way to escape. I had to understand this calling because it had already consumed me. There was no turning back at this point.

Lisboa veered off the main Avenida and turned into a parking lot outside one of the gleaming high-rises that lined the waterfront. She stopped the engine and turned to me. "This is it," she said, pocketing her car keys and opening the side door. I got out the other side and followed. Compared to the historic disarray of Santa Teresa and the poverty of the *favelas*, this glass building oozed modernity and wealth. We followed a perfectly manicured pathway to the shining double doors of the condo's entrance, the sun glinting off the glass and momentarily blinding me.

"I called ahead," Lisboa was saying as we opened the doors and entered the cool air-conditioning of the sleek, minimalistic lobby. "So he is expecting us."

I had no time for my eyes to adjust from the bright sunlight to the dim blackness of the interior. But I could hear their voices clearly.

"Ah, you came down to meet us." Lisboa's voice registered relief as she approached the silhouetted figure of a man coming out of the elevator. "Clara, this is where you will be staying for a while. Please trust me." Lisboa's eyes implored me as I turned to look at the man standing there. His stance, his commanding presence, his musical voice, his eyes...

I drew in a sharp breath as I once again found myself staring directly into the dark brown eyes of Eduardo Soares.

7

W**HAT ON EARTH WAS GOING ON?** I watched as Lisboa embraced Eduardo. I thought Lisboa disliked Eduardo, that she felt resentful of his power in the *terreiro*. Yet clearly a close relationship existed between them that Lisboa had kept well hidden. Eduardo then turned to me, his face a well-concealed mask.

"Hello, Clara," he said with practised ease, looking at me directly. There were so many unspoken words in his gaze. The last time we'd seen each other was at the Odún ceremony, where we'd made love across the firelight. We'd talked that night. And I'd felt a strong bond. But then he told me to go back home where I belonged. The bitterness rose in my throat. I did not want to meet his gaze.

"Eduardo," I acknowledged briefly, glancing away. Lisboa turned to face me, questions in her eyes.

"Come," she said, taking my arm. "Eduardo, take us up to your suite. Let's not stand here anymore."

We entered the elevator and waited silently in the dark mirrored interior as we rose to the penthouse suite. Clearly, Eduardo had wealth. Did university professors really make that much money? The elevator doors opened to reveal not a hallway, but an entranceway. The entire floor appeared to be Eduardo's suite. I absorbed the rich, mahogany interior, the row of dark panelled glass along the wall, the African masks, and the crystal chandeliers. I allowed my feet to sink into the silky Persian carpets and breathe in the floral scent of freshly cut flowers displayed on the grand dining room table. But Lisboa was unfazed. Clearly, she'd been here many times before. She swept past the luxurious dining room and went straight into the living room, collapsing on the smooth, black leather couch.

I followed Lisboa, my eyes drawn to the row of windows with a beautiful view of a shimmering blue ocean and a white, sandy beach. I walked to the window and stood there a moment. No wonder Eduardo was able to finance the *terreiro*. But where did all his money come from? Eduardo came to stand behind me.

"Please," he said politely. "You've had a long night. Why don't you come sit here beside Lisboa?" His hand touched my shoulder. I turned and met his eyes. They were inscrutable. Why was he being so kind and gentle?

I nodded and allowed Eduardo to lead me to the couch as if I were in a trance.

Lisboa patted the space beside her and smiled. "Come, come, *querida*. It's been a difficult night, *não?*"

I sat down, my legs jittery from exhaustion and too much caffeine. I sank thankfully into the softness of the leather and closed my eyes for a moment.

"You rest. And I will get something to eat and some tea," Eduardo said.

"Such a dear. That would be perfect." Lisboa's voice sounded so calm.

I kept my eyes closed until I could hear Eduardo's footsteps returning. The welcome aroma of steeped tea and warm bread filled the air. I accepted the steaming cup of *maté* tea and bit into the hot-buttered toast. The butter melted in my mouth, and the bread slid effortlessly down my throat. I hadn't realized how hungry I'd been. We were silent as we ate. Then Lisboa turned to Eduardo.

"We must tell her," she said simply. I caught the look that passed between them and my confusion only increased. What were they not telling me? I felt the old panic return. Lisboa's expression was full of concern. What did Eduardo have to do with any of this? The expression on his face was anything but reassuring. He looked away from Lisboa, rubbing his jaw absently. He shook his head.

"Eduardo," Lisboa said, reaching out to take his hand. But he stood up. His gaze slid over to me, his expression now fierce. His eyes were dark and full of unconcealed desire. He looked like he could devour me. I felt myself respond instinctively. Then, to my surprise, he laughed. He ran his fingers through his short hair, allowing the coarse strands to curl, and he laughed again. A bitter-sounding, ironic laugh that was anything but humourous. Lisboa stood and walked over to Eduardo, breaking into rapid Portuguese as her hands danced in the air.

I strained to understand the words. *What had come over him? Why did he look at me that way? What on earth was wrong with him?* I could understand enough to realize that Eduardo was arguing with Lisboa, telling her that he couldn't do it. I couldn't stay there. Lisboa finally threw her arms up in the air and turned to face me. "I'm sorry, Clara, for this. I do not know what has come over this man. My dear friend has gone *louco*." She turned back to Eduardo as she raised her hands in the air again, circling his head. "Completely *louco, sim?*" She gave an enormous sigh and then stormed out of the room, leaving Eduardo and me alone.

Eduardo stood there, an immobile statue. I didn't know what to do. On the one hand, I was still furious with him for making things so difficult for me in Brazil. But ... just seeing him again, looking into his eyes ... all I could think of was how much I wanted him. I didn't understand his resistance to the palpable connection between us. But I wanted to understand. And so I stood up.

"Eduardo." I touched his arm. He didn't move. "Lisboa brought me here for answers. Whatever happened between us, it's not part of this. I don't understand what's going on, but if this is about what happened..." My words trailed off as his eyes met mine. He grasped my hand, which rested gently on his forearm. The strength of his grip was astonishing. He leaned toward me, and I felt my heart start to race. Was he going to kiss me? No, instead he turned his gaze back out the window again. But he didn't let go of my hand.

"I have not made things easy for you, Clara," he said quietly.

I laughed. "No, you sure haven't." There was silence as Eduardo continued to look out the window. "What I don't understand is—why?" I wanted him to turn around. To look at me. I wasn't just asking why he'd made it so difficult for me to do my research. I was asking why he was so determined to ignore our connection. And he knew it.

He finally turned around. "There is so much you don't understand."

"Then tell me." I was tired of this constant evasion. "Just tell me, damn it! You keep saying I don't understand. That it's too dangerous. What the hell is going on? And, come on, Eduardo. You know this is about a lot more than simply research."

Eduardo stood back. "Yes, I do." He didn't say anything more. I felt my anger rise.

"Just admit it, Eduardo. Admit you want to have sex with me." Wow. Where did that come from?

Before I could stop it, I felt the strength of Eduardo's arms around me, the pressure of his lips. His kiss was fierce. Almost desperate. His tongue probed my mouth while his arms pinned me against his chest. It scared me. And yet, I felt the same desperation. The same need to be together, to be united. Every time he kissed me, I was transported to another time, another place. It was Eduardo who pulled away.

"Damn it, Clara." He shook his head, swearing in Portuguese. "Have you no idea? Do you not know who you are? Clara, at some level, you must know."

I couldn't respond. I stood there, feeling exposed somehow. I *did* know. I knew deep down that I had been called to Brazil, to the Odún. And that I'd been fighting the call for years. But

I still didn't understand what it all meant.

"Well, why don't you tell me then? Tell me who I am. Because as far as I can see, I'm nothing special." The words came out in bitterness, and I realized too late how insecure it made me sound. Years of my father telling me just that had taken their toll.

"Nothing special?" Eduardo came to me, holding me close and gently stroking my hair. It felt good to be in his embrace. "*Minha querida*, you are the saviour."

The saviour? I remembered what Catalina had said about the prophecy. What was this? How could it be true?

Lisboa returned to the room at just that moment. Eduardo glanced up and nodded, pulling away from me. "Clara will stay here."

Lisboa approached us, her arms extended. "I knew it, of course." She smiled.

I turned from Eduardo to look directly at Lisboa. "I need to know what's going on. You can't hide anything from me anymore," I said resolutely. I saw Lisboa and Eduardo exchange a glance, and Lisboa gave an almost imperceptible nod.

"Eduardo, I think this may require a great deal more tea, no?" Lisboa said.

"Or a shot of whisky." Eduardo's voice was darkly humourous.

Lisboa gave Eduardo a look. "You and me. We will need to talk, hmm?"

"Hey, a shot of that whisky sounds pretty good to me," I joked, but part of me was serious. I could have used a stiff drink.

Eduardo nodded. "I'm not surprised after the night you've had, Clara." The look in his eyes was now one of concern. I needed to feel his warm embrace again. I couldn't understand my mixed emotions. I only knew that at that moment I wanted to close my eyes and press myself against the hardness of his chest, feel the soft fabric of his shirt against my cheek, and inhale the sweet scent of sugared tea on his breath.

"Eduardo, why don't you make another pot of tea, and I'll

sit with Clara." Lisboa took my hands and led me back to the couch.

"Lisboa…" I began.

Lisboa nodded, her eyes weary. "*Pobrecita,* such difficulties. If only it could be easier, *não?*" Lisboa sighed, staring off into the distance for a moment, still holding my hands. She turned back to me and looked directly into my eyes. "Clara, you know I have told you before what powers you have."

I nodded. "The *axe.*"

"Yes, the *axe.* But there is more. Remember how I spoke of those Macumba murders?"

Nodding, I felt a tiny chill pass through the air. But I wanted, I *needed,* to understand.

"They've been going on for years now. But it has gotten so much worse in the past couple years. Politics and religion in Brazil, they are one and the same, *sim?* During the dictatorship, Odún went underground. But then, after almost twenty-one years, Brazil had democracy again. Democracy, ah yes."

I nodded. "I was here during the dictatorship. In that last summer. I remember how crazy it was."

"Yes, you were here before. I forget that. And it was the first time the drums called to you."

I nodded. Lisboa looked thoughtful. "Well, you were here during a time of great change. As it is now. With democracy comes the electoral process. The politicians quickly realized the benefit of befriending the *mãe de santos,* hmm?" Lisboa shook her head. "Yes, a beneficial relationship was established." Lisboa turned to look at Eduardo, who brought in the pot of tea and placed it on the table.

"Yes, a finely tuned, perfectly functioning system. I'm sure none of this is news to you." Eduardo caught my eye while Lisboa reached over and carefully refilled the three teacups.

I shook my head. "I knew about the relationship between the *terreiros* and the politicians. I guess with each *terreiro* having potentially hundreds of initiates, that's a lot of votes in one go. But even though the politicians establish the relationship with the *mãe de santo,* how is the *ogun* connected?" I directed my question to Eduardo, who I knew was the *ogun* for Lisboa's *terreiro.*

He smiled. "Well, I like to think I hold all the political power, but we know who really does." He looked at Lisboa with one eyebrow raised. She swatted at his arm.

"Yes, Clara, in the majority of the *terreiros* it is the *ogun* who typically makes the political decisions or at least appears to be doing so. He's the political face of the *terreiro.* Other than initiate fees, he also provides the majority of the funding for the *terreiro.* But the *mãe de santo* holds all the power." She gave Eduardo a wink.

"And you never let me forget that!" Eduardo took a seat beside me, and I felt his presence keenly, the way his leg rubbed against mine, the way his arm brushed my hand briefly. I told myself to focus on the conversation.

"But now," Lisboa continued, her voice darker, "the Macumba sects have become more powerful. Odún is about white magic and female power. We gain energy from nature, from the goddesses of the forest, the trees, the ocean, the wind. Macumba is all about black magic and male power. And they use their powers...." Lisboa glanced around the room, her voice suddenly becoming soft. The breeze from an open window brushed against my cheek, startling me.

"The powers of Exu..." she filled in. I instinctively sank deeper into the couch, as if to protect myself. I thought of those yellow eyes haunting me, the eyes of Exu. Was I being haunted and tormented by the Macumba?

Lisboa nodded. "Yes, they use Exu to fulfill their evil plans. But they are slaves to him."

Lisboa was silent for a moment. All I could hear was the sound of her teacup tinkling against her plate as she raised it to her lips. She took a small sip and waited. Pulling herself out of her reverie, Lisboa sighed dramatically again. "Drink,

drink," she exclaimed, indicating that I should finish all my tea and have some more. She lifted the teapot to refill my already brimming cup, but I just shook my head. Eduardo stood up and walked to a silver bar cart in the corner. He filled three crystal whisky glasses, eyeing Lisboa and me as we nodded and smiled. He returned, handing each of us a glass. Then he went back for his own glass, drinking it down in what seemed like one gulp. I knew just what it would feel like to kiss his whisky-soaked lips, feeling his tongue dart into my mouth, tasting the acrid flavour of the smoky whisky while I pressed my lips against his. How on earth was I going to live in this apartment without wanting him so badly? I took a sip of the strong brown liquid from my own glass, allowing the burning sensation to slide down my throat. It only took a few minutes to feel the warmth spread throughout my whole body, threatening to ignite my lusty thoughts even more. I needed to concentrate on what Lisboa was saying. This was important.

"So," Lisboa continued, "they use fear and intimidation. They suck people in. Poor people. People with little to lose and much to gain. People who must pay initiation fees in Odún but can be initiated into Macumba for nothing. And they have slowly destroyed over half of the existing *terreiros* in Rio. The poor are now going to Macumba for sustenance and hope, and no longer to Odún. Yet once they cross over, there is no turning back. They are trapped forever. And if they do try to go back to Odún..." Lisboa stopped, and Eduardo filled in the blanks for her.

"Only a tiny percentage of the murders end up in the papers. The ritualistic murders are deliberate, meant to instigate and perpetuate the fear. But death means nothing in Brazil. Especially the death of the poor."

"So they're killed? Just like that?" I bit my lip. I understood the brutality of a society in which "cleaning up the streets" meant the "disappearance" of homeless children. I thought back to the article I'd read about how the federal police reported close to 5,000 children murdered in Brazil between 1988 and 1990 and I was once again horrified. It was still difficult to comprehend.

Eduardo nodded. "Life is fleeting. But death is constant." He glanced away.

"So that man, Lisboa, who threatened you.... He mentioned the Macumba." I was trying to understand everything and fit the pieces together.

"Clara, I have the largest remaining *terreiro* in Rio. We are still powerful. And they want to destroy us. But I am not willing to back down, no matter what." Lisboa put down her whisky glass a little too forcefully, and the liquid sloshed over the side onto the coffee table. I just stared at it blankly. So I understood now the threats and the fear. But I knew there was more to it than that.

"What else have you not told me?" I asked, determined to hear everything.

"I've been doing some research." Eduardo's voice was low, its musical tone softened by the severity of the conversation. "Things have been escalating. You know about Velho?" I knew it would come back to Rio's mayor. Ever since I'd seen that picture of Bento Velho in the paper, I had suspected that he was central to everything. That blank look in his eyes, despite the cagey smile on his face, spoke volumes.

"Yes. I asked you about him the other day. Remember, Lisboa?"

Lisboa nodded. "*Sim*. Clara, I wasn't ready yet to tell you. I didn't want to get you involved."

"But clearly I am involved. So what about him?"

"Clara, I've been researching the Macumba. Undercover, so to speak. And I've seen him." Eduardo paused. He seemed anxious. I'd never seen him spooked by anything. He cleared his throat and went on. "We have reason to believe he's the leader of the largest Macumba sect in Rio."

I stared at Eduardo in shock. "Rio's current mayor is a Macumba lord?" I repeated.

Lisboa placed a finger on my lips. "Hush," she whispered, glancing around the room. I felt the tension; the room vibrated with nervous energy. "They're everywhere."

I shook my head. "Who?"

Both Lisboa and Eduardo were silent for a moment. Then Eduardo looked directly into my eyes. "You've witnessed it. You've experienced it. You know the power of the gods. The power of Macumba is the same. If Exu is doing their bidding, there is no escape."

I shivered, wishing I had a sweater to pull closer around my body. Eduardo noticed and draped his arm over my shoulder, pulling me against his chest. I felt his warmth and security. It felt good. It was what I'd needed. What was going on? How had I managed to become involved in something so big, so strange? And in a country where magic and rituals were part of everyday life?

"Clara, we must stop him."

I clung to Eduardo's body, trying to block out the fear. "But he looks so perfect in all the pictures. He's got the good looks. He's from some aristocratic Brazilian family, isn't he? I mean, he's wealthy, and he's always travelling around the world. He's well-known, a celebrity even."

"I know he's the one responsible for the murders. But he's clever. He makes it appear as if it's a subculture cult committing these acts. He's even spoken against it, saying he'll clean up the streets of Rio." Eduardo sighed, running his hands through his hair. "The people don't know. They think they voted for one man, but what they got is someone entirely different. We need to expose him; otherwise he will destroy not only Odún, but also Brazil itself. His power extends far. There's talk that the president may be impeached. We might just be looking at Velho as our next president. We will become a nation of terror once again."

I pulled away from Eduardo's embrace. "Why are you telling me all this now? Lisboa, you waited three weeks to even tell me that you are a *mãe de santo*. And you." I poked Eduardo in the chest. "You've been trying to get rid of me from day one. And what about that dead chicken, huh? I saw Chico hiding in the bushes the next morning. What about that?"

Lisboa glanced at Eduardo, her eyes questioning. Eduardo sighed. "Yes, I will admit, that was my doing."

"Eduardo!" It looked like Lisboa was going to whop him behind the ear. "How could you frighten Clara like that?"

Eduardo just shook his head. "It was wrong. But I was desperate." He glanced up at me, imploring me with his eyes.

"And to have a young boy do your bidding. Really, Eduardo." While Eduardo and I stared each other down, Lisboa was fuming. Eduardo was the first to look away.

"Lisboa, please. I know it was wrong. But you have to understand my position. At the time I felt that the only solution was to have Clara leave the country. I didn't understand yet." The room fell silent for a moment.

"Well, I suppose it's good news in a way. It means the Macumba lords didn't send it." I sighed. Lisboa nodded abruptly.

"Quite right. Well then, we'll put it behind us." She gave Eduardo a stern glance.

"But as I was saying, why now? Why are you finally telling me everything now? Eduardo even admitted how badly he wanted me gone. What's changed?" I stared from Lisboa to Eduardo, demanding answers.

Lisboa reached out again to clasp my hands. "Because you have the power of *axe,* Clara. For whatever reason, the gods have sent you to us. We've tried to deny it. We didn't recognize it at first. But now we know." Lisboa's voice was calm and dark. I'd never heard her speak like that before.

"Know what?" I whispered, already knowing the answer.

"That you have been sent here for a reason. You are here to stop it. To save the Odún."

I shook my head, a hysterical laugh bubbling in my throat. Oh, no. Not this again. I pulled out of Lisboa's grasp and stood up. "That's ridiculous," I said. I couldn't even look into either Eduardo's or Lisboa's eyes. But I could hear Eduardo trying to reach me.

"Clara, every era has a saviour. Whenever the Odún has been under threat. And it always survives. History repeats itself. We've been waiting for your arrival. We just didn't recognize that it was you. We didn't expect a foreigner. A student." He stopped, noticing my anger.

"So I'm the chosen one, hmm? Chosen by the gods to save Odún from disaster." I threw my hands into the air. I couldn't hear this anymore. I'd entered my own nightmares, and I couldn't seem to wake myself up. I strode over to the window, wanting to block everything out, to escape. I stared at the ocean, a great blue expanse, the line of high-rises edging the waterfront like crystal jewels. Such a dramatic landscape with so much beauty. And so much ugliness. I thought of Catalina. I touched the cool glass, leaning my head against it in exhaustion.

"A saviour. What does that even mean? I don't believe in saviour fairy tales. It's never just one person." I turned around, suddenly feeling like I needed to speak up. I was tired of being led around, of waiting for everyone to tell me things. Eduardo came to stand beside me. I felt his hand caress my cheek. I leaned in to his touch. I couldn't seem to stop myself. How are you involved in all this, Eduardo? The lover of my days and nights. How do you fit into this magical and surreal picture?

"Clara," he whispered, placing his arms lightly around my shoulders. I sank back into his embrace. I didn't want to think anymore. But I knew I couldn't stop now. It was time I started to take control of my own destiny and start writing my own story. I wasn't just a vessel of the gods. I had agency. I had an identity. And I needed to start figuring out who the hell I really was and stop trying to be what others wanted me to be.

"I'm not a saviour. Maybe I have something. I don't know. Something powerful, who can say for sure? But this whole idea of one person coming to save the world ... I don't think so." I stood straighter, moving out of Eduardo's embrace. Maybe it was the alcohol. I wasn't sure. But I suddenly felt like I had a lot I needed to say. "Maybe there's a prophecy. And a history. But it's never just one person who saves the day. It might sometimes seem that way in the end. But it's everything that happens before and between. All the people who come together. Like both of you. It's about community. So don't call me the foreigner who comes to save Odún anymore because I'm tired of being identified as an outsider, and I'm tired of having to live up to some singular saviour complex." I looked at them both, my shoulders back, my face determined.

I could see both Lisboa and Eduardo smiling. Eduardo looked at me with pure admiration. He had looked at me with longing before, and maybe even love, but now there was something more. Respect. "Yes, Clara. You're right."

Lisboa nodded. "The prophecy talks about the saviour, of course, through the ages. But we all know it's more than that. The saviour story is a good one, no? Everyone likes it." Lisboa smiled at Clara, acknowledging what she had said. "Odún has always been about the strength of community. That's what it is. The strength of women coming together." Eduardo raised an eyebrow. "And sometimes men can join us too," she added with a laugh. But then she was serious again. "Clara, I should apologize to you. All this time, I kept thinking, why would the gods choose this young Canadian girl? And you know, it was only my own jealousy. I might have the power of *axe*, but I will never possess what you do. I have never had the power of dreams or prophecy. The way you dreamed of Catalina..." She shook her head. "That was really something. And I do need to stop talking about you as a foreigner. What does that mean anyway when we've all had multiple lives? When the Odún pantheon is about multiple reincarnations and identities?

A black Brazilian woman in one life and a white Canadian woman in another. How can we break down identity and talk about it as one thing, when our very belief system suggests we can be and have been everything?"

I nodded, feeling stronger somehow. I felt for the first time that my voice was being heard. And that I was finally starting to figure out who I needed to be in all this. Maybe things didn't make sense yet, but somehow, with Lisboa and Eduardo by my side, at least in that moment, I felt good. They both put their arms around me, and we hugged. I felt overwhelming love for both of them, and I realized how in just a few short months I had come to feel more connected to Eduardo and Lisboa than I ever had with anyone else before. I needed to allow these connections to happen. I needed to allow myself the freedom to love.

"Well, I'm done," Lisboa stated, yawning and waving her arms. I was suddenly exhausted as well. Eduardo touched my shoulder gently, noticing my tired eyes. I downed the last of my whisky, and he took my glass and placed it on the table. He put his arm around me again, and I let him walk me across the living room and down the hall to a small guest bedroom. Eduardo continued to hold me as he led me to the bed, where he told me to rest. And when I closed my eyes, I felt the reassuring touch of Eduardo's lips brushing mine. I allowed the blissful unawareness of sleep to take over, praying that this time, there would be no nightmares.

8

THE THICK, MOIST HEAT OF THE JUNGLE *surrounded us. The sound of the macaws and the howler monkeys. The feel of the bristly mat and the prickly undergrowth beneath. The scent of smoke and crushed earth. And the sensations. Wild and intoxicating. The feel of his tongue sliding down my abdomen, stroking, caressing, gliding toward my centre. His arms, the sinewy muscles holding me tight as I wrapped my body into his. The feel of his skin next to mine. His whispered words of love in Nagô, spoken in his musical voice. The taste of his salty skin as I nipped at his ear and ran my tongue along his throat. I caressed his smooth head as his tongue licked and circled my clit, making me explode with sensation, my climax coursing through my entire body. He came back up, trailing kisses along my thighs, my stomach, my breasts, my neck, the sweet hint of rum and cane sugar on his breath. His tongue darted into my mouth, each thrust matching the movement of our bodies. I wanted to feel all of him. I wanted him inside me.*

I reached down to caress his cock and heard his groan. His hands cupped my breasts, his mouth tugging at my nipple. I allowed myself to feel every sensation—the warm breeze blowing across my face, the sweat dripping down my forehead. I looked directly into his eyes and stared into his soul. "Zumbi," *I whispered. His dark brown eyes held me mesmerized as he guided himself into me.*

He filled me in one swift motion. We were both so eager, so ready for this. I raised my hips to meet his every thrust and pushed my body upward. I wanted him even more. Nothing could satisfy my hunger, my driving need for him. I loved the feel of his weight on top of me, his smooth dark, glistening skin and his strong chest muscles. I pushed on his shoulders, indicating that I wanted him to go deeper. He flipped me over so I was on my knees, my backside raised high. I pushed my ass into the air and allowed my breath to escape as he thrust his penis deep into me. He thrust again and again, each thrust becoming more fierce and intense. And I met him thrust for thrust. His hand wrapped around my hair, and I pulled myself up so I was now sitting upright, his cock still hard inside me. His hands moved over my breasts, pinching the nipples while his tongue darted in and out of my ear. "Ife," his dark voice whispered. I heard my own cry blending with those of the howler monkeys. And finally I felt the intense release shake my entire body.

But, in the next moment, the sensations crashed together and created pandemonium. The screaming, the stench of burning fires, the heat, the chaos. He was still inside me, and I couldn't understand what had happened. Suddenly we were torn apart. Cruel hands circled my wrist and yanked my naked body away from my King. I cried out in fear, shocked and confused. I looked into the eyes of my tormentors and realized it was all over. We had been discovered. Palmares was being raided and destroyed. I turned my neck to glance one more time at my husband and saw the pain in his eyes. He knew it, too. It was the end for both of us.

I WOKE IN A RIVER OF SWEAT. My sheets were soaking wet and wrapped around my body so tightly that I felt suffocated. My breath came way too fast. I untangled myself from the sheets and sat straight up in bed, trying to calm my racing heart. I took several deep breaths and looked around the simple room for reassurance. The dream had been so real. It had felt so real. I had been there. I could still feel the heat within me, the moistness of my climax between my legs. The lingering sensation of his hard penis still deep within.

I forced myself to count to ten, to inhale and exhale deeply. Finally, my breathing seemed to calm down a bit. I stood up on shaky feet and decided to find the kitchen for a glass of water. I noticed someone had left a clean T-shirt on the bedroom chair. Relieved, I took off my rumpled-up clothing and put on the T-shirt instead. It smelled of fresh laundry, and I inhaled the scent of normalcy, touching the cotton and thinking that the T-shirt must belong to Eduardo. The condo was eerily silent. It appeared that both Lisboa and Eduardo had left. I glanced at the living room clock, realizing I'd slept for nearly the entire day. The shimmering lights of Rio dotted the waterfront with their brilliance. I stood for a moment in my bare feet, just staring out the expansive window at the view. Rio at night glittered like a cut diamond. I turned away from the window and padded over to my original destination. After gulping down a tall, cool glass of water, I sat at the kitchen table, too numb to do much of anything else.

What did all these dreams mean? Were they some kind of message? Why was I being sent to these places and made to feel all the sensations? And what about Eduardo? Zumbi's dark brown eyes were Eduardo's. But his skin was smooth and black, his bald head shiny. I thought of how it felt to touch Eduardo's short thick hair, running my hand along the bristled texture. Eduardo was strong and lean. His skin glistened darkly, his chest hair tickling me when I ran my hands along his body. Zumbi was thick and fierce, his muscles bulging and his skin smooth. Their bodies were so different, but they were the same. I knew it. It was Eduardo's soul. It was always Eduardo. Why did he enter my every dream like a shadow that followed me everywhere? And what about me? Was I Ife? I could feel everything she felt. I made love to

Zumbi in Ife's body, feeling the strength in her muscled legs and wide hips, feeling the pull when Zumbi held her thick, coarse hair. I understood now what Lisboa had meant. How could I be an outsider when in a past life I had been a black woman and an escaped Yoruba slave who became a Queen? How can we think of any identity as rigid in a paradigm of multiple lives? Even in only one life we take on so many different personas, as I was quickly learning.

Sighing, I decided to look for some answers on my own. *Zumbi. Ife. Palmares.* Clearly, I was dreaming about a place that actually existed. All of my dreams were different versions of reality. I knew a little bit about the escaped slave kingdom from the seventeenth century, but not enough. There was a reason my mind kept taking me back there. A message I needed to understand. And I knew that everything was somehow connected to the Macumba murders.

I couldn't very well leave the condo. Not now, not at night. I was supposed to be in hiding, after all. But surely Eduardo would have some reference books on Brazilian history. He was a professor after all. Maybe he had a library in this monolithic mansion. Feeling like a sleuth, I wandered around the condo in my bare feet, amazed at its size. It was like a floating palace in the sky, decorated with rich fabrics and dark wood furniture. Sure enough, when I looked down a hallway off the living room, I caught a glimpse of a small study lined with bookshelves. Aha, the library. I walked down the hall and pushed the door open all the way. Clearly, this was where Eduardo liked to spend his time. This was the most lived-in area of the condo. Books and magazines were strewn across the sofa. A large mahogany desk stood in the corner, an imposing black office chair before it. Papers, documents, and files were everywhere, covering the desk and side tables, barely leaving room for the lamps that lent a warm glow to the space. The entire area exuded maleness.

Amazing what you could learn about a person just by being in his home. The rest of the condo was sterile. But not this room. It was filled with a warmth and openness I'd rarely witnessed in Eduardo. He was still such a mystery to me. I knew nothing about him. We were connected in such an esoteric way, and yet in reality we had barely any connection at all. Other than physical, of course. But the physical was a memory. A memory of a previous life? Is that what all the dreams were about? I needed to find out.

I started scanning the bookshelves, trying to find anything relevant. Probably a book on seventeenth-century Brazilian history would be the most useful. I was fascinated by Eduardo's collection of books. I believed that you could learn so much by what books and magazines people read. I noticed he had a series of Brazilian news and economics magazines. But he also had a number of anthropology journals and articles. I would love to read his work. Of course, most of it would be written in Portuguese. I was surprised to find a selection of literary authors from around the world. Impressive. So Eduardo liked to read fiction, as well. We shared that in common. Ah, there it was. He had a whole section on Brazilian history, and most of it was in English. I had my choice of books.

I grabbed the closest English history book and sat on the sofa, scanning its contents. Perfect. A whole chapter about the freed slave kingdom, Palmares, and its rebel king. I scanned the information quickly, absorbing every word. Zumbi was the rebellious nephew of Ganga Zumba, the first king of Palmares. When Ganga Zumba agreed to a settlement with the Portuguese administration for the freedom of Palmares, his nephew, Zumbi, disagreed. He did not believe in submission. Nor in securing protection only for themselves when the rest of the African community remained enslaved. Zumbi wanted to continue fighting for the freedom of the people. And so, when Ganga Zumba mysteriously died, Zumbi became the next rightful King of Palmares. With his Queen by his side. Queen Ife.

I sank back into the plush softness of the sofa. What did this mean? How could I have possibly dreamt about names and places I didn't know? In the dream, I had been Queen Ife. I'd felt everything. I'd seen everything through Ife's eyes. I'd even thought Ife's thoughts. It was as if I'd gone back in time and relived that period in history. I read on, wanting to know and understand everything.

Zumbi did continue to fight. He was a brave and strong military man, passionate about his beliefs. And Ife fought right beside him. Until the day the Portuguese finally discovered the location of the largest Palmares community. An enormous raid destroyed everything. I thought of the dream—the smell of fires burning, the screams, being torn from the arms of my lover. My realization that it was all over. It was the end. I'd gone back to the night of the raid in my dream. I had been there.

But why? What did this mean? I continued reading, my eyes glued to the page. Ife was captured that fateful night. But Zumbi managed to escape, although not for long. Betrayed by one of his most trusted friends, he was discovered and captured again. I read the final, cold sentence. King Zumbi and Queen Ife were both beheaded on the morning of November 20, 1695. *Beheaded.* I shivered.

November 20. I thought about that day, about whether there was anything significant there. What had I been doing on November 20 of last year? Immersed in my studies, I'd been starting to prepare for my upcoming trip to Brazil in February. I'd been organizing my notes, trying to establish contact with the Universidade Federal do Rio de Janeiro and to define my thesis. Yes, I was almost sure of it. It would have been right around that time that I'd first made contact with Eduardo. It might have even been that exact day. With a sudden feeling of urgency, I jumped off the sofa and raced to the guestroom. I dug through my purse for my daytimer. Sure enough, there it was. *November 20, 9:30 a.m. phone meeting with Dr. Eduardo*

Soares, Professor of Anthropology, Universidade Federal do Rio de Janeiro.

I could remember the day clearly. I'd been nervous. I remembered dialling the number with shaking fingers. And then the conversation had been so brief. I remembered hearing his musical voice for the first time. But his words, even then, had been cold and functional. He'd been polite enough, but that was about it. I'd been having dreams and nightmares on and off for years. Ever since I'd started studying Odún in undergrad. But now, I remembered vividly that it was the night of November 20 that I'd had my first visionary dream. Now I understood why Lisboa's home had seemed so familiar. I'd dreamt about it that night. I'd been there. I bit my lip as the realization struck me. How could I have forgotten? Yes, I could see it clearly now. I'd been in the bedroom, with the silky white curtains blowing in the breeze and the scent of the bougainvillea tree drifting across the room from the open sliding doors. I'd been there with my lover. That was the first time I'd dreamt of my phantom lover. My dream that night had been much like the waking vision I'd had upon arriving in Lisboa's home that first time. Why hadn't I made the connection sooner? But again, what did it all mean? My phantom lover beneath the white, satin sheets was not the king of Palmares as in the other dreams. He was someone different. I tried to remember what he looked like. Something beyond his deep gaze. And all I could visualize was a tall, broad-set, light-skinned man with dark, wavy hair that fell into his hazel eyes as he looked at me.

I sighed. I couldn't make sense of it. Obviously the home in Santa Teresa didn't exist in the seventeenth century. So what time period was that? Was it another past life I was dreaming about? Was this my unconscious mind taking me back to all my previous selves? But why? I knew that the Odún practitioners believed that when there is discordance, it makes your reigning Orixa stronger. Was that what this was all about? Perhaps, because of my violent death in the seventeenth century, my reigning Orixa couldn't rest and thus continued to haunt me. But again, what did any of this have to do with the Macumba murders? I went back to Eduardo's study to read some more. But, once I got there, I found myself simply staring at the pages blankly until I felt a presence in the room. Startled, I glanced up. Eduardo stood in the doorway. I'd been thinking about him all night and all day. And now, there he stood. Who was he, really? And how did he fit into my life?

"I see you slept all day," he commented, walking toward the couch. I nodded. I wasn't ready to talk to him about my dreams and visions. To admit my seemingly intimate connection with him. To say to Eduardo that I had a strong feeling we were lovers in past lives. That perhaps we'd been lovers all along, following each other through the generations. Which meant, of course, that we were meant to be together in the deepest sense. No, I certainly wasn't ready for that yet. My feelings for Eduardo were still so raw, so confused. He had treated me so indifferently and yet made love to me with such conviction. I needed to understand him better before I could start discussing eternity and soul mates. So I decided not to tell him about Palmares and what I'd just been researching.

"How are you?" Eduardo looked at me with an intensity I couldn't ignore. The question was far from a casual "How are you doing?" The concern in his voice was palpable.

I shook my head, glancing away briefly. I didn't even know how to act around Eduardo anymore. Not that I ever did.

"I slept really well. I definitely needed that," I answered, trying hard not to meet his gaze.

Eduardo touched my face gently and turned my chin so I looked at him directly. "Clara, I want you to know…" he hesitated, and I waited. His eyes bore into mine, and I felt as though our souls were merging. But what we communicated with our eyes remained unspoken in words. He sighed and broke the intense gaze. "I know this must be difficult for you," he finally whispered, lightly tracing my cheek with his finger. I wanted to tell him everything. Everything I felt. Everything I thought could be true. But I just couldn't do it. It wasn't in me to give so much of myself. Or to reveal my emotions like that.

"I've been looking at your book collection. Very impressive." Eduardo laughed. "Yes, I love to read."

"Well, I do, too. I wasn't surprised to see Gilberto Freyre's *The Masters and the Slaves*. But you have some great literary books, as well. Like stuff by Jorge Amado."

"Aha. I don't strike you as the literary type?" He raised one eyebrow, and I couldn't help but laugh.

"Actually, you do. And I shouldn't be surprised. Amado does talk about the Odún in his work. And Freyre's ideas in the 1930s created Brazil's whole concept of a racial democracy, didn't they?"

Eduardo whistled. "Indeed, they did. And we've been living with that fallacy ever since."

"Most of the Odún initiates are black, aren't they?"

"As opposed to white?" Eduardo winked at me. "Not sure if those divisions even exist here. Only politically. But yes. It's really a religion of the north. Salvador da Bahia. It came here with all the migrant workers hoping to find a better life in Rio. And the majority of the practitioners would self-identify as black."

"And did they? Find a better life?"

Eduardo came and sat down beside me, resting his head against the back of the couch. I was uncomfortably aware of the lemon scent of his aftershave, the feel of his bare arm against mine, the distracting sight of his strong hands. His nearness brought back vivid images from my dream. I saw, felt us together again—the taste of him, the feel of him on top of me.... I made myself focus on the conversation because I didn't want to lose myself again. I wanted to talk to Eduardo.

"I think you know the answer to that. Most of them live in the *favelas*. Or work as nannies or maids. But you're right.

These are the people who come to the Odún. As you know, it is a religion of women. Until things change, they have few other options for power in this country of ours." Eduardo sighed. "Desperate people hoping to find answers."

I smiled. "I guess we're desperate then, huh?"

"I guess so." Although Eduardo smiled, I could feel the tension. Yes, we were desperate. But what an interesting thing for him to say. I wondered how he reconciled religion and academia.

"So how do you self-identify?" I asked.

Eduardo looked at me curiously. "I'm black, Clara. And I would never for a moment hesitate to self-identify that way."

I nodded. I understood the racial politics in Brazil, the racial democracy that in reality meant a racial scale of light to dark with descending access to resources and privilege. Eduardo was dark-skinned, but he could technically "pass." And yet he self-identified as black. I knew that for Eduardo that was a political stance, and I admired him for it.

"Have you ever loved a white woman before?" I couldn't seem to help myself. Since we were opening up the race discussion, I wanted to know.

Eduardo laughed, pulling me in closer. "Ha ... I thought we were both supposed to be anthropologists breaking down racial constructions?"

I smiled, realizing that I really just wanted to know if he'd ever fallen in love before.

"And what about you?" he teased.

I turned my head and smiled slightly. "Have I ever fallen in love? Maybe," I responded coyly. But it wasn't true. In fact, the thought of falling in love terrified me. I expected him to laugh, but he didn't.

"Odún also has some powerful wealthy patrons," he pointed out, turning serious again. "But it used to have more. Things have been changing. Odún is meant to be a religion of resistance, of the people. It's meant to break down class and racial divides. But of course it's political, like everything, and it depends on the *mãe de santo*. Like anything, some of the *mãe de santos* are just in it for the money. It can be very lucrative."

I nodded, resting my head on his shoulder. It felt good to be sitting together talking. I wanted to learn more about this man.

"So what is your favourite book in your library?" I asked.

Eduardo leaned back, thinking for a minute. "Now that question is too difficult. I have too many I love."

I laughed. "You know, I originally thought that I wanted to be an English major. Until my dad..." I shrugged, deciding I didn't want to bring up the subject of my father at that moment.

"Clara," Eduardo sat up, "why don't you tell me about your dad?" How did he know it was a sore topic? "Earlier today, when you told me you didn't think you were anything special—why would you believe that?"

I didn't want to broach the topic. Talking about how my father managed to make me feel like a failure was not something I wanted to share. But Eduardo seemed to know this. It was as if we knew each other without even needing to speak the words. What was the point in concealing the truth?

"My father's an oil executive, although I have no idea what he actually does. All I know is that he's in some kind of management position and makes a decent amount of money. But he was never home when I was a kid. And I was okay with that." I stopped, not sure if I wanted to continue. But Eduardo's presence gave me a quiet reassurance. "Anyway, I guess he's a competitive person. Type A personality or whatever. I'm an only child. So all the pressure was on me to follow in his footsteps. He was happy enough when I went to university and when he thought I would get a degree in business. But when I switched my major to Anthropology, he practically disowned me. He always managed to make me feel like I wasn't doing enough." I stopped, shocked that I'd blurted out all that.

"You must be a strong person, Clara. To have faced all that opposition and still do what you wanted."

"I never thought of it that way." I often felt so weak inside. As though I had to make up for my weakness with outward strength. What Eduardo said made me look at things differently.

"Our parents can put a lot of pressure on us." Eduardo uttered those words as if he knew from personal experience.

"Eduardo, where are your parents? Are they here in Rio?" It seemed incredible to me that I didn't even know this basic information.

"Yes. My father works in finance. We are what you might call one of Brazil's aristocratic families. Kind of like our mayor."

I shook my head. "You mean, you ran in the same social circles as Velho?"

Eduardo nodded. "Why do you think I know him so well? I grew up in that elite political world. But I left all that when I entered academia."

"But you still have the wealth." The words just came out.

He looked at me and smiled. "Yes, indeed. An inheritance from my grandfather. I have been fortunate."

He'd obviously come from generations of money.

"But I have also learned what wealth can do. I have no intention of throwing it all away. Clara, I have never claimed to be anything other than what I am. I give generously to Odún because I can afford to do so. I believe in a more equal society, and I do what I can to make that happen. But I do own this penthouse suite, and I won't be hypocritical and not admit that I recognize my good fortune."

I nodded. I understood what he was saying. I fought every day for social justice and equality. I was always trying to think of alternatives to capitalism and debating different political systems. But at the end of the day, I too came from a family with privilege. I might not be in contact with my parents, but I couldn't deny that I'd had a comfortable upbringing. "So you broke away from your family then?"

Eduardo nodded. "A necessity. I couldn't be an *ogun* and have my family's support at the same time."

"But what about your mom?"

Eduardo smiled gently, his expression sad. "My mom passed away."

I held his hand. "I'm sorry," I said, wanting to know everything about this man.

"When my dad married my mom, my grandfather was so angry." He shook his head and I waited for him to continue. "She would darken the family," he'd said. "She came from the north, from Salvador. She had the most exquisite voice. And she was so beautiful. She moved to Manaus to become an opera singer. When my father went to hear her sing one night at the Amazon Theatre in Manaus on a business trip, he fell in love." Eduardo looked up and we smiled at each other. "But then she got sick with cancer when I was twelve and she was gone."

I gently stroked his face. "That must have been so hard."

Eduardo was quiet for a moment. "Do you miss your family?"

I was taken aback by the question. But yes, I realized that I did. Despite the problems with my father, I still loved them. "Yes, I do," I said quietly. "Especially my mom. You know, sometimes, when I get scared…" I bit my lip and saw Eduardo looking at me.

"Ah, *minha querida*. I wish I could take it all away. I wish we could just be meeting like two ordinary people falling in love." He gently kissed my hand.

"But isn't that what we are?" I looked up into his eyes, and I felt that rush in the pit of my stomach. I couldn't push away my feelings anymore. And I didn't want to. I wanted to feel Eduardo again. I wanted him to be my lover in reality again. Not just in my dreams.

"Eduardo." I reached out and touched his lips gently. He pressed his hand against my finger and then sucked gently on it, the pull of his lips on my fingertip mesmerizing. He was in another place and so was I. Neither of us could stop the inevitable. He let go of my finger to bring his hand behind my neck and pull me forward so his lips could meet mine. The kiss began sweetly, our lips meeting in a gentle dance, our tongues circling. But as his other hand reached over to caress me and bring me further into his embrace, the kiss deepened and increased in intensity. It was like the dream, and yet it wasn't. I was not Queen Ife, and he was not Zumbi. Yet the connection was the same. The incredible bond. The feeling I had had from the first moment we'd made love that night of the Carnival. As if we had done this a thousand times before, and each time it only got better.

We didn't speak. We just fell into each other's embrace. I no longer felt that this was wrong or that we should stop things. This was exactly where I should be, where I wanted to be. In the arms of my eternal lover. Eduardo's kiss became more demanding as he caressed my breasts and his hands ran down my entire body. I shivered with the sensation. He lifted my T-shirt over my head in one smooth motion. I gasped as the warm air hit my skin. He pushed me gently back against the couch and rained kisses along my breasts and abdomen while his hands caressed my body and then reached down to take off my panties. He pushed my legs open, and I lost all comprehensive thought as his tongue proceeded to dart expertly around my clit. Eduardo had once again reduced me to a mass of sensation. I could feel everything, just like in my dreams. The moist air from an open window brushing against my exposed nipples, still wet from Eduardo's tongue; the smooth texture of the couch behind my back; the feel of Eduardo's strong arms and the riveting sensation of my building climax. I couldn't stop my cries of sheer release as I felt the waves of my climax build and descend.

I could hear Eduardo undoing his fly and the thunk as his pants hit the floor. I opened my eyes and just stared at his body. He had raised himself above me, and he was quickly undoing the buttons on his shirt. In the next moment, he took my arms and raised them above my head. Then he sucked fiercely on my nipple while he teased me with the feel of his hard cock.

"I can't imagine you wanting me more than I want you in this moment," he whispered. "But I like to hear you beg for it."

I nodded, losing all sense of anything. I was desperate and wild and intoxicated. "Believe me, I'm begging."

Eduardo nudged his penis further, just edging the tip into my centre. I squirmed and raised my hips to get him to go deeper but he continued to edge his way in slowly. I heard my breath start to come in frantic pants. "Eduardo." I could feel my insides melting and my whole body shaking from need. He finally urged himself fully inside, and I sighed as his cock filled me. But then he pulled out again.

"I need you now," I said, any sense of decency and politeness long gone. Why was he teasing me like this? But it was deliciously intoxicating as well. Eduardo leaned back, taking his grip off my hands and releasing my arms. In one swift and surprising movement he lifted me off the couch and managed to turn me around so I lay on top of him.

"Now, my dear Clara, the power is all yours." I smiled. I took his penis in my hand and guided it smoothly deep inside. Then I raised myself up and fiercely rode him like there was no tomorrow. I arched my hips backward and leaned my hands behind me so I could feel him as much as possible. With all the teasing and build-up, it didn't take too long for both of us to climax. I felt Eduardo tense and release deep within me. I heard him cry out as he reached to pull me closer.

I fell against his chest, inhaling the scent of sweat, sex, and musky cologne tinged with the Rio night air, feeling the steady rise and fall of his breath. I did not want to move. I felt so completely satisfied and protected and ... happy. I allowed that word to sink in to my brain for a moment. Happy? When was the last time I'd felt that elusive emotion? It had been so long that I couldn't even remember. And yet there it was. Lying there like that, enveloped in Eduardo's protective embrace, I felt like I finally had the strength to fight the demons of the universe.

I could hear Eduardo's breathing slow and become more even. I moved over so I could snuggle against him more comfortably and realized he'd fallen fast asleep. Almost giddy with spent pleasure, I rose quietly and went to the guestroom to get a blanket. I came back, threw the blanket over both of us and surprised myself by falling asleep once again.

9

THE AIR WAS THICK WITH INCENSE, *the smell intoxicating and cloying at the same time. Dark, musky, yet sweet. I breathed it in, inhaling everything. The smoke from the candles, the smell of diesel from the open door leading to the street outside, the sweet scent of the honey offerings mixed with the acrid scent of blood. The smell of sweat as hot bodies surrounded me. I swirled beneath the light, my bare feet hitting the simple wooden floor. The dancers weaving and swaying before me were dressed in a rainbow of colours. The whites of their eyes gazing from behind dark faces. And the beat of the drums. The persistent rhythm varying in only slight degrees, carrying me higher and higher to the stars. I allowed myself to become lost, to absorb my surroundings and become one with my Orixa. I felt the peace, the descending calm as my goddess entered my being. I allowed the release, the ultimate freedom as Oxala took over.*

But something was wrong. Even as I heard the voice of Oxala begin to speak wisdom to the people, I could sense the fear. I could taste it on my tongue. The people were not listening. They were distracted. It wasn't just about the drums and the incense. There were other sounds. Sounds that didn't belong. The sound of rushing feet. The sound of a door slamming. The bright lights suddenly blinding me. And the voices.

"This is an illegal establishment. We are shutting it down immediately. Who is the mãe de santo *here?" The cold, hard*

voices. Oxala lost her glorious power as the drumbeats ceased and it allowed me to return. I felt dizzy and disoriented. The heat, the chaos, the beams of light cutting across my face. A man was gripping my arm, pulling me up. I had collapsed on the floor. I needed a moment. I needed to think. But the strength I'd needed to become Oxala had drained me, left me empty. I struggled to breathe within the confines of so many bodies. I pulled my head up to look around.

It was total chaos. Running, screaming, crying as the military pushed my people out of the building, twisting their arms and pushing them to the ground. I felt the bile rise in my throat, the scream that would not be released. The day of reckoning had arrived. It had to come to this. I cried silent tears for all my devotees. For all the ones I would no longer be able to save in the future. I stood tall and looked directly at my captor.

"I am ready. You can take me now." His hard, cold eyes stared into mine, and he laughed.

"So you are the great Mãe Ahmara?" His voice was a snicker.

I stood tall. I searched the room, wanting, needing to find Ignacio. Where are you, my love? And then I saw him. He was across the room, his dark eyes glued to mine. I saw the look of sadness, of desperation, of total capitulation. But not fear. Even in a moment such as this, fear was not the emotion shining out of Ignacio's eyes. We held each other's gaze. We both knew this was the end.

"I have strict instructions for you." The man roughly pulled me forward. "Nothing but a blood-eating puta." He spat at my face, and I turned my gaze away from Ignacio. I didn't want to see the pain in his eyes. "You think you can save everyone." He laughed. A cruel sound. "Some people are not worth saving. A new society. That's what Vargas wants. A new order. Cults and devil-worshipping *putas are not going to be part of it."*

I was silent as he continued to pull me forward. I allowed myself to be pushed out the door and relished the feel of the *moist night air hitting my face. The man pushed me to the ground, and I caught a glimpse of silver metal. I lay there, clutching my crucifix. All the great saints and goddesses would protect me. They would make my death swift and painless, and take my soul where it belonged. I waited for the moment to arrive, calling softly to Oxala and to all the goddesses and gods of the Odún pantheon for strength.*

"Are you the great Mãe de Santo Ahmara?" he asked again, pulling my head up by my hair and staring directly into my eyes. I looked into an empty soul, knowing my answer would be my death sentence. And then I saw him. Ignacio. He was pushing through the crowd, trying to reach me. His eyes told me to wait. To let him save me. To not answer the question. But I had no choice. If I stalled, Ignacio would die as well. There was nothing he could do for me now. And so I sent him all my love. I smiled at him, allowing the tears of regret and love and hope to spill down my face. We'd dreamed of so much together. We'd tried to save the Odún. And we'd succeeded. But we had both known that our time was limited. We had both known that this was the inevitable end. But at least if Ignacio survived he could continue the mission. Without me. And so, just as I saw Ignacio escape the crowd and stride toward the man, I nodded. I stared into his dead black eyes and said, "Yes, I am Mãe de Santo Ahmara."

I AWOKE COUGHING AND CHOKING on my own fear. I'd pushed out of Eduardo's arms and was sitting up straight on the couch, confused and disoriented. I still felt the impact of the bullet as it hit my chest. I tried to calm the frantic beating. My ears were still ringing from the drumbeats, my mouth dry with the bitter taste of smoke and incense lingering on my tongue, my eyes still absorbing the flashes of colour, the images. The bright dresses, the swirling bodies, the deadened eyes of the military man, the dirt at my feet, the crucifix. I touched my hand where the indent from the crucifix remained.

"Clara," I heard Eduardo whisper, his hand reaching up to stroke my hair. I turned around and met his concerned gaze, staring into the same eyes as Ignacio's.

"Eduardo." I touched his cheek. He caught my hand and studied my palm.

"What is this?" he asked sharply, sitting up straighter and outlining the crucifix. It was there, like a bloody red marker. A sign of my fate.

I sighed. "There's so much we need to talk about."

Eduardo continued to lightly trace the crucifix. "There's a lot you haven't told us, isn't there?" he asked.

I nodded. "Eduardo, I've been so confused. I have never understood any of this." I pulled my hand out of his grasp and held it protectively in my lap. "This…" I indicated the mark on my palm, "and so many other strange, inexplicable things." I shook my head.

"It's all part of it, Clara. It all makes sense within the pantheon." His eyes were dark as he looked at me intently. "That cross is the mark of the saviour."

I bit my lip. "I know," I said. "It's also the mark of death." A small laugh escaped my mouth along with the words.

"No, Clara, it doesn't have to be." Eduardo tried to meet my eyes, but I wouldn't look up. I just kept shaking my head, not wanting him to see the fear on my face. "Listen, Clara. History doesn't have to repeat itself. We can change things this time. We can change it for ourselves forever."

I turned abruptly. "So you know, then?" I whispered in surprise. Eduardo knew about our linked destinies? He knew all this time that we were soul mates?

"I suspected," he said. "But I didn't know for sure. I definitely knew you were the chosen one, but I wasn't sure what role I had to play. I knew we were connected. But now, I'm starting to think…"

"It's not like that, Eduardo. We're not chosen. I think it's more about linked destinies. Not just me. Or you. The prophecy talks about a chosen couple. All through history, it's always been a couple linked through destiny and time for generations. Who knows how far back we go? But it's everyone, isn't it? Maybe in our past lives we've been the leaders, but it's not like we could ever save Odún on our own. But I do believe we've been linked for a very long time. Maybe going all the way back to Africa and the Yoruba." I couldn't believe what I was saying. What I was starting to believe. But this reality made everything clear. It made sense.

Eduardo nodded. "Yes, I believe you're right."

We looked at each other, the realization almost overwhelming. A few short months ago, we were strangers. To now discover that we'd been linked through time as soul mates, destined to be together forever ... well, it was a little much for anyone to fully comprehend. Not only was there the reality, but there was also the responsibility of our deep connection. It was terrifying.

"I've felt it from the beginning," I said softly.

Eduardo nodded, not saying anything for a moment. We weren't touching. I held my marked palm securely in my lap, my other finger circling the indent. Eduardo sat rigidly on the couch, his hands resting against the edge. It was as if we were afraid to touch, afraid to unleash the magnitude of our bond, the intensity of our connection. I couldn't help thinking how much easier it was to think he'd just been an exciting one-night stand at the Carnival. But, even then, he'd been so much more. And I'd known it.

"That first time..." I began.

"Making love in that filthy back alley..." Eduardo shook his head ruefully.

"No, it was magical. And that first moment, when we came together..." I smiled shyly at Eduardo, "I felt like we'd been together a thousand times. It was so familiar." I reached out and touched Eduardo's hand.

He held himself so stiffly. "Clara, I've been cursing myself for that."

I stared at him in surprise. "But why? If we're destined to be together, that night at the Carnival was inevitable. It was meant to be."

"You have no idea how I've been struggling. Trying to ignore you, forget you. Clara, I've been so cruel...." He held my gaze. "I'm sorry for that."

I shrugged. "Well, yes, you were kind of mean," I teased. But when I saw his torn expression, I stopped. "Eduardo, this is so huge and so confusing. Neither of us could possibly know how to act. We're talking about the forces of eternity here." Even as I said it, I could hardly believe it.

"Eternity." Eduardo whispered the words. We were both silent for a moment.

"All we can do now is move forward," I said, wanting to take away the torment from Eduardo's eyes.

"But we're not empty vessels, Clara. We may be linked to Odún, and we may have this connection through time, but we are still in charge of our own destinies. I refuse to accept that our fate has already been determined and that we're just vessels doing its bidding." His voice was hoarse.

I so hoped he was right. But I wasn't entirely convinced. So far, I had felt like a vessel, carrying out an ancient and predetermined plan. Could my own actions make any difference?

As if reading my mind, Eduardo said, "Yes, our actions can make a difference. We don't have to blindly follow history. We don't have to be sacrificed, Clara." He looked directly into my eyes, and covered my hands with his.

"So you know about Zumbi and Queen Ife?" I asked. Eduardo nodded. "And what about the great Mãe de Santo Ahmara?" Again, Eduardo nodded.

"It's all part of the history. Part of the great folklore—the stories we tell around the smoke of the fires."

"Then why didn't anyone tell me?" I tore my hands away and stood up. "I've been tortured by nightmares. All revolving around Palmares. And last night I dreamt of Ahmara. Everything would have made a lot more sense if someone had told me about this earlier." I turned around, trying to push down my anger, my fear, my feeling of once again being controlled by other people, other forces.

"Clara, you never told anyone about your dreams."

"Oh yes, I did. I told Lisboa."

Eduardo was silent for a moment. "Lisboa didn't know who you were in the beginning. She didn't know whether you carried the forces of good or evil. Just as the prophecy talks about the chosen crusaders, there are the chosen lords who hunt us down."

"How could Lisboa possibly believe that I would destroy the Odún?" I could hear the anger rising in my voice.

"In the time of Palmares, it was Zumbi's best friend who betrayed him. His best friend who was the lord of destruction. One can never know." Eduardo's voice was gentle.

"Eduardo, I need a drink." I'd gone from the world I knew and understood to this … this magical, surreal place where reality was founded upon bits of folklore and spells, and dreams and nightmares were becoming hidden clues to a pre-determined destiny.

I flung myself back down on the couch while Eduardo stood up to get me something to drink. I didn't care what time it was. Night and day seemed to be all mixed up. I supposed it was early morning, judging from the reddish glow emerging from behind the living room curtains. The view would probably be spectacular. I stood up and made my way over to the window. I opened the heavy, velvet curtain and took in the early morning view of the bay, the dark water still reflecting the lights from the surrounding high-rises. For a moment, my mind was blank.

I felt Eduardo's presence beside me once again. He pushed a glass into my hand. "It's a mimosa," he said. "Seemed appropriate. Better than whisky, anyway."

I laughed and took a sip. The fizzy champagne slid down my throat, the bubbles tickling my tongue. I sighed. "Perfect," I said, turning to face Eduardo again. "Okay, I think we need to start sharing everything we know without holding anything back."

Eduardo nodded. "I agree." He took my arm and gently led me back to the couch.

I curled up in one corner, taking sips of my mimosa. Eduardo sat beside me, and I noticed that he carried a heavy mug, no doubt filled with coffee. Probably a better idea than champagne and orange juice, but the mimosa was calming my nerves.

"Tell me about the dreams," Eduardo said softly.

I sighed, placing the nearly empty glass down on the coffee table and leaning back into the plush sofa. I realized I'd never really discussed my dreams with Lisboa. Not in detail. The only one I'd actually shared with her was the nightmare about Catalina. "They started in Toronto."

"Were you already a graduate student?"

"Yes. They began shortly after I started studying Odún. But they weren't nearly as vivid. I thought I'd just been reading too many books about possession and it was getting to me." I laughed weakly, thinking back to eight years ago. "I kept thinking that if I could find the right apartment, the dreams would go away. I moved five times that first year. By second year, I gave up trying to run. I lived alone in a studio grad apartment. I'd decided to remain in Toronto and finish my Master's thesis. All the other students had gone home for the summer, so I felt all alone in the middle of a huge city of people." I remembered the bustling traffic of downtown Toronto, the empty faces that passed me on the street, the blistering heat that made it almost impossible to even sit outside and read.

"So you ignored the dreams at first," Eduardo prodded when I fell silent, lost in my own memories. I shook myself back.

"Yes, yes, I did. I figured they would go away once I finished my thesis and resumed my life again."

"But it didn't happen that way?"

I bit my lip, staring off into space. "No, it didn't. The dreams only got worse and they started to interfere with my studies, my life. I went straight from my Master's into my PhD, studying—guess what?—Odún." I met Eduardo's eyes briefly. "I never really understood my fascination with Odún. From the moment I'd first heard those drums during my first trip to Brazil eight years ago, I've been mesmerized. I chose it as the topic for my undergrad honours paper, then for my Master's research paper, and then for my PhD dissertation. I've been living with it ever since that first day." My mind took me back. Before the Odún had consumed me, I'd danced to the drums, thinking it was exotic and fun. Never for one minute thinking any of it could be real.

"It's this whole destiny thing that's bothering me. I was being driven by something I didn't even understand." I shivered. "To think that the work of the past eight years hasn't even been my own initiative. I've just been steered forward by some…" I waved my arms in the air, "some force."

"Don't doubt yourself, Clara. You may have been called to Odún. But you are the one who did all the work. Do you remember any of the dreams? It may help us. There may be clues there." Eduardo's voice was calming, soothing.

I tried to rein in my emotions. The horrible realization that the sacrifice of my life, my family, my friends, everything I'd left behind in the pursuit of academia hadn't even been my own doing, that all along I wasn't an agent of my own actions, terrified me. I had lived such an isolated life in Toronto, managing to alienate nearly everyone. My mom was the only one who was able to pull me back every once in a while. And I hadn't even bothered to call her and let her know I was okay.

"Eduardo, I've given up everything. My parents, my friends…" I turned my head away, determined not to cry.

Eduardo nodded. He reached out and stroked my hair gently. "I know, *minha querida*. It's part of the prophecy."

"The prophecy!" I spat out. "I thought we already said it was a fanciful story. When are you going to tell me about this prophecy, anyway?"

"When you tell me about the dreams." Eduardo's voice was quiet but resolute.

I nodded, rubbing my eyes briefly. Okay, maybe what I thought I'd been working on for the past eight years was in fact not the reality I'd imagined. My past lives had led me to be mesmerized by Odún, but no one had forced me to be consumed by it. No one had forced me to become a living hermit, literally possessed by my own studies.

"I even went to see a psychic." I laughed again, thinking how crazy that had been. I'd needed answers so desperately. I had been so convinced that I was slowly going insane.

"And what did she say?"

"She was terrified. She told me I was trying to fight something. And that I should listen to the warnings in my mind."

Eduardo nodded. "Very accurate. She knew what she was talking about."

"So the dreams are warnings?" I asked.

"Yes, in a way. My guess is that you're probably dreaming about your past lives, and that your previous selves are trying to send messages through your subconscious. You remember the whole idea of the universal soul in Odún, right?"

"I know. The concept that every individual has a personality soul in the form of a reigning Orixa, but also a universal soul. So, in my dreams I'm tapping in to the power of this universal soul? Tapping in to the universal subconscious mind and finding my previous personality souls in the process?" Could this be true? I felt like I was finally gaining some clarity.

"Exactly. Now tell me about the dreams. I know how hard this is, Clara. I've been going through it, too. I guess I had the ancient knowledge to fall back on. But for you, everything was new."

"I don't need your pity, Eduardo."

"This isn't pity, believe me. It's understanding."

I smiled at Eduardo. I needed that. Now was not the time to think about where else my life could have led. It was not the time to regret past decisions, or to think that I'd just been following a predetermined destiny anyway. "They started with Palmares, the freed slave community in Brazil. In the dreams, it's like I'm there. It's as though I actually am Queen Ife."

"Because you are. She's taking you back. She's taking you into her own mind. After all, she is you, just in a different time period."

I tried to wrap my brain around that one, but it was still a little difficult. "So I am there. But then why don't I die?"

"Because it's only your subconscious that travels. Queen Ife is still the physical form of your personality soul for that time period. It means you can feel the sensations and sometimes even bring a bit back, but you can't be killed. You can only be killed in your own time period."

"How reassuring," I mumbled. "I dreamt of the night Palmares was discovered." I felt my cheeks get hot just thinking about that particular dream. Remembering the hard feel of Zumbi's body. Eduardo looked at me quizzically. "You were there," I said simply.

The look Eduardo gave me sent shivers through my body. He knew exactly what I'd dreamed. "And we were torn apart from each other's arms," he finished. "Must have been a heated dream before the nightmare part began."

"It was." The dark look in Eduardo's eyes made my stomach muscles tighten. I wanted him again. Just being near him made me want him inside me. "So you're Zumbi, just as I'm Queen Ife. And you're Ignacio, as well."

Eduardo nodded, getting up. I smiled, knowing exactly what he was thinking and how he was trying to distract himself. I just wanted him to kiss me again so we could stop talking and just enjoy our desire for each other. "Of course, we never look the same. Our physical forms change. But yes, our souls remain the same. So you're saying you dreamed of the Mãe de Santo Ahmara and Ignacio."

"Yes, that was the dream I just had. I dreamed about the night of the raid."

"The raid of 1945."

"I don't know anything about it. I was swirling around in a trance possessed by Oxala when the military barged in. The man shouted something about Vargas wanting a new order. A new society. And I guess Odún *terreiros* were not intended to be part of that new society." I knew a bit about Brazilian history, but I hoped Eduardo could fill in the details. My glance held his.

"*Querida*, the force between us. It's so powerful. You're like a drug to me." He strode the few steps toward me and kissed me firmly. I leaned into his embrace, caressing his lips, wanting his tongue to dance with mine, wanting to feel his arms holding me. But, just as swiftly as he had kissed me, he pulled back, shaking his head. "I could make love to you all night." He looked at me fiercely, his eyes dark. I felt my pelvic muscles contract. His gaze slid down my body. I licked my lips, and I could see his half smile.

"The *Estado Novo*. Yes," he said emphatically, returning to our conversation. "It lasted from 1937 to 1945. Getulio Vargas created a dictatorship that he called a new order. It was supposed to be about industrialization, about taking the nation from the sugar barons and providing it with a profitable future and a middle class. But this meant destroying anything he didn't consider progressive. Odún houses were one of those things. Next to the time of slavery, it was the worst period of Odún persecution in Brazilian history."

"And we were there," I said in awe as pieces of the puzzle started to fall into place.

"We weren't just there, Clara. The great Mãe de Santo Ahmara is legendary. She saved hundreds of lives. She used her *terreiro* as a refuge for the persecuted and helped them escape the government. Odún initiates were all marked as communists. Anyone who was different was a "communist," of course. All the other Odún houses were destroyed, but she somehow kept hers alive. There's never been a more impressive or greater *terreiro* in the entire period of Brazilian history. And her lover, Ignacio, was right there by her side. Until that night, of course. He tried to save her, but he was too late."

"So what happened to Ignacio? Now that I know Ahmara was shot and killed that night."

Eduardo gave me a sad smile. "I know, Clara. The fates of our former selves weren't the greatest."

"So he died, as well. I mean, obviously he can't still be alive if you're his new reincarnation." I shook my head, thinking how insane it all was.

"Yes, he was captured later that night. He was thrown into prison and…" Eduardo stopped as he glanced away. "It's not a pretty part of the history."

"Was he tortured?"

"He died in prison, refusing to give up any names of the people they helped. He and Ahmara were true to their word right to the end."

"I just don't understand, Eduardo. How could I have been studying Odún for so long and have no idea about this folkloric history?"

Eduardo shrugged. "It's not exactly something you'll find in a textbook. Of course the lives of Mãe de Santo Ahmara and Ignacio are documented. And Palmares. This is Brazilian history, after all. But the whole story of the Odún crusaders is just that. A story. No academic would have tapped in to that part of the culture. But every worshipper knows about it."

"It all makes sense. Everything. All the questions I had in my mind, I'm slowly getting answers for. I just don't like the answers." I held Eduardo's gaze. "I suppose I must have lived in Lisboa's home in the 1940s. That must be why it was so familiar to me. It was my home."

Eduardo nodded. "Did you dream about the house?" I could feel the tension between us. As if he knew my thoughts and dreams because he had been there too.

"It was my first dream. And then, when I came here, I was drawn to Santa Teresa and obviously to that particular ad for room and board. And the moment I entered, I fell into a kind of waking trance. I knew where everything was. My mind took me back, I guess to the way it had been. That's why I was surprised by the different décor. And I dreamed of you, of course."

I bit my lip, remembering how those heated dreams had tortured me. My secret lover coming to me through the lacy curtains in the dead of night. "Just like Romeo and Juliet. But why would you have had to sneak in through the window?" I laughed. "If I was the great *mãe de santo*, would my lover really creep up a balustrade?"

"I imagine you were dreaming about a younger version of the great *mãe de santo*. Apparently, Ignacio and Ahmara were childhood friends who eventually became lovers. And yes, the history books do say that Ahmara lived in her childhood home that she inherited when her father died. Her home in Santa Teresa."

The laughter died in my throat. There was no point fighting it. What seemed impossible or implausible before was now becoming far too real. I could taste the fear rise up in my throat. Eduardo sensed the shift in my mood. He reached out and touched my face gently. I reacted instantly. I wanted this man. I looked up and could see both affection and desire in his gaze.

"It's going to be okay, Clara."

"Is it?" I asked, wondering if anything could ever be okay. "Eduardo," I said matter-of-factly, "I don't want to get my head chopped off."

Eduardo glanced at my serious expression, and I was surprised to hear him laugh.

"I'm serious. How can you laugh about that? All of our

past selves died horribly. I don't want to die, Eduardo. I may be all for the cause, but I'm not ready to give up my life. I'm too young. I have too many things to do. I..." I welcomed Eduardo's embrace. He pulled me forward, stroking my hair and holding me close against his chest.

"Clara, I won't let anything happen to you."

But I pulled away. "You can't stop it, Eduardo. You're part of it. You've never been able to save me in the past. Why would this be any different? And I've never been able to save you, even when I gave up my life trying."

The look on Eduardo's face was resolute. "It's like I said before. We're not just vessels. We are individuals with our own choices to make about our future. I don't believe that our destiny has already been written. Maybe some part, because we are part of this greater vision. But I, for one, have no intention of being sacrificed, and I won't let it happen to you, either. We're going to change things, Clara. This time, I want us to live out our lives together. This time I don't want to see us torn apart."

I stared at Eduardo. *Live out our lives together.* I couldn't deny the strength of my feelings for Eduardo, but we hadn't even said we loved each other yet. I realized in that moment that I did love Eduardo. I had always loved him, and I always would. "Okay. I'm ready to create the future." Eduardo pulled me close again, and I felt the shift. He lifted my face and traced my lips with his finger.

"Ah, *querida,* I need you so much." I sucked on one finger, my eyes meeting his dark gaze.

"I just want to feel you inside me," I whispered. He pressed his lips firmly against mine and kissed me deeply. I wrapped my arms around his neck, pulling his chest close to me.

"I need to feel you. All of you." His warm breath tickled my ear, and my body responded instantly. He took my hand and led me to his bedroom. My heart was pounding. All I could focus on was my own building desire. The drapes were closed, blocking out the early morning light. I stood beside the bed, looking at Eduardo. I wanted to see his beautiful naked body. He took off my T-shirt, running his hands over my breasts, leaning down to kiss each one. I leaned my back against the wall, allowing myself to surrender to the sensations. His hands smoothly caressed my stomach and hips, and then his fingers entered my already very wet vagina. "You're definitely ready," he whispered into my ear.

"Yes," I murmured, my back arching as his fingers pressed against me, teasing me and making me insane with need. My hips moved involuntarily as I pushed against him, wanting more. I felt my climax rising, and I leaned helplessly into his shoulder. Suddenly, he lifted me up, and I wrapped my legs around his waist. I loved the solid strength of his biceps flexing as he carried me.

"I want you on your hands and knees," he murmured.

I felt my insides contract. He positioned me on the bed, my arms forward, my ass exposed. My breath was now coming in quick gasps. I felt the smooth texture of the silk sheets against my cheek as I waited. I felt him moisten his fingers again before they entered me. "I love how wet you get," he groaned softly. Then, I felt his tongue dart into my vagina from behind, expertly circling my clit and licking me everywhere. I moaned, struggling to keep my hips still as my climax built in waves of intense pleasure. "I need you inside me," I whispered hoarsely, shocked by the desperate sound of my own need.

"Soon, *querida*. Soon." His voice was dark and husky as well. He continued to lick me and then I felt the edge of his cock stroking, teasing, my labia. He rubbed his penis along my rigid clitoris, but still he wouldn't enter me. My hips were rising on their own, my body desperate to feel him.

"Now," I cried, needing him so badly.

In the next moment, he entered me swiftly from behind. I inhaled my breath sharply. The sudden sensation of him filling me was overwhelming. He entered me hard and started pumping into me fiercely. I held on to the bed sheets, feeling my entire body being consumed. I wanted him to go as deep as possible, and my body responded by meeting his every thrust. I felt him go so deep into me that my orgasm seemed to rock me from the inside as my entire body shook. I felt the waves of my climax take over, my muscles contracting with exquisite force. And in that same moment I heard his moan as he came inside me.

In the next moment, he pulled me close, coming to lie down on the bed beside me. I wanted him near and so I pulled his entire length against me, luxuriating in the feel of his naked skin against mine.

"Mmm," I murmured, reaching up to kiss him gently.

He smiled, touching my cheek. "Ah Clara, what you do to me." He sighed, pulling me close into his embrace. It was still early in the morning, and it didn't take long for Eduardo to fall asleep again. I listened to his gentle breathing and felt completely safe.

10

I OPENED MY EYES LAZILY. I yawned and stretched, still caught within the afterglow of our lovemaking. I leaned over to find Eduardo, but he'd already gone. I didn't want to get up just yet. I just wanted to bask in the glorious sensation of the cool bed sheets, the light breeze from the fan brushing my hair and the memory of Eduardo's kiss still fresh on my lips and skin. We'd had such a heated discussion. So much passion, so many emotions. We were connected in incomprehensible ways. I knew Eduardo couldn't save me. But, together, we could work in unison to save each other.

The passion of our lovemaking had been unlike anything before. With the new knowledge of our soul mate connection, I'd felt all the forces of the universe bringing us together. The memory of Eduardo's kisses, the feel of his arm muscles beneath my fingers, and the sensation of him moving inside me, in a rhythm established centuries before, made me sink deeper into the sheets. Ahh. But I couldn't exactly lie there forever, going over every last detail.

I sat up, looking around Eduardo's room. Red velvet curtains blocked out the sun, leaving the enormous suite in murky darkness. I lay in a king-size bed that barely filled the empty space of the cavernous room. A Moroccan-looking red silk rug was spread out across the floor, leading toward a marble fireplace mantel. I stood up and walked over to the fireplace. It seemed strange somehow, given how hot Rio had been since

I'd arrived. I'd been here for over three months now. Pretty soon the weather would start to cool and the Brazilian winter would begin. The last time I'd been in Brazil was in August. But it had been an unseasonably hot August, so I had yet to experience the cold in Brazil. Time seemed to be moving so quickly. I'd had no contact with anyone in Canada since I arrived. Not even with my advisor. I didn't even know if I could finish my PhD at this point. Everything had become so strange.

I noticed that Eduardo didn't have any pictures on his fireplace mantle. I was hoping that his room would reveal something more personal about him. I loved him. I felt it deep inside. But I didn't understand him. And I didn't really know him at all. I thought about our conversation that morning. We had basically pledged ourselves to each other for eternity. Could love really be so powerful? I knew what I felt in my heart. But my mind told me otherwise.

I had never fallen in love before. I'd always been so careful, so protective. Sometimes I'd worried that my parents' marriage had made me jaded. They might have been happy in their own way. But as much as I loved my mother, I hadn't been able to see her as anything other than weak. And maybe that was my secret fear. That I would become like my mother. And yet, maybe there was a strength there that I hadn't recognized. The strength to raise a daughter. To love her. To give her financial security. If my mother had divorced my father, I wouldn't have had that comfortable middle-class existence. And, as much as I derided it and wanted to escape it, I had benefitted from that suburban Calgary upbringing. I suddenly felt a respect for my mom that I'd never felt before—respect and appreciation. It made me want to see her and to tell her how much I loved and admired her, something I'd never done before.

I sat back down on the bed, feeling a little dizzy. I needed food. I couldn't remember the last time I'd had a proper meal. And a nice, long hot bath. It seemed like day and night, dreams and reality, were all blending. I glanced at the bedside clock. It was past noon. My internal clock was completely off. I entered the marble bathroom, looking forward to a nice long soak in the deep tub. I let the warm water run and stepped in, adding some bath gel for bubbles. As I lay in the warm water, my thoughts drifted back to Eduardo, and I couldn't help wishing he was in the tub with me. I imagined him running his hands down my back and cupping my breasts as I leaned against him, the soapy water covering both of us. I imagined feeling his hard cock pressed against me as he kissed my neck, before massaging my shoulders and gently soaping my back and arms. I washed my hair, wishing Eduardo would come in. But he didn't. Sighing, I stepped out into the now steamy room and wrapped myself in a fluffy white towel. It felt good to be relaxed and clean. My feet padded across the lush carpet, and I realized that while I'd been sleeping Eduardo had placed some new clothes on the bedroom chair. I smiled, pulling on cotton panties and a simple white dress. Very sweet and practical. My stomach grumbled. I was absolutely starving.

Just as I went into the kitchen in search of some breakfast, I heard a knock at the door. Eduardo didn't appear to be anywhere so I decided to go and answer it myself. I could hear Lisboa's voice as I opened the door.

"*Olá!* Is everyone still sleeping inside?"

I opened the door, laughing. "Just about, Lisboa. I woke up not so long ago."

She turned to me, placing both hands around my face. "Ahh, but it is good, *não?* I'm happy you slept well. Now we will have lots of energy." Lisboa seemed uncommonly enthusiastic. I watched as she swept past me and entered the living room. "Where is Eduardo?" I shrugged my shoulders. "No matter. It's you I came here to see. So…" With her usual directness, Lisboa turned back to me, her expression one of determination. "Are you ready to continue your studies?"

I stared at her in confusion. My studies? Didn't we have

larger and more pressing concerns right now? "What do you mean, Lisboa?"

Lisboa gave a dramatic sigh. "You have all the answers, Clara. We just need to get them out."

I watched in silence as Lisboa sat down on the couch with a flourish, spreading her floral skirt around her. She proceeded to take some cowrie shells out of her purse and place them carefully on the coffee table.

"Lisboa, I haven't even had breakfast yet."

"Breakfast! How can you be thinking of breakfast when we have the fate of the entire Odún pantheon upon our shoulders." Lisboa continued to lay out the shells, seemingly unfazed. "Go, go. Get a muffin," she called out, not even glancing up.

I went back to the kitchen. Lisboa seemed to suddenly understand exactly what needed to be done and she wanted to get down to business. I grabbed a muffin and a glass of orange juice, and returned to the living room. There was something almost feverish about Lisboa's actions.

"Are you okay, Lisboa?"

Lisboa glanced up, her eyes bright. "Dear child, I have never been better. Do you realize that I am connected to this? That I am actually part of the crusader myth?" Her voice held awe and incredulity.

I smiled and nodded. "Yes, you must be connected somehow. I dreamed about your home, after all. It's where I lived as the Mãe de Santo Ahmara. And from the moment we first met, we had a..."

"A connection. *Sim*! I knew it then, and I know it now. But it is exciting, *não*? To be part of history. To be creating the future." Lisboa appeared drunk with the reality of her own involvement.

"Yes, I suppose I could look at it that way," I said, wondering why my reaction had only been one of fear and disbelief. Lisboa stopped arranging the shells and suddenly looked directly at me. She smiled, and I was relieved to see the old Lisboa again. "Clara, do you realize that we have been friends for generations?" Her warm brown gaze held mine. As I nodded, Lisboa reached out and took both my hands. "I'm so sorry, Clara, if I ever doubted you. I should have trusted my own instincts from the beginning."

"But you did, Lisboa. You took me in, you welcomed me into your *terreiro* as an initiate."

Lisboa nodded. "Yes, but it took me a while. Well, that is in the past." Turning back to the cowrie shells, she pointed at the larger one in the middle. "You are the answer, Clara. That means everything is already inside you. We just have to coax it out."

I felt a tiny prick of fear. What exactly did that mean?

"We have kept your reigning Orixa silent. We have been afraid to give her a voice. Her power is so strong that I didn't want it to consume you until you were ready. But now…" Lisboa hesitated.

"Now you think it's time to give her a voice? Am I ready, Lisboa?"

"I no longer think we have that luxury. We need to hear her words. We need her help. She must be released, Clara."

I shivered, even though it was perfectly warm in the room. "Do you mean allowing myself to be possessed?" There was silence for a moment. I could hear the clock ticking in the corner, the distant sound of traffic, the cadence of Lisboa's nervous breath.

"Yes, Clara."

I sank back into the couch. Was I ready for this? They'd warned me so many times about not allowing my Orixa to take over until I understood it completely, until I'd gone through the proper training. I'd barely begun my training. I felt that there was still so much to learn. But maybe Lisboa was right. My reigning Orixa had been trying to reach me in other ways, through my dreams, my nightmares, my waking hallucinations. She'd been constantly sending messages. Maybe I should give her a direct voice. Maybe we would get some answers. Find a way to combat the rise of the Macumba.

"In my dream, she was Oxala. I remember feeling it. I remember the sensation as I let go and allowed her to take over."

Lisboa leaned forward, her gaze intent. "Then you've already been possessed, Clara."

I shook my head in confusion. "But it was a dream."

"You know that your dreams are reality. Your former self is taking you back. You are in her head. That means you were directly possessed by Oxala." Lisboa's voice held a note of nervous excitement. "Oxala," she said again. "I knew it. I just knew it had to be Oxala."

I didn't feel nearly the same excitement. "Oxala is the strongest goddess, isn't she? Kind of like the Christian Jesus?"

Lisboa nodded. "Yes, yes, she is. She is the strongest of them all. Very few have Oxala as their reigning Orixa. But with your level of *axe*, well, it makes perfect sense."

I tried to get caught up in Lisboa's enthusiasm, but I was too filled with fear.

Lisboa continued to hold my hands, noticing my hesitation. "*Querida*, it will be okay. I will be here the entire time. It is all meant to happen this way."

"Just as I'm meant to die some horrible death at the end, Lisboa?"

Lisboa didn't say anything. She just looked away. I could see all the excitement, the enthusiasm, drain from her body. It was like a torch had been extinguished. Lisboa's shoulders drooped, and her magnificent brown eyes appeared lost. I couldn't stand the silence.

"It's okay, Lisboa. We won't talk about it."

"It is not okay, Clara. I've already spoken to Eduardo. We are going to create a new myth this time. We are going to change the crusader story." Her voice held conviction, but her eyes remained tired and sad.

"Tell me what I need to do, Lisboa."

Lisboa nodded and turned back to the cowrie shells. She carefully picked up each one, whispering incantations in Nagô, the language of the Yoruba African slaves. I sat down on the carpet across from her. I waited, watching the intense concentration on Lisboa's face as she held all sixteen cowrie shells cupped in her hands. In the next instant, Lisboa took a deep breath, and, as she released the air in a loud gush, she threw the cowrie shells into the air. Her eyes closed for a moment. I listened to the soft tinkle of the shells as they landed on the table's smooth wood surface. When Lisboa opened her eyes and studied the position of the shells, she nodded. "As I thought," she whispered. Almost brusquely, she swept the shells off the coffee table and stood up.

"Lisboa," I began, expecting some sort of divination.

But Lisboa only shook her head. "We have what we need to know. You are correct. It is Oxala." Her words sounded strangely ominous.

"But..." I was at a loss for words. I wasn't sure what I had expected. The last time we'd attempted a divination it had been far more dramatic. Lisboa had transformed into Yemanja, her reigning Orixa, and an element of fear and intensity had entered the room. This time I'd felt nothing. Something was very wrong.

Lisboa swept her skirt aside and spread out an enormous leather bound book filled with bright pictures of initiates. "We must begin, Clara. We have little time." She pointed to a page that featured a photograph of all the initiates dressed in white, and with white beads around their necks. The room was filled with white lilies. Beeswax candles were placed carefully, lighting up the dusty floor. And around the candles were lines drawn with chalk, creating a sacred triangular space for each initiate.

Although intrigued, I wanted some answers first. "Lisboa, tell me what you saw. We must be completely honest with each other."

Lisboa sighed dramatically. "Ah, Clara. No one is able to divine the future. The future has yet to be created."

"Don't give me that, Lisboa. You and I both know a certain element of destiny exists or we wouldn't be sitting here now."

"That is the ultimate question, *não*?"

I could see I was getting nowhere. "I know you saw something and you're just evading my questions. I need to know to protect myself. To protect the Odún." I willed Lisboa to look me directly in the eye.

Lisboa finally turned to me. "Yes, Clara, I saw that your Orixa is Oxala. The shells told me that much. But I saw nothing else." Lisboa's tone was blank.

"But that's impossible."

"Not impossible, Clara. It has happened before." Lisboa stopped for a moment, obviously wanting to phrase her words carefully.

"Lisboa, we must promise to tell each other everything. No more secrets." I stood up and went to sit beside Lisboa. She lost her calm exterior and took a shaky breath.

"It's good news, Clara. It means your future cannot be divined because it has yet to be determined."

"But isn't that the case with everyone's future?"

"Not according to the Odún pantheon. We are free agents. Choice does exist. But there are certain pathways available to us. In any given divination, the various possibilities will reveal themselves with the strongest energy veering towards one possibility. That one possibility becomes the divination. It is why a divination is not always correct. Yet in your case … there are no possibilities."

I didn't like the sound of that. "What does that mean?"

"It means that the future is completely open. There is no energy veering in any particular direction. Put simply, Clara, the future is yours to create." Lisboa smiled.

"Then why didn't you say so right away? This is a good thing, right?"

Lisboa nodded. "Yes, though somewhat disconcerting."

I noticed the abruptness of Lisboa's actions. The way she turned her gaze away and started busying herself by flipping through the pages of the initiate binder. There was still something left unsaid.

"Lisboa..." I needed to know everything.

Lisboa shook her head, sighing again. She placed both hands on the binder and moaned. "*Ai, filha,* can you never let something be? Do you not think I would tell you everything if I felt you needed to know? Perhaps some things are simply better left unsaid. Please, Clara. Leave it be." Lisboa's voice was a desperate appeal. But I couldn't leave it alone.

"No. Tell me."

There was silence for a moment. Finally, Lisboa looked at me. "There are two possibilities when no future can be divined. One is that the future is yet to be created..."

"And the other?" I felt the familiar fear rise in my throat.

"That there is no future to divine."

I heard my sharp intake of breath. I felt it in my chest. "You mean I die."

Lisboa said nothing. "Technically, if you were going to die, I would read that in the cards. This emptiness, it is unusual. But yes, it is a possibility. But only one possibility, Clara. As I said before, this could be very good news. It means that the predetermined destiny has already been altered. It means you can make a difference. The path is open." Lisboa's voice was determined, full of passion. I knew I'd begged for the answers, but the fear of death was so real.

"I'm scared, Lisboa." I'd always been terrified of death. I had rejected my Catholic upbringing and I no longer had the reassurance of any faith to make me feel better. I didn't believe in a heaven or hell. But with everything that had happened to me recently, I supposed I had to believe in reincarnation. How could I not? And wasn't that reassuring? Somehow, it wasn't. My future was a black hole. I could either consume it with determination, or be consumed by it. The choice was mine.

Lisboa gave me a sympathetic look. "I know. Sometimes, you should let me spare you. There is so much within you. Yet you charge ahead so blindly." Lisboa's words were kind. But I had to disagree.

"You can't protect me, Lisboa. No one can."

Lisboa didn't respond with reassuring words. "But I can guide you, Clara. I can help you along the way." She indicated the cowrie shells, the pictures of the initiates.

I nodded. "Okay, let's start." My voice was far more enthusiastic than I felt.

"First of all, you need to know about your Orixa. I will teach you everything I know about the great Oxala. Of course, in the original myth, they say Oxala is a male deity. That he only dresses as a female because he tried to gain access to the portal of death and this is his punishment."

"The portal of death?"

"Ah, so much to learn, Clara. Where to begin? Yes, the portal of death is the gate to the afterlife. It is protected by the goddess Nana. Only her female followers are allowed to pass through. So, according to the myth, Oxala thought he could fool Nana by dressing as a woman, but she caught him. His punishment was to be portrayed as a woman from then on." Lisboa laughed briefly. "Ah, but that is the original myth, no doubt conceived by the great male *babalaos* in the time before Odún was ruled by the female sign and the *mãe de santos*. We no longer believe in that myth. Oxala is a great female deity and has always been thus. If the Catholic Church wishes to equate her with Jesus Christ, I see no conflict in her being a woman. Hmm?" Lisboa gave me a sly smile.

"I love that. How it's all about the strength of female energy." I smiled. "So what does Oxala do?"

"Do? Clara, she is the great one. She is the daughter of Olurun, the almighty god, who created heaven and earth in four days and returned to the celestial realm, delegating authority over the human race to his daughter, Oxala. She is the epitome of good. She is purity personified. She is the force that combats all evil."

"It all makes sense. My mission is to fight against evil. To fight black magic and the Macumba."

"Exactly. Come now. Look at these pictures." Lisboa pointed to the binder again. "These are pictures of all my initiates who have Oxala as their reigning Orixa. As you can see, there have only been four. And that is over twenty years of being a *mãe de santo*. They were all significant, strong individuals."

I studied the pictures. "Are they all wearing white because it is the colour of purity?"

"Yes. White is the colour of Oxala. Do you see the glass of water carefully placed beside each candle?"

I looked closer and did see the glasses of water. "Yes."

"Again, water is pure. It draws all evil within its pure emptiness and cleanses it. And the lilies, of course, pure and white, surround the room in blessing. And do you see those chalky white lines?"

Again, I studied the picture. I'd noticed those lines before. "Yes. Are they creating a sacred space for the initiates?"

Lisboa smiled. "I can see you are a quick study. Yes, the lines are drawn in white, of course. They keep Exu out of the triangle of faith and protect the initiate while she is possessed."

I suddenly felt a chill. I wrapped my arms around my body and sank into myself. I felt the icy wind brush my cheek like a warning, and I shivered.

"Clara?" I could hear Lisboa's concerned voice, but I was too caught within myself to respond. It was like a cold whisper in my ear, the icy tendrils of evil pulling me close. I could hear the low whispering, the insistent rhythm of words surrounding me until nothing else existed. What was happening? I seemed incapable of pulling away. The insistent, low rhythm increased in tempo and became louder, more powerful. It was no longer a cold whisper in my ear. It seemed to fill my entire head. It seemed to consume me. I drew upon my inner energy, whatever reserves I had. I felt so weak. So cold. I wasn't sure if I could fight it. I wasn't even sure if I wanted to fight it anymore.

"*Uma é Satanaz ao inferno...*" The low incantations slowly transformed into words until I could hear the strange language screaming in my head. I raised my hands and started to scream to block it out. I had no idea what I was doing. I just wanted the horrible words to stop. And then I felt strong pressure on my arms. Someone was holding me down, preventing me from hurting myself. I was aware of someone calling my name in a deep, reassuring male voice. And I could hear very softly a different sort of incantation. Different words being spoken. Rhythmic, as well, yet soothing. I clung on to those words, desperately trying to block out the terrible din.

"Oxala, *minha mãe!* Oxala, *minha mãe! Tem pena de mim, tem dó! Se a ronda do mundo é grande, O seu poder ainda é maior!*"

The phrases continued in a constant sequence, rising and falling and slowly drowning out the other more sinister words. The terrible pounding in my head started to fade. I started to relax, letting my muscles release their terrible tension. I felt myself melting into solid arms, allowing myself to be protectively embraced. I could hear the reassuring male voice, followed by a female voice, chanting the same phrase over and over again. And finally, finally, I came back. I opened my eyes, not sure what to think or what had happened. I was completely exhausted.

"Oxala, *minha mãe.* Oxala, *minha mãe.*" I looked into Eduardo's eyes. He was repeating the words intensely, his entire face masked with concern. I could see his enormous relief the moment our eyes met. "Clara," he whispered. I nodded. I wasn't quite ready to speak. I felt a larger presence in the room. Something far greater than myself or Eduardo or Lisboa. It was a strong and comforting presence, and I didn't want it to go away.

"Oxala?" I felt a gentle touch on my cheek. Faint yet distinct. I reached my arms out to embrace it, but the fleeting touch had passed. The presence had left.

"Eduardo?" I looked into Eduardo's eyes again. I was tired. So very tired. He nodded, his fingers gently tracing my cheek.

"I'm here, *minha querida*," he whispered. I had no energy. I couldn't even respond. I only wanted to sleep. I wanted to lose myself in blissful oblivion. And, in the next moment, all was darkness.

11

I WOKE TO THE COOL SENSATION of a wet cloth on my forehead. I opened my eyes, even though it was an enormous effort to pull myself out of the warm and comforting sleep.

"Clara, please, you must wake up." I could hear Lisboa's insistent voice and feel Eduardo's gentle touch.

"Okay, okay. Can't you let a girl take a break?" I smiled at both of them and saw the relief on their faces.

"Oh, Clara!" Lisboa rushed over and nearly smothered me in a hug. Meanwhile, Eduardo didn't seem inclined to let go of my hand.

"Okay. I'm all right." I disentangled myself from Lisboa and let go of Eduardo's hand to stretch. My entire body felt stiff. "Tell me what just happened."

I noticed that Lisboa refused to meet my gaze and Eduardo didn't say anything.

"A nice cold glass of water. That's just what you need," Lisboa pronounced a little too jovially. She went to the kitchen and returned, handing me the water. I took a sip, the refreshingly cool liquid sliding down my throat.

I sighed, shaking my head. "Was that Exu?" I asked point blank.

Lisboa looked stunned, but Eduardo just nodded. "Yes," he answered. He turned to Lisboa and added, "There's no point trying to protect Clara from the truth anymore. She needs to know everything if it's to be an equal battle."

Lisboa pursed her lips and was silent for a moment. Then she turned to look directly at me. "Eduardo is right. We are in this together."

She sat beside me on the couch. "And yes, it appears that the Macumba are using Exu to get to you. They are sending him your way."

I tried not to shiver. Eduardo grabbed a throw blanket and wrapped it around my shoulders. Then he sat on my other side and held me in his arms.

"It was the lines." Both Lisboa and Eduardo looked at me. "When you showed me those white chalky lines drawn around the initiates. To keep out Exu," I explained. Lisboa nodded. "I remembered the ashes. The black ashes I saw around Catalina..." I paused, glancing at Lisboa. "And around you."

Lisboa's face turned white. Eduardo looked at her in alarm. "What are you talking about, Clara?" he asked.

"That day, when the man came to see you. You collapsed, Lisboa. And, when I found you, there was a triangle of ash around your body. Just like with Catalina."

Lisboa nodded, her voice expressionless. "Yes, it is the triangle of death. It means Exu has claimed you as his own."

Eduardo stared at Lisboa. "Why have you not told me this? How could you have kept such a thing hidden?" His voice was angry, but I knew it was only out of concern.

Lisboa sighed. "I am marked. We cannot change that reality. I have been doing my salutations to Yemanja every night, and she protects me. She will continue to do so." Lisboa's words were resolute and suggested no opposition.

I knew that the Macumba were using Exu as their power source and claiming their victims. Once the circle of ashes appeared, it was believed that the soul of the individual within the ashes then belonged to Exu. "But it can be reversed," I said.

"Yes, the power of the Odún gods is strong. Yemanja will protect Lisboa, just as Oxala has always been protecting you." Eduardo gave me a small smile of reassurance.

"Then I must draw upon that power. I must open myself up to Oxala."

Lisboa clapped her hands. "As I've been saying. Now, let us prepare you for initiation. But first, the cleansing bath."

I glanced at Eduardo with a small smile. "You are in the best of hands," he pronounced, kissing me lightly on the forehead. "Clara, I need to go again now."

"Where are you going?" I asked, wishing Eduardo could stay by my side. He always seemed to be disappearing, coming and going from the condo at all hours. I couldn't help wondering what he was doing.

Eduardo didn't answer immediately. "There's been some unrest, Clara. I need to clear up a few things. But you're okay now?"

I nodded, even though I had more questions. Eduardo gave me another kiss, this time gently on the lips. I felt my desire rise instantly. I wanted him to stay. I wanted to feel his body close to mine again. I felt slightly rebuffed but decided to let it go. I would ask him more later. I glanced up to see that Lisboa was in the kitchen, busy filling a vase with water.

"Now, I think the best thing to do first is rid your body of any lingering evil influences," she was saying as she placed the vase on the counter and reached over to grab a loaf of bread. I continued to observe as Lisboa rummaged around in the cupboards, cursing in Portuguese. "Surely, the man cooks once in a while, *não*?" she was muttering. "Olive oil. Should it be so difficult to find?" Finally, a shout of success as she found the olive oil in a bottom cupboard.

I just laughed. I'd read about cleansing baths for initiates, but I didn't know exactly what to expect. "I have no idea what you're doing, Lisboa."

"Ah, but you will soon." She took down four white china bowls, then went to the fridge and pulled out some grape juice and uncarbonated mineral water. "Thank goodness," she mumbled. "Ah ha!" I went to sit at the kitchen table, hoping to have a moment to relax, since Lisboa seemed to be preoccupied anyway. I wasn't sure if she was going to prepare a bizarre lunch, or if these items were meant to be used in my cleansing bath. I sincerely hoped it was the former and not the latter. I didn't relish the idea of bathing in olive oil and grape juice.

Triumphant, Lisboa's head appeared from underneath the sink, where she had managed to also find some beeswax candles and matches. "We are ready now," she announced.

I stood up a little reluctantly and helped Lisboa carry the items to the living room. Lisboa cleared everything from the coffee table and covered it with a white tablecloth. "We should be doing this on a Sunday during the waxing moon ... but alas." She sighed. "We must protect you now. Exu has too much power."

I shivered again and decided that I was grateful to Lisboa. As implausible as these rituals seemed, I had felt the reality of Exu's power and I was afraid of it. I wanted Oxala's protection. I believed in the energy of the gods. I wasn't so sure whether or not I believed in the earthly rituals to trap this energy. But I intended to take it all very seriously.

I watched as Lisboa placed the three bowls on the cloth in a triangle that pointed to the back of the altar. "To capture the *axe*," she explained. Then she carefully placed some pieces of bread in one bowl, poured olive oil in anovther, and then grape juice into the third. "These are all Oxala's favourites. You must know Oxala's likes and dislikes if you are to gain her protection." She then placed the fourth bowl in the centre of the triangle and filled it with the mineral water. "Again, for purity," she whispered.

I watched as Lisboa went to her purse and retrieved a piece of white chalk. I felt my stomach slide uncomfortably. Suddenly, the ritual went from being a strange sequence of actions to something that actually held meaning. I knew the power of what I was dealing with, even if I couldn't explain or define it.

"The most important part," Lisboa said, as she carefully drew a white triangle around the bowls. "This is to keep the power of good within." I nodded. Lisboa then glanced around the room. She took some white lilies from their place by the window and set them in a vase filled with fresh water. She placed the vase at the back of the altar.

"Now we begin." She lined up the six beeswax candles in front of the altar and proceeded to light them. "Now we will begin the chant. I will say the words in Portuguese, and I will tell you what to say in English."

I was surprised when Lisboa handed me a carefully folded piece of paper. "The words are written there. We will call upon Oxala with our chanting, and she will appreciate the effort we have made to bring together all of her favourite things."

I nodded again. I was too afraid to speak. Lisboa had been so busy and so clinical with the preparations. She stopped for a moment and held my hand. We sat down together on the plush rug before our created altar. Fear was so much a part of my life now. I wished desperately that I could learn to control my terror of the unknown. As if reading my thoughts, Lisboa turned to meet my gaze.

"Clara, I believe in you. I believe you have far more strength than you give yourself credit for. A weaker person would have run away long ago." She gave me a small but encouraging smile that calmed me.

"I'm ready," I whispered, unfolding the white paper. I looked at the words and began to chant. "*Oxala, my mother. Have pity on me. If the world forces are great, your power is even greater.*"

I could not say how long we sat there like that, both of us chanting. I blocked out the sound of Lisboa's voice in order to concentrate on the words I spoke. I repeated the chant over and over and over again until my voice became hoarse and my eyes started to water from the burning candles. The light scent of beeswax filled the air, mixing with the heady aroma of the white lilies, creating an almost suffocating sweet smell. The candles added heat to the room, and soon I could feel the sweat dripping down my forehead. I stared at the water as I chanted, desperate for just one sip. But I didn't stop. I couldn't stop. It was as if some other force had taken over. The longer I chanted, the more I seemed to sink deeper within myself. I was not transported; I did not hallucinate. I was not taken away to another time period. But I did go deeper and deeper into my own thoughts. Who I was. Who I had always been. My past lives, my present life, my future life—all blending and becoming one. I was part of this greater pantheon, and I felt my deeper soul, the personality soul, as Lisboa had called it, connecting with that greater, primeval, and universal energy source. I could feel myself tapping into the *axe*, the energy of generations. The energy of the universe.

I became vaguely aware of my own voice echoing silently in the room. The shadows of sunset appeared on the walls, and soon only the flickering light from the candles touched my face. Yet I didn't feel exhausted. I felt renewed. I felt powerful. I felt confident. I felt as I had never felt in my entire life. And the one thing I most definitely did not feel was fear. My insecurity, my difficulty believing in myself, it all stemmed from fear. Fear of failure, fear of disappointment, fear of loss. Fear that if I ventured out too far, I wouldn't be able to come back. Fear of my father's disapproval. The loss of fear also meant the loss of this terrible insecurity.

It suddenly occurred to me that maybe this was exactly how it felt to die. This pure sensation of oneness with the universe. Of complete and utter peace. Of energy and vitality and happiness. I no longer felt afraid of death. I no longer feared the future, or the present, or even the past. I could accept myself for who I was. The fear and insecurity that had been stifling me, which I'd been carrying around like an unwanted piece of heavy luggage … lifted. It was gone. I never heard the voice of Oxala. But I knew Oxala was there. I knew it was Oxala who gave me this strength. Who gave me the freedom and courage to look deep within myself. And, as the shadows of night overwhelmed me and the last candle burnt out, I felt the gentle and reassuring touch of Eduardo's hand on my cheek, drawing me out of my chanting. And I realized that in vanquishing fear, I was able to embrace the greatest power of all—love.

I looked at him, my eyes wide, my soul bare. "I'm not afraid anymore," I whispered. I saw him nod, and I could swear there were tears in his eyes.

"Come, Clara," he whispered, helping me up. The room was dark and smoky, the lingering and cloying scent now gone. I was relieved and exhausted. The energy had disappeared, but the feeling of complete peace and inner confidence remained. I was vaguely aware of Eduardo carrying me to his bed and lying down beside me. And, as I snuggled in his embrace and fell into a blissful sleep, I realized I had never been happier.

I WOKE EARLY THE NEXT MORNING to the delectable aroma of coffee and bacon. And the gentle feel of Eduardo touching my hair. "*Minha querida*, you are awake."

I smiled. "Yes, and if you're not making that coffee and bacon, then who is?"

Eduardo laughed. "Someone needs a good cup of strong coffee. How about something else first?" He kissed the tip of my nose.

"Oh, no. I need that coffee and bacon first." I stood up, grateful that Lisboa had brought over some of my things. I stepped into my slippers and bathrobe, giving Eduardo a quick kiss. "But don't worry, you better be sticking around for a while today." I gave Eduardo a look, and he laughed.

"Do you have special plans for me?"

I wiggled my butt as I walked to the door. "Just wait and see."

"You can't tease me like that." He approached me, his chest bare, his eyes dark with want.

I laughed. "I think teasing you might be kind of fun."

Eduardo groaned, pulling me back toward his naked chest. "Oh, I can think of way more fun we can have." He surprised me by kissing me firmly and then cupping my ass and bringing me toward him so I could feel his cock pressed against me, removing the bathrobe in one quick motion. I allowed myself to melt into his embrace as he trailed kisses down my neck. "I can't seem to get enough of you."

I felt myself moan just slightly as his hands moved into my panties, feeling me. "You're so wet and ready for me." He inserted two fingers, expertly building my climax. I leaned into him, running my hands along his muscled chest and enjoying the feel of his hard and angular body so close.

I smiled, pushing his chest slightly. "On the bed. This time it's my turn." He kissed me again and lay down on the bed.

"I'm all yours."

I looked at his naked body, admiring his perfectly chiselled muscles, his hard chest, the line of dark hair down his stomach to his pubic area. I loved looking at his erect penis, wanting to touch him. I climbed on the bed and put my knees on either side of his body, balancing my hands on his chest. And then I nibbled his ear and licked his chest and trailed kisses down to his thighs, all the while looking at him and meeting his intense gaze, enjoying his moans.

"Yes," he was whispering. I took him in my mouth, enjoying the feel of him, letting my tongue swirl over the tip and then down his length. I loved how he felt and tasted. And I loved his soft words of encouragement as he gently took my hair and held it back. And then I held his penis in my hand with Eduardo whispering, "Yes, put it inside you." And I did. I wanted him to fill me again. I leaned my body back, letting my hips rise and fall while we moved in perfect rhythm. And then just as quickly, he managed to flip me over, and suddenly he was on top, staring into my eyes with such deep intensity as he entered me. I wrapped my legs around his waist, urging him deeper. He lifted my legs above his shoulders, and I cried out as he moved so deep within me that my building orgasm washed over me in waves. We moved onto our sides, and, as my legs wrapped around him, I pressed my body into his, and together we climaxed at the same time, my head pressed against his shoulder and our moans blending together. We held onto each other as our muscles contracted, and, as I let my orgasm slowly subside, I didn't want to move. He stayed inside me even while he went soft, and we continued to clasp onto each other, both of us unwilling to let go. As if by remaining united, we could hold on to this moment forever. Slowly, he pulled out and I shifted slightly so that I could lie beside him, our legs intertwined, my head resting on his chest. He stroked my hair, my face, and my neck gently, tenderly. I kissed his cheek and burrowed my head into his neck.

I loved this man. I knew it with such incredible ferocity, and it shook me to the core. I didn't need to hold back with him. I could allow my emotions and my passion to be released, and it was okay. He felt exactly the same way. I didn't want anything to break our magical spell. Except, maybe, the intoxicating smell of coffee!

I looked up and smiled. "You're amazing, you know."

He raised an eyebrow. "Am I? You didn't always think so."

I lightly punched his arm. "So, seriously. Who's down there making coffee?"

"Yes, I will admit it. I have a woman who comes here twice a week to look after things. But before you say anything, I pay her good money."

"I didn't say anything."

"But you were going to. I know you."

I glanced up. His casual comment had caught me by surprise. We were acting toward each other with the familiarity of a long-time couple. And it was completely natural. He was right. He did know me. And maybe I knew him more than I realized.

"Come on, let's go eat. I'm starving."

As we gorged on a huge American-style breakfast of eggs,

and bacon, and toast and jam, we found ourselves chatting comfortably. "So you still own a yacht?" I asked. Eduardo had been telling me about his childhood, spending his summers in Europe or Argentina. When his mother died, his father had disappeared into a world of work and travel that no longer included him. But when he got older, he escaped by buying a yacht with the inheritance from his grandfather and sailing around the world. It sounded glamorous, but also sad.

"Yes. You know, Velho's been on that yacht. I used to throw some good parties."

I wasn't sure what to say. Eduardo had this entire life, this other existence before he renounced his family and chose to pursue academia.

"You don't talk about your mom a lot." I touched his arm softly.

He nodded. "Yes, I was lost for a few years. I think all that partying ... it took me a while to find my way back after she died. You know, I am not sure where I would be today without anthropology. It grounded me. Made me want to learn about something beyond the narcissism of my own life. To understand things better. Why we do the things we do. My mom would have loved that. She was always a bit of an outsider, leaving her beautiful world of opera and music to be the proper political wife for my dad. She would have loved you."

I smiled, looking into his beautiful eyes and saw the depth of feeling there. I could see how much he had loved his mom. "I wish I could have met her," I said.

Eduardo leaned over, pulling my chair closer and kissing the top of my head. "Me too," he whispered.

"You know, I understand what you mean about anthropology. It changed everything for me, too. Coming here to Brazil changed everything." My discovery of anthropology had led me to a new world of knowledge as well, taking me out of my previous comfort zone and helping me to understand different belief systems and ways of thinking. Studying anthropology really did provide a completely different and more open way of seeing people and the world.

"Eduardo, what are you really doing? I mean, you talked about undercover work. Are you still part of that circle?"

The intimate mood broke. Eduardo was silent. I could hear soft samba music and the noise of a vacuum cleaner. I waited. "Clara, you need to know something about me. I will do whatever it takes to bring this man down."

"Including becoming part of his inner circle?"

"I was already there. I only needed to get back into it again. They have no idea. It's the best way to really understand the man. To see whom his associates are. To keep a close eye." Eduardo paused. "Clara, I just need to catch him one time. I need proof."

"What kind of proof?"

"I don't know yet. But something to prove unequivocally to the public his true identity as a Macumba lord."

"And what about me? What am I supposed to do during this time? Aren't we supposed to be in this together?" I stood up, too jittery to remain seated.

Eduardo stood as well and held my shoulders. "Clara, you need to be here right now. With Lisboa. She will be here soon. You need to use this time to learn. You need to be ready."

"Ready for what?"

"They're planning a raid soon." Eduardo looked at me. I knew I wasn't going to like his next words. "Lisboa's *terreiro*."

I bit my lip, a nervous tic I couldn't seem to get rid of. I tried to remember the strength I'd felt the night before as I had whispered the incantations. The confidence. I needed to hang on to that.

"Clara, you need to be ready to fight."

LATER THAT DAY, I sat on Eduardo's couch sipping a special tea blend Lisboa had prepared. I was now fully immersed in the initiation process. Lisboa had arrived not long after breakfast.

Eduardo had said he had some errands to run. I knew it had to do with Velho, but I hadn't pressed. Lisboa had prepared the cleansing bath that I should have taken the day before. And it did involve olive oil and grape juice. My skin had never felt so smooth and sticky at the same time. Fortunately, I had been able to shower afterward. The bath had been relaxing, though. I'd lain there, inhaling the sweet incense and allowing my body to unwind in the warm water. Now I sat curled up on the couch, wearing my loose cotton PJs and sipping my tea. It had a slightly bitter but not unpleasant flavour. The taste of the goddesses, as Lisboa had described.

I'd lost track of the days, the amount of time I'd been in the condo. My sleep schedule had been so unusual; I didn't seem to function by day or night anymore. Time just was. Lisboa said isolation was part of the initiation process, so, in an ironic way, my captivity in the condo was a good thing. But it did feel strange to never set foot outside. I wondered how long it would remain like this. I was starting to feel housebound. Opening the curtains to let in shafts of sunlight, and to gaze at the world outside where sunbathers lazed on the sand, children jumped in the waves, and couples walked hand in hand along the boardwalk, only enhanced my feeling of isolation. I no longer felt part of the outside world. It was as though I'd entered another reality, one in which magic and goddesses were present and more powerful than the mundanities of everyday life. Oddly, it was precisely the everyday that had kept me sane for the past few months. And now all that had changed.

I turned on the television, desperate for some connection with the outside world. But what I saw made me wish I'd remained in my isolated universe. There was Bento Velho in all his glory. Smiling and holding up a banner for the new children's hospital. He was giving a speech on the importance of family values. The future generation. Even on television, I could see the emptiness in his black eyes, despite the grandeur of his words. I struggled to catch snippets of the Portuguese. "... Captivates his audiences ... promises a new future for Rio ... children are the future ... respect our children...." Everything he said was wonderful. After so many years of repression of the youngest of Rio's citizens, the throngs of poverty-stricken children joining *favela* gangs for survival, here was a politician who would finally address the problem. And yet, according to Eduardo, it was all a front. He was dressed in a crisp sapphire business suit, looking elegant and poised and saying all the right things. But there was something wrong, terribly wrong. I looked closer, almost dropping my teacup as I stood up and edged toward the television. I studied his bone structure, the fine angles of his face leading to a strong, square jaw, the way his forehead rose to a receding hairline. And then he turned and looked directly into the camera, his smile wide. I gasped, feeling as if a hand had reached directly into my body and squeezed my heart. I could hardly breathe. I was transfixed by those black eyes that appeared to be looking directly at me.

"The future is ours to create ... and create it we will. Nothing will stop us." His teeth gleamed; his voice was triumphant. And yet those eyes ... deadened eyes. I knew this man. In the next instant, he turned away from the camera and faced his audience, once again continuing with his exalted plans and pausing for the cheers of his devoted followers. I went back to the couch and sat down, able to catch my breath again.

"Now you've seen him." I heard Lisboa's voice, but I couldn't respond immediately. She sat down beside me on the couch. "You've seen his eyes then."

"Lisboa, it was almost as if he could see me. Through the TV. That's crazy."

Lisboa shrugged. "Remember, Bento Velho is not human. He is evil personified. I have no doubt that he can transmit his *axe* anywhere. Radios, televisions—they are all conduits for energy sources."

I couldn't help thinking it made no sense at all. But I knew those eyes had stared directly into my own, and the message he had sent had been meant for me. Nothing would stop him.

"But he is human, Lisboa. He's the mayor of this city."

Lisboa shrugged. "Evil takes all forms. Yes, of course he is human, Clara. He has a human form. But his soul—it is ancient. Just as your personality soul is united with purity and goodness, his is united with darkness and destruction."

"So we're born either evil or good?"

"We are born with a universal soul that unites us with our destiny. But this destiny can be altered. The future is one of many alternatives. It is not a solid form, already in existence. Nor is the past. It is all a continuum."

I wondered why we tended to think of the past as being fixed. If the future is yet to be created, then so, too, is the past, I thought. What happens and what happened are two sides of the same coin. I liked to think of time in this way. It made anything seem plausible.

"Lisboa, do you know where Eduardo went?" I had to ask.

"I know the myth, Clara. I know you are connected. I knew from the moment you met each other. Although back then I didn't realize you were soul mates. But no matter, it is still love, *não*? In all its complicated forms." Lisboa sighed, imparting her usual dramatic flair.

"But he's out there, socializing with Velho's circle. Isn't that dangerous?"

Lisboa clicked her tongue. "Yes. He tries to catch Velho red-handed, to use your expression. But Velho is too careful. He keeps his bones hidden well." Shaking her head, Lisboa took a sip of her tea. "I fear we must move ahead more quickly than we planned, *querida*. Velho is afraid. He knows that his time is running out, and he's getting desperate. People are becoming agitated. Too much money being spent. Too many scandals. And yet, even so, people throng to hear him speak." Lisboa nodded toward the discarded morning paper, where I saw yet another picture of the popular politician surrounded by a glorifying entourage. "They talk about him as though he is a new symbol for Brazil. He has that power, you see. Evil has always been able to mesmerize and captivate the masses. He knows what they want, and he gives it to them. But even charisma cannot hide a failing economy."

Before I could respond, Eduardo walked through the door. In a few quick strides he crossed the room and enveloped me in his embrace. "Clara," he whispered, holding me close. I loved the feel of his arms circling me. But we had so much to discuss. I pushed him away gently. "What's going on, Eduardo?"

He looked at me and then at Lisboa. I felt myself tense. Something was wrong.

"We need to move fast. Velho has all his pieces in place. He's determined to wipe out any opposition, and that includes the *terreiro*, Lisboa. He plans to raid it the night after tomorrow."

Lisboa sank back against the cushions. "So soon," she whispered.

Eduardo nodded. He continued to hold me close. "I was there. At the hospital rally. And when he turned his eyes and faced the camera, I knew something had happened. I felt it. Clara, I was so worried…"

"I'm okay, I'm okay. But tell me what we need to do."

"It's time," he said simply.

I looked from Eduardo to Lisboa and back again. And I knew exactly what it was time for. "I'm ready," I said with a calmness I certainly did not feel. "I'm ready to be fully initiated into the Odún."

12

I IMMERSED MYSELF IN THE SOUND of the drums, listening carefully, attempting to identify the changing rhythms and patterns. I stood in the tiny alcove at the entrance to the main initiation hall. I shivered. The nights were starting to cool a bit. I wore only the loose, white cotton dress of Oxala. I fingered the heavy, white beads around my neck, anxious and excited at the same time. A breeze from the open door brushed against the back of my neck, drying the rivulets of blood left over from the chicken sacrifice. I felt bare and exposed, standing there like that, waiting. I'd already shaved my head as part of the initiation process. I had sat very still on the metallic chair in that damp room as Lisboa had carefully cut and shaved all my long hair off. It was to allow the power of *axe* to enter through my head, the belief being that, by exposing my body in the most pure form, I was allowing Oxala easier access. But, at that moment, it only served to make me feel vulnerable and naked.

I knew this was the moment I'd been waiting for. This is what the past eight years of my life had been about. It had been about a process of unification with my deeper self, with my personality soul. A unification that would finally be complete tonight. It was a symbolic rebirth. An awakening into a new form of myself. A better form, at peace and at one with the energy, the *axe* of the universe. The initiation process would give me power, and that was precisely what Lisboa and Eduardo counted on. Oxala would lead the way. Oxala would guide us and tell us what to do. But the strength would be coming from me, from inside myself, where my soul and the universal soul of Oxala were united.

Even though I'd conquered my fears and insecurities that long day in the smoky candlelight of our makeshift shrine to Oxala, I had not conquered my feeling of vulnerability. But I felt so much stronger than I had a year ago, even a few weeks ago. I thought of the day I'd arrived in Brazil, so naïve and full of optimism. I'd had no idea what world I would be entering. It felt so long ago, even though it had only been a few months. I was a different person now. I smiled, realizing that this was precisely how I *should* feel. I'd been studying Odún for years, but I'd never truly believed in it. I'd believed in infinite possibilities. And I still did. There couldn't be just one way of measuring and identifying the universe. The universe was far too complicated for anything that simple. And, as far as I was concerned, human beings didn't have the capability to properly grasp the meaning of our own existence. But what I'd witnessed, what I'd experienced, made me believe in an energy force that was far greater than anything I'd ever imagined. You could give it a name and identity, call it *axe* like in Odún, and create a ritualized structure for your belief system. You could believe in goddesses and gods that hold and control the energy—whether it's the holy trinity of Catholicism or Oxala of Odún—but the energy forces are the same. The only aspect that changes is the way human beings label and identify this energy.

Standing there in that alcove, I suddenly felt at peace. I'd been on a long journey, one that had begun on that first trip to Brazil, when I had witnessed the drums of Odún for the first time. A journey that could very well end tonight. But all the uncertainty, the confusion, the fear ... it had evaporated. I still felt anxious, but there was also a strength, a belief in myself that hadn't existed before. I could do this. I *would* do this. I no longer needed to question the bizarre reality of my situation. It all made sense. It was part of a larger picture of the universe. And tonight I would draw on my inner strength and allow myself to become one with the *axe*.

"Clara?" Lisboa rushed over to my side. "Are you okay?"

I nodded, shaking myself back to reality. All my senses needed to be awake, alert. I needed to be fully in the moment. "I've never been better, Lisboa." I smiled, and Lisboa, in turn, sighed with relief.

"Well, thank goodness for that. The way you were standing there, I thought the goddesses had already claimed you." She shook her head.

I reached out and grasped Lisboa's hands. "It's going to be okay."

Lisboa's eyes were bright with unshed tears. She simply nodded. "*Sim*. Now then…" She glanced around, observing the hall to see if everything was in place. "I believe we are ready." Her voice was calm, but I could tell by her frantic movements that Lisboa was terrified. And fear was not something I'd seen often in my friend.

I glanced around the room, my eyes searching. "Where's Eduardo?"

"He will be here. Now, you remember the drum rhythm for Oxala and the dance just as we practiced?"

"I've gone over it so many times in my head. Don't worry, Lisboa." The drum rhythms were complex, with only the slightest variation identifying the different gods. I had to wait until I heard Oxala's particular rhythm, and then I would enter the room, dancing Oxala's dance. There were other initiates that night who would come before me, so there was still some time. Lisboa noticed me shivering.

"*Querida*, you are so cold. Come, come…" She indicated the tiny room just off the alcove. "Wait here until we begin." She brought over a warm blanket and waved toward the kettle. "And make yourself a cup of tea. Relax." Lisboa smiled at her own words. As if I could possibly relax. "Or at least make yourself comfortable. I will give you plenty of warning before it is time."

I nodded, welcoming the security of the blanket. Wrapping it tightly around my shoulders, I filled the kettle with water. "I'll be fine, Lisboa."

With a nod and a wave, Lisboa left to look after the other new initiates. As I waited for the tea to boil, I peeked into the hall. Still, I couldn't see Eduardo. He should have been here by now. Where was he? I tried to stifle my concern, but it was becoming difficult to do so. What if something had happened? What if the Macumba lords had...? I stopped that thought before it could progress any further. He was probably delayed. I had initially wanted to come with him to the ceremony, but Eduardo had been the one to hesitate. He felt it was important for me to arrive with Lisboa. To have time to concentrate entirely on the evening ahead and not be distracted by anything. It had seemed like a good idea at the time. But now I realized that all I wanted was to be in Eduardo's arms. It didn't matter that we'd only known each other a short while in this life. I felt the connection of generations and I loved him. Startled by the shrill sound of the boiling water, I went to pour my tea. I only knew that I felt closer to Eduardo than any other person in the world.

"Clara, your hair..." I turned around, relieved to hear his voice. "But of course, the initiation."

I touched my shaved head. "Yeah, it feels weird." I didn't say how vulnerable it made me feel. I put down my teacup and reached out to Eduardo. "I'm so happy you're here."

"Clara, of course I'm here." He touched my head gently and held me close. "It does make you look different."

"But you love me all the same, huh?" The words just came out. Eduardo looked at me, his expression serious.

"Yes, Clara, I love you."

I looked into his eyes and felt the saltiness of tears on my face.

"Clara, what's wrong?"

I shook my head, wiping the tears on my sleeve. "It's just …" I knew exactly what it was. "Hearing you say it like that. That you love me. Eduardo.…"

We looked at each other. I knew he was waiting for the words. Waiting for me to say that I loved him, too. But I just couldn't do it. I didn't understand what held me back. I did love him. I realized the strength of my love in that moment, as I looked into his eyes. I knew ours was a primordial love. An eternal love. And yet, in this lifetime, I had spent so many years protecting myself, closing myself off to love, seeing love as a distraction, a weakness. I couldn't simply open up immediately and expose my heart and soul like that. No matter how much I wanted to, or how much I knew it to be true. I tried to tell him the truth with my eyes. But I just couldn't say the words out loud. And then the moment was gone. The brief moment in which he'd expected to hear the words. When it didn't happen, there was nothing else to say. Nothing else that could be said. And I just stood there as he nodded briefly, his face suddenly closed off, his expression once again inscrutable.

The possession drumming had begun. The first set of initiates danced into the hall, and the ceremony was under way.

"I have to go now, Clara."

"I know."

I could feel Eduardo's hesitation. He didn't want to leave me. But he had no choice. He was the *ogun*. He had to return to his rightful place. And this was one thing only I could do. Only I could be possessed by the energy of the universe. As Eduardo left and I stood in the alcove alone, I attempted to find solace in the warm liquid sliding down my throat, but I couldn't ignore the dark feeling that seemed to take over. Why was it so difficult for me to say those three simple words, "I love you"? The drums suddenly sounded sinister. The air was cold. The incense choking. I knew this was the night. Whatever was going to happen would happen in the next few hours.

"Clara." Lisboa rushed over, her voice anxious. "It is time to get ready. Your moment of initiation is about to begin."

I felt the air draining from my lungs. I stood mutely for a moment. Lisboa reached out and touched my shoulder.

"You are strong, Clara. I believe in you."

Her words were few, but they shook me out of my moment of dread. I told myself I'd prepared for this, and I was ready. My mouth had suddenly gone dry. I took one more sip of tea and nodded.

"Okay." I shook off the blanket, put my teacup down on the counter, and went back into the alcove. Peering into the large, open hall, I could see that the night of initiation was in full swing. The first set of initiates for Yemanja were already in the midst of their possession, the whites of their eyes glinting off the neon lights. Smoke from the sacrificial fires outside entered the hall and left an acrid smell in the air. As the room filled with people, the coolness of the night disappeared. The drum rhythm varied just slightly once again, and all the initiates danced onto the floor, their war cries raging, their bright red skirts swirling like flames. The drums of Oxala would be next. I would be the final initiate. And I was the only voice of Oxala that night. Where all the other initiates had the relative oblivion of numbers, I would be dancing alone. Lisboa grasped my hand briefly and gave me a small smile. "You are ready, you know," she said with absolute certainty.

"*Obrigada*, Lisboa." I squeezed my friend's hand and then let go reluctantly. As much support as Lisboa could provide, I ultimately had to do this by myself. As I stood there, focusing on the drum rhythms, I felt my heart start to beat faster in anticipation. The initiates had fallen into their possession, joining the swirling bodies of Yemanja, so now the entire hall looked like a convulsing mass of colour and sound. An intricate eternal dance, linking all forces of the universe. And soon, I would become a part of it.

And then I heard it. The insistent, low beat of Oxala rising. Different from the chaotic and frantic sound of Ogum's discordant rhythm. Oxala was the ultimate goddess. Her drum rhythm was refined, controlled. A singular, low, and continuous beat. I allowed myself to hear it, to let it fill my soul, to become one with it. Unlike that night, months ago, when I had sat in this very hall and fought the pull of Oxala with every bit of my being, tonight I would stop fighting. Tonight, I would allow the energy of Oxala to take over completely. And I knew I was ready. I was no longer terrified at the thought of total surrender. I welcomed it. I trusted that Oxala would take me where I needed to go.

I found myself in the middle of the open dance floor, swirling and absorbing the sound, the incense, the feel of my bare feet hitting the rough wooden slats. The neon light touching my eyelids as I closed my eyes. The images and the colours still reflected behind my lids. I hadn't even felt myself move away from the alcove. It had just happened. I felt my body swaying, sinuously and sensually. I felt myself becoming one with the *axe,* letting it fill my head and move deep inside. I felt the same kind of incredible energy that I'd experienced that day at the shrine, whispering my incantations to Oxala. Oxala was coming to me. She was sliding within me, filling me with her power. I heard my own voice, startling and sharp, crying out. Yet I had no control over it. I was losing myself. I felt it. That sensation of being enveloped. The heat, the sweat now pouring down my temples as I danced and danced and danced. The insistent drumbeat that had now altered slightly to become a rising and falling cadence. Discordant yet beautifully harmonic at the same time.

And, as I swirled and danced and allowed the energy of Oxala to fill my soul, I opened my eyes one last time. The neon lights were harsh and bright, and at first all I could see was a blur of red and white and moving bodies. And then I caught his eye. I looked directly at Eduardo. With the eyes of Oxala.

I was no longer myself. I'd been absorbed. I could no longer feel my feet hitting the ground, or the smoke stinging my eyes, or the sensation of my arms swaying and my body moving. I was floating in a void of nothingness, no longer part of myself, yet also not outside myself. But I felt so calm, so peaceful. And I stared at him. Eduardo looked back. His eyes dark with unspoken words. "I love you," I whispered in my mind.

And then something happened. I was still looking into his eyes, but I could feel again. Every sensation had been heightened. And I was no longer looking at Eduardo. I was looking into Ignacio's eyes. I was the great Mãe de Santo Ahmara. Oxala had taken me back to 1945 again. To the same night. The night of my death. But this felt different than the dreams. The dreams had taken on a slightly murky, disconnected quality. Images had been hazy; events had been blurred. The dreams had been vivid and real, but not in such stark colour as this. I looked around the room through Ahmara's eyes. The space was filled with writhing bodies in various states of possession, their skirts swirling, their eyes vacant pools of white, their backs arched, and their arms reaching to the heavens. They hit the dusty floor with bare feet, the fires from outside lighting up the dark room. And that was all it was. A room. Corrugated tin deep within the *favela*. It was Ahmara's secret *terreiro*.

I felt my arms moving, my feet lightly striking the ground, my face flushed. I touched my hair and felt the tight curls. I touched my face and felt the wide cheeks, the full lips, the high forehead. I touched my body, moving my hands in slow motion, feeling my wider curves and smooth hips that swayed with such lightness of rhythm, such sensuality. I absorbed the rhythm and the movement. And, as I stared at Ignacio, my eyes dark and hot, I moved my body in a slow and seductive pace. I realized Ahmara had allowed me to take over. Ahmara had surrendered and given me the power. Instead of being the one possessed, I was the one doing the possessing. And yet, Ahmara had done so willingly. But she was still there. I felt her presence. I could look into her thoughts, her mind. We were one and the same for just that brief span of time.

And, as I danced, I felt the influence of Ahmara's thoughts overwhelm me, taking over. Suddenly, I could see everything. Everything that was in Ahmara's mind. All of her memories, her thoughts, her dreams, her hopes, her fears. It all blended into one. I felt myself spinning, falling, sliding into a zone of swirling images and ideas. It felt like my brain had been slammed with an overload of information. Blurring text and sounds and voices all intermingling and coming together. I held my head, begging it to stop. And then it all slowed, and the images and words cleared, although everything still moved in hyper speed, like a movie on fast-forward. The movie of Ahmara's life.

I could feel her in her mother's womb, the moment of her first cry, being brought home to the house in Santa Teresa with the bougainvillea tree. Growing up and feeling things other children didn't feel. Sensations and callings. Going to the *terreiro* for the first time and being told that she was being called by the goddesses. The initiation process, a blend of sensation and fear and colour and light. Ahmara had felt all the things I had. She had been afraid, as well. And, over the years, she had managed to conquer that fear and become a strong and independent woman leading her own *terreiro*. The moment she met Ignacio. Just a boy living on the same street. Growing up together, playing the same games. Until one day the physical attraction appeared. The secret rendezvous. Ignacio climbing the bougainvillea tree and meeting his lover. Brushing aside the lacy curtains and making love on the white, satin sheets. I felt it all. The incredible passion, the love. I revelled in it. And then the dark moments. Vargas' rise to power and the dictatorship. The closing of the *terreiros*. I felt Ahmara's determination. The conquering of her own fears to protect the Odún and her initiates. And then the images stopped. The jumble of voices and sounds ceased, and I found myself back again.

And, as I danced to the differing drum rhythms, I held my crucifix in my hand. The crucifix that had left the red imprint in my palm. The red imprint that had appeared on Ahmara's palm at the moment of her death. And then I realized. Ahmara had known she would die that night. Just as I could read Ahmara's thoughts, so too could she read mine. And so, by going to her that night, I had warned Ahmara of her impending death. Yet she had done nothing to stop it. She had simply accepted it as her destiny. I felt myself falling once again into oblivion. Destiny....

When the blackness disappeared and I opened my eyes once again, I breathed in the smoke from burning fires and felt the warmth of the flames caressing my cheek. Someone had passed me some food. I swallowed, allowing the nearly rare meat to slide down my throat. Instead of gagging, as I normally would have, I took another big chunk of red meat, letting it ooze between my fingers as I brought it to my mouth. It was a feast. We hadn't eaten properly for days, and I was starving. The food tasted divine. My eyes glanced upward. There he was. My King. My lover. My eternal destiny.

He turned to look at me, his gaze intense as always. "The night is only beginning," he whispered in Nagô. I met his gaze, my stomach clenching with anticipation. Just as before, I could feel all the sensations. I could taste the meat and even feel the blood as it dripped down the side of my mouth. I could smell the smoke and hear the sounds of calling voices and activity in the Palmares community. And, as I looked around with Queen Ife's eyes, I realized that once again Oxala had taken me back to the night of my death. I heard a cry at that moment. A sound escaping my lips that I hadn't intended to make. It was Ife. She was crying. I found myself bent over, the tears coursing down my cheeks. Ife was struggling to come back. She didn't want to die that night. Yet Oxala would not allow it. "I'm sorry," I said in my mind, hoping that Ife could hear me. I could feel such pain. Such keen and horrible pain slicing through her body. Zumbi held her in his arms, his face a mask of confusion. He rocked her back and forth, yet I could say nothing. There were no words of reassurance.

I begged Oxala to let her go. To allow Ife to mourn the realization of her own impending death. To give her those precious last moments with Zumbi. It all seemed too harsh, too cruel. Would this be my destiny, as well? Is this why Oxala took me back to my previous lives? Was this the message she was trying to send out? That I had to accept my fate, whatever it may be? That there was no use fighting it? I felt the pain course through my soul. I cried along with Ife. Together we mourned for all that had been, all that could be, all that was. I could hear Ife's voice telling me something. Telling me to fight it. Not to accept my fate. It was too late for her, but not for me.

"Please, please," she begged me. "At least give me the knowledge that in some future self, I will be allowed to live out my destiny with my true love. That there will come a time when we will no longer be torn apart. That we will grow old together." And as I lay there on the sandy earth, listening to the crackling of the flames, feeling the warmth of Zumbi's arms around my shoulders, I promised Ife that I would do my best. I would try to break the sacrificial curse. And then I felt it. A slamming into my very bones. The entire world was spinning out of control. I was careening, a speck in the void of eternity, floating, falling, disappearing into nothingness. Was I entering a black hole? Had I disgraced Oxala with my promise?

But then I fell. Hard and fast, landing with a thud on the black cement. And, once again, my battered and bruised body was alive with sensation. The gravel rubbing against my bare leg, the thin line of blood running along my thigh from the fall, the moistness in the air, the din of traffic nearby, and the sound of voices. Dark, sinister voices whispering the same incantations to Exu. "*Uma é Satanaz ao inferno...*"

For a moment, I hid within myself. I stayed exactly where I'd fallen, wrapping my legs close to my body, paralyzed by a feeling of dread so strong that I didn't have the energy to face it. I was myself again. My thin dress barely providing protection against the dark night, no longer able to hide behind my long hair. I closed my eyes, buried my face in my arms, and prayed to Oxala. Begged Oxala to take me back. Take me away from this horrible place. I wanted the reassurance of the drums, the comforting gaze of Eduardo telling me that everything would be okay. But I knew that it wouldn't be okay. It wasn't okay. And I couldn't hide here, a shadow within myself, my body dancing and careening uncontrollably in the *terreiro* while my soul evaporated beneath the watery glow of a streetlight in a dingy alleyway of Rio de Janeiro. That simply wasn't how the story was supposed to end. But I couldn't keep the images and sensations away. Ife's searing pain, Ahmara's stoic acceptance. I didn't want to be like either of them. I didn't feel heroic, but nor did I feel resigned. I simply wanted to live. And, in order to live, I had to face whatever was out there.

I opened my eyes and made myself observe my surroundings. I blocked out the sound of the chanting, not allowing it to take over as it had before. I kept Oxala close, relying on her strength and energy. And Oxala did not let me down. I was definitely back in Rio de Janeiro in my own time, but clearly far from the initiation *terreiro*. I looked for any identifying markers, because if this was anything like the dream, Oxala had brought me here for a very specific reason. I was clearly in a back alley, the stench from the garbage rising off the pavement. I stood up, my legs shaky and almost buckling beneath me. I took a deep breath and a few tentative steps forward. I was in the same place. The exact same place where Catalina had nearly died. And then I felt the choke of fear and terrible foreboding. Is that why Oxala had sent me here? Was I meant to rescue someone? Who was it this time?

And then I heard it. The terrible, agonizing sound of pain and fear and defeat. The cry of helplessness. But it came from a child. I inhaled my breath sharply, dreading what I was about to witness. I moved closer, knowing that I should move a lot faster, but somehow my legs wouldn't cooperate. But I didn't have to go far. Just around the corner, I could see them. A group of men all dressed in black, their faces covered with ghastly bright masks, chanting the same dark words over and over. They circled the prone figure on the ground, their masked faces whirling with sinister colour. And, as their bodies merged and parted, I could see the black triangle of Exu surrounding their victim. And, as I stood there, needing to know who the victim was, feeling that horrible dread and bile rise in my throat because somehow I knew the answer even before it was revealed, I saw him.

I couldn't look at his face at first. I could see that he had been ritualistically cut just as Catalina had been. I felt tears come into my eyes at the absolute cruelty. I couldn't accept the reality. But there he was. And then I forced myself to look at his face, into his eyes. Because I knew that there was no time to waste. And Chico stared back at me, his terrified eyes showing a spark of hope. I nodded and tried to tell him that I would be back. I wouldn't let him die this way. Poor Chico. So eager to please. So tough and so brave, growing up poor and vulnerable in the *favelas* of Rio. Why on earth would they choose a child for their macabre rituals? What purpose would it serve? And why Chico? And then my gaze shifted. And I understood.

I felt his eyes boring into me, sending darkness to my very soul. And that's when I looked at him for the first time. That's when I finally gazed directly into the yellow eyes of evil, the eyes from my nightmares, my visions. The yellow eyes that had possessed me that night in the mirror. The eyes of Exu. The eyes of Bento Velho. And, as our gazes locked in a macabre and dreadful dance of will, he smiled triumphantly.

13

"**C**LARA, CLARA." I COULD HEAR Eduardo calling my name in his deep, soothing voice. I wanted to sink into that reassurance. I wanted to remain in that spot, hearing the low sound of Eduardo's voice whispering in my ear, knowing he was near, knowing I was safe, at least for that moment. If only I could suspend time and hang it there like the edge of a half moon. But that was impossible. I knew I had to open my eyes. I knew we had to hurry if we were to rescue Chico.

"Chico," I whispered, finding my voice hoarse. My throat felt tight. My eyes felt heavy, and my head was buzzing. I tried to raise myself up and immediately fell back into Eduardo's arms, overcome with dizziness.

"Hush, it's okay, Clara," Eduardo was saying, gently stroking my forehead.

No, I needed to tell them about Chico. He was being tortured at that very moment, and we had to go to him. I had made a promise. But I couldn't seem to talk, let alone move. I forced my mind to relax for a moment, to adjust to the shock of removing myself from my trance. But I kept my eyes open. I looked around, seeing all the concerned faces. The lights hit my pupils and sent daggers into my already aching head. The fires must have died down, because I could no longer smell the smoke. In fact, even with all the bodies, the open hall felt cold, and I was shivering once again. I noticed Eduardo indicating to Lisboa to bring a blanket, and, when he draped it over my shoulders, I sank within the protective embrace of the wool. My entire body felt beaten. My limbs were weak, my muscles like rubber.

They had stopped the initiation process. There were no drums. The incessant beat that had kept me spinning and dancing had died. It was silent. All except for the hushed tones of concerned voices. All the mystique had disappeared. Without the fire and incense, the drums and dancing, the room was just a simple hall with lights and a wooden floor. We were the ones that had created the magic.

I willed myself to gain back some energy. I had to tell them about Chico. I knew how important this moment was. It was the deciding factor in the future of our lives, in the future of Odún. Given the significance of the moment, why did it feel so impossible to even keep my eyes open? Why wasn't Oxala giving me the energy I needed? Why take me to all those places only to have me return too exhausted to even lift my head? What do you want of me, Oxala? I felt the tears running down my face. Silent, watery tears.

"Clara, you've been dancing for hours. We knew how important it was for Oxala to reach you, but I just couldn't allow it. Clara, I had to stop it. I'm sorry." His expression was torn, his face a mask of pain. "I don't know how my actions may have altered destiny, but I couldn't allow it to go on any longer. Clara, your face was so pale, your body going everywhere. I didn't know how much longer you could last. Your physical form was deteriorating before my eyes. I couldn't just watch it happen."

I listened to Eduardo's words, my eyes open but my body unable to respond. I couldn't understand his sorrow. Why was he apologizing?

"I took you out of your trance, Clara. I stopped the drums." He ran a finger along my cheek. "Without the drums there is no dance. And then I watched you collapse like a rag doll. Your whole body just sank to the floor." I heard Eduardo choke on his own words. He turned to Lisboa, who brought a glass of water. I looked at my friend, who appeared as stricken as Eduardo.

"Clara," she said simply, a tiny smile on her face.

Eduardo lifted my head while Lisboa brought the water to my lips. I drank in the liquid; the cool water was heavenly as it slid down my parched throat. I took several sips and then breathed in deeply. I had to shake this. I had to fight back. I had to tell them about Chico.

"Chico." I pushed his name out, more forcefully this time. A tiny bit of energy seemed to be returning to my body.

"Chico?" Good. Eduardo had heard. I nodded, my eyes trying to tell him what my voice couldn't. Both he and Lisboa stared at me in confusion. "You had another vision, and this time it was Chico?"

I nodded again. I took another few sips of water, and prayed. Oxala, please give me the strength. Give me the energy and the power to do what must be done. And I started to feel my energy return. Bit by bit, feeling entered my body. And with feeling came pain. But at least I was able to move again. I no longer felt paralyzed. My toes and my legs were tingling, a sharp pain from my previous fall burning my thigh. My arms were heavy, but I was able to push up slightly. And then the energy seemed to rise within me, to come from my heart, which started to pound with a steady beat rather than the erratic pulse I'd felt before. The energy rose up through my throat and into my head.

"Yes," I found myself saying, hearing the power of my voice return. Thank you, Oxala. "Eduardo, we have to go." Now that the heaviness had lifted from my limbs, I pushed Eduardo away and started to get up.

"Clara, please. I'll find Chico. You rest here." Eduardo tried to stop me, but I was determined.

"Eduardo, Oxala is giving me the power. This is what it's

all about. This is what we've been waiting for." I turned to Eduardo, my eyes bright, my face determined. And I saw him smile. That brilliant, beautiful smile of his.

"You're back," he said simply, taking my arm and helping me to my feet. The others stared in shock. Some of them holding their crucifixes and praying to their reigning saints and Orixas. They all parted, allowing Eduardo and me to move quickly through the crowd, Lisboa rushing behind us.

I could hear Lisboa's voice in the background. "*Ai Deus! Ai Deus!*" She was muttering, nervous and excited and terrified all at the same time. "Clara, watch yourself. Be careful."

I turned around when we reached the entranceway. "We're going to change history, Lisboa," I announced, giving Lisboa a confident smile.

Lisboa laughed and clapped her hands together. "Clara, I believe you will."

But just as we passed through the doors, I realized Lisboa needed to be there, too. She had been there from the beginning, and somehow she was part of this whole plot. "Lisboa ..."

"It was the same vision, but with Chico this time," Lisboa said, her voice calm. "In the same location."

"That's right."

"I will be there," she said simply

I wasn't sure how to respond. "I don't want anything to happen..." I began, but Lisboa cut me off.

"Clara, I will be there as I always have been. Now, how can I allow my initiate to take the most important journey without her great *mãe de santo* there for support? No, impossible. Lisboa will be there." With a flourish, Lisboa lifted her skirts and waved at the congregation of people as she followed us into the dark night. As we left the bright lights of the *terreiro* and walked deeper into the woods, I felt my heart starting to beat faster again. I couldn't know the future, but I did know that this was the moment of my showdown with Bento Velho. At last, we would meet face-to-face.

We reached Eduardo's car, the tires deep in the forest mud. Lisboa's car was parked just a short distance away. Eduardo opened the door for me and went to the driver's side. I stood there beside the car, looking at Lisboa. I had the strangest sensation. I didn't want to let go. I knew somehow that this moment was crucial. Would I ever see my friend again? But Lisboa just smiled in response, acknowledging the look on my face. I could only guess what it might have been.

"Clara, here you are worrying about an old lady. You've come so far, *minha querida*. I am so proud of you. Now you go with Eduardo. You take the power of Oxala deep within you, and you fight." Lisboa nodded, as if the whole thing were a simple matter. Then she softened, reaching out to touch my hand. "I will be right behind you," she whispered.

"Okay." I felt my throat tighten once again.

"Now, go." Lisboa laughed, and the strange, almost surreal sound of her laughter echoed with the night cry of the howler monkeys, eerie and startlingly loud in the black air. With her usual flourish, Lisboa spun around and went to her own car. I wondered if this would be the last time I would hear her wonderful laughter. I thought of everything Lisboa had done for me: taking me into her home, giving me access to the Odún, trusting me, accepting me into the very recesses of her life. I could never thank her enough. I wished I'd had that one extra moment to do so. But there was no time to waste. Besides, why wouldn't I see Lisboa again? I needed to focus on the task at hand. Saving Chico.

I got into Eduardo's car and turned to face him as he eased the tires out of the mud, and we made our way along the gravel road to the main highway, heading back to Rio. I noticed Eduardo's hands were white on the steering wheel. His actions were quick and erratic.

"He's going to be okay, Eduardo," I said softly.

"If anything happens to Chico because of me..." He couldn't even finish the sentence. "You know, I found him in an alleyway. He'd been cut up pretty bad, but he was a tough little guy. Didn't want any help. I took him to the hospital and made sure he got something for his cuts. Then I told him I had a job for him. If he could be my gopher, run around for me doing errands here and there, I would pay him more money than he probably saw in a month. But he had to stay clean and stay out of the *favela* gangs. He agreed." Eduardo paused, shaking his head. "That was two years ago now."

"That was a good thing you did." I reached out and touched his arm lightly. "He's the bait, you know. They won't kill him. They can't. Velho needs me to be there."

Eduardo looked straight ahead at the road. "I know." His words were clipped.

In that moment, I felt that he was unreachable. I knew he was distancing himself. Closing himself off. Maybe it was his way of dealing with the moment, with the possibility of a future in which we could not be together.

I knew I had to reach out to Eduardo. I had to let him know the extent of my love. That through my dreams and hallucinations I'd seen Ignacio and Zumbi, and I'd witnessed a love unlike anything I could ever have imagined. A love so deep and abiding that it crossed time and eternity and remained strong. I felt it whenever I looked into Eduardo's eyes. And now, I realized how crucial it was for Eduardo to feel *my* love. We would need to be united if we had any hope of defeating Bento Velho.

"Eduardo," I said softly, still touching his arm.

Eduardo concentrated on the bumpy road, winding and curving through the forest. The headlights lit the trees, turning them into living, dark green shapes, crawling and moving beneath the pale light of a dim moon. "I know," he repeated, only this time his words were soft. He glanced over at me. And in his eyes I saw his love.

But I needed to say the words out loud. "I love you."

Eduardo reached out and held my hand briefly, kissing it

lightly before turning back to the steering wheel. He smiled. "I know what it took for you to say that."

"How can you know me so well?"

"Clara, our souls have been united for generations. I think there must be some subliminal memory."

I nodded, smiling, as well. But then I could feel Eduardo closing himself off again. "I'm driving you to the hands of your tormentor." His words were short. "If our love is so strong, shouldn't I be protecting you? Shouldn't we just forget about destiny and curses and everything else and take off? Right now?" We veered off the gravel road, and I could see the lights of the city ahead. Soon we were back on the main highway, having left the safe, dark green refuge of the forest behind.

"Eduardo, you know we can't leave Chico." I winced as he brought his fist down on the steering wheel. I felt him accelerate to a frightening speed. "We don't want to be stopped right now," I warned. I could see Eduardo was fighting a battle within himself. "Eduardo, please, it has to be this way."

"It doesn't have to be anything!"

We reached the turnoff to the Avenida Atlantica. I marvelled at the beauty of the night. The moonlight was magical, the stars shining like jewels in the black velvety sky. "Open the window." Eduardo stared at me in confusion before hitting the automatic button. As the open window allowed the cool, moist sea breeze to enter the car, I stuck my head out and inhaled. I felt the salty spray hit my cheeks and the wind slap against my face. I felt the glorious freedom of my shorn hair, the night air rushing over the top of my head and igniting all my senses. I allowed myself the ultimate freedom. My mind ran wild, my senses absorbed, my tongue tasted the humidity while my hands reached out to touch the sky. "I'm breathing in Yemanja!" I cried to the wind. "And Oxala and all the other Orixas who are converging to bring us energy." And I felt them surrounding me, their soft caressing voices, their energy, their support carried on the wind.

And then we arrived. I heard the soft thud of the ignition being turned off. The swirl of wind and water and energy remained with me, though, even in the sudden silence within the car. Eduardo had closed the windows, and we sat there like that for a moment.

"This is what it's about, Eduardo. They're all with us. They surround us. We're not fighting this alone."

I was shocked to see tears in Eduardo's eyes. He touched my face gently and brought his lips to mine in the sweetest of kisses. "The Odún has been part of my life for so long, Clara. And yet I've never inhaled the *axe* as you just did. I've never witnessed anything like it before." We just looked at each other, communicating with our eyes. "Clara, I don't want to lose you." His voice broke on the last word, and he turned his gaze away.

I reached out and pulled Eduardo toward me. "Now this time you listen to me, Eduardo. I feel so renewed, so strong. But I can't do this alone. I need you there beside me. I know it's going to be different this time. All the signs have indicated that it will be. We're not going to lose each other. As long as we believe that, we'll remain together. And I'm not talking about being together in the celestial realm. I'm talking about here, right now. Living our lives out right here in Rio de Janeiro. Who knows, maybe you'll come back with me to Toronto?" I smiled slightly, and Eduardo just continued to look at me. "The point is that both Ahmara and Ife believed that they were going to die. It's a cycle, like everything is. And I perpetuated it by going back in time to warn them of something they couldn't change." I looked pointedly at Eduardo. "No one has come to warn me." And for the first time I saw a bit of hope in his eyes. "I need you."

Eduardo leaned forward and kissed me fiercely. A deep, desperate kiss during which he pulled me roughly into his embrace, his hands running over my entire body. "I want to take you now," he whispered. "Hard and fast. And remember this moment." My body responded as I returned his kiss, my hands reaching out to touch his face, his arms, his chest. I wanted to touch every part of him. My desire was sharp and overwhelming and desperate. We broke apart just as suddenly, our breathing ragged. I pulled my dress back into place, and we looked at each other in silent and complete understanding.

"Okay," he said simply. With that, he opened the door and I got out on my side of the car. We walked toward each other, and, holding hands, we faced the demons that awaited us.

THE ALLEYWAY STANK OF ROT, the humidity in the dark night air carrying the stench into our hair and clothes. I took a deep breath, squeezing Eduardo's hand. This was definitely the spot. And then we heard it. That horrible, deep, repetitive chant. "*Uma é Satanaz ao inferno, inferno, inferno...*" I shook my head, knowing that I had to block it out once again. But this time it felt more powerful. Louder, the cadences longer, the rhythm more beguiling. I knew I couldn't succumb to it. This was only the first test. Surely, I could at least pass this one. I could hear Eduardo's voice. "Focus, Clara. Focus." And I did. I started whispering, "Oxala, Oxala, *minha rainha,*" and my repetitive words blocked out the sinister voices. I knew Oxala was there. Oxala had never left my side.

We walked forward slowly. I could no longer hear Chico's cries. My stomach tightened, and I felt that familiar sensation of horror rise up in my throat. But I pushed it back down. I had to do this. And, this time, I had Eduardo by my side. We looked at each other. He didn't need to say anything.

We rounded the corner, and there stood Velho. Tall, proud, completely confident in his stance. He knew I was there and he turned to look at me as we stepped into the alleyway. His eyes bored into my skull, as though he was trying to tear the very thoughts from my head. But, for a moment, I refused to return his blatant stare. For a moment, I closed my eyes and whispered one more time to Oxala, feeling the strength and energy of Eduardo's grasp, knowing that I wasn't alone. And then I opened my eyes and met his yellow gaze directly.

It was the first time I'd ever faced Bento Velho directly. This wasn't a vision or a dream. My soul wasn't being transported here while my body remained elsewhere. No. This time I was here. Body and soul. There was no protection. No shield. Nothing to propel me away and save me from an imminent death. And, as I looked into his all-too-familiar eyes, I felt myself being pulled in all directions. My mind took me on a dizzying journey. Once again I entered my previous selves. In a swirl of colour and sounds and raw emotion, I felt the moment of both their deaths once again. The very final moment. Ife lifting her head, tears streaming down her face, realizing that this was the end. Looking up into the eyes of her beheader. Seeing the yellow eyes of Exu staring back just as he raised the axe. And Ahmara, so strong and accepting. Looking directly into the eyes of the man who would fire the final lethal shot. Staring at him wilfully, refusing to back down. Determined to die with dignity. Both women had died gazing at the same yellow, evil stare. The eyes are a window to the soul, and in that yellow gaze nothing existed. No shred of humanity. No glimmer of anything at all. Velho had no soul.

He was smiling. A cold rising of his thin lips. Looking at me in triumph. "I've been waiting for you."

The spinning and the visions ended. I found myself back again, hearing Velho's voice, staring into his deadened eyes. And I felt nothing. Those eyes that had tortured my soul and provided so much fear—now that I gazed into them directly I could see how truly lifeless he was. How could I be afraid of something that was already dead? And so I smiled in return.

"As I've been waiting for you." I walked closer, standing nearly a foot away, my stance equally proud, my face a blank mask. Eduardo let go of my hand and stood just a step behind. Somehow, he must have sensed that I needed to do this. I needed his strength, and his energy and presence gave me courage, but, ultimately, this was my personal battle with Bento Velho. A battle that had lasted for generations. A battle that I was determined to win this time.

I could see Velho's slight start, which he quickly attempted to hide. He was surprised by my reaction. And then he laughed. The sound echoing in the eerie night, piercing and sharp. "So this is how it is to be?" His voice was caustic. Almost teasing. "Ah, I've waited so long. Anticipating this moment. Wanting to savour it." His tongue darted out, his voice becoming a low, sensual drawl. His thick Portuguese accent slowed the words and made them sound like liquid honey coming out of his mouth. "A shame, really." He shrugged his shoulders. "Such beauty, such promise..." He took a few steps forward, his hand reaching out as if to caress my cheek. It was a seduction. Evil's greatest weapon.

But I would not allow myself to be beguiled by his smooth voice and eyes that had miraculously turned to satin. Why would he bother? Why even try to seduce me? What did he need? As if reading my thoughts, he pulled a sharp knife from behind his back. "At least in the other lifetimes you were a foe to be reckoned with. Ife..." he sighed, touching the tip of the knife lightly against his neck, running it along his collarbone. A thin trail of blood followed in the knife's caress. He managed to make the act look sensual. "So much life, so much resistance. Ah, but she couldn't accept her fate. She fought to the end." And with gleaming eyes, he cut open the artery in his neck, smiling and rejoicing in the blood that streamed down his body. Great, thick gobs of red that seemed to spread like larvae, covering his shoulders, his arms, running down his stomach and thighs. "Ah, the delight..."

I continued to stand there. I was determined not to express emotion. Not to be horrified by the spectacle. I felt Eduardo's comforting presence. I could almost hear his whispering voice telling me that it's all a show. Exu could alter reality. Make you see things that weren't even there. Make you believe things you never imagined you could. But if you continued to look closely, if you held your ground and fought back using your own power, you would see the truth.

And so I did. Whispering my incantations to Oxala, standing my ground, not letting my expression betray my chaotic emotions, I started to see. There stood Bento Velho. And he was just a man. Flesh and bone, just like me. His power came from his multiple reincarnations and the energy of Exu, but ultimately he wasn't any different than me. We were both simply human beings unusually connected to the forces of the Odún pantheon, but human all the same. And, once I could see that, once the mystique had disappeared, I could look directly into his eyes and see that they were no longer yellow or even black. They were brown. Brown eyes that could reflect nothing back because he was so filled with evil that nothing else existed within.

I knew that if I believed in myself and my own strength, no amount of trickery could affect me. Because that's exactly what Exu was. Smoke and mirrors. Evil was an illusion. The real force, the true *axe*, lived within Oxala, the great goddess. That kind of energy would always win out in the end.

I didn't say anything. I gathered my strength, continuing the incantations to Oxala, the repetition creating a slow, building momentum. And I watched the show. "Then there was Ahmara. The great *mãe de santo*. Now, she understood the way of the universe." He stopped, waiting for my reaction. Yet still I said nothing. I could tell he was surprised, clearly having expected me to be more affected by his words. He sought my gaze once again. "Ahmara knew it was her end. What joy…" he paused. He threw down the knife, and in his other hand I could see the cold gleam of black metal.

The images swam before me. I tried to focus on seeing Velho as just a man, standing there with his dull eyes and grand theatrics. I forced myself not to see the blood, not to let the eyes of Exu haunt me. But Velho was strong and combined with the energy of Exu. I felt the images start to blur. I couldn't stop myself from seeing Exu's haunting eyes, piercing my soul, laughing at me. "Smoke and mirrors, smoke and mirrors," I repeated. I needed more energy, more *axe*. I watched as he raised the gun and pointed it directly at me. I heard the sound of the catch releasing. I tried desperately to will it away. To realize that none of it existed unless I allowed it to. But the gun was real. There was no denying that. And it had nothing to do with spiritual powers.

"But you, Clara..." His face wavered before my eyes, his expression almost soulful. "You're like a little lamb." His voice was soft. I fought it. I fought with everything I had. And I could feel both Eduardo and Lisboa sending energy my way. "It will be so easy." And then he laughed again. "No challenge at all. A little boring, in fact, *não?*" He twirled the gun around his index finger and let it drop to the ground. "No, I think we should have a little fun first. Let's not end things so quickly. I've been looking forward to this for far too long."

Still I said nothing. I took a deep breath. I turned around and glanced at Eduardo. I looked into his eyes for just a moment, and I saw the strength of his love. And then I realized the truth. It wasn't about the power of Oxala. Or even the strength of the Odún Pantheon. This was about love. The eternal love between Eduardo and me. And how the strength of that love was enough to fight any sort of evil. It was our love that created the connection. That made everything possible. And then I felt it. At last. The surge of energy. The strength. The power. The belief in myself and the realization that I could do this. That I *would* do it. It was Eduardo's love that made me realize the infinity of possibility. The freedom of life itself. And the strength in allowing oneself to feel that freedom. And it was Lisboa, standing nearby, giving me her strength. It was the strong combination of our female energy—Lisboa, myself, and Oxala—combined with the forces of powerful love. Love for Eduardo, love for Lisboa, love for

Oxala. I was capable of so much more than I ever thought possible. Giving in to love, giving in to the energy source—it wasn't weakness. It took strength to love. The fear was swallowed. It evaporated into the night. I felt the positive energy of Eduardo and Lisboa. I felt Oxala rise within me. I felt the *axe* of all the goddesses and the living elements of the universe—the trees, the ocean, the sky, the stars—converse within me. And then I raised my arms.

"This time it is you who will fall." I felt powerful. I felt sure of myself. I knew we would defeat history. We would alter our fate. I felt almost a quiet reassurance in my knowledge. As if this had been our destiny all along. I watched as the *axe* swirled around me, the trees swaying, the leaves flying, the garbage from the street rising into the air and cloaking Velho's henchmen, blinding them. I stared into the eyes of evil, seeing only emptiness once again. His body had become a thin shadow. His antics were over. His game had ended. And his followers knew it. They cried and flew in all directions as the cement ground rose to engulf them. In the face of truth, evil lost its power.

"Fools! Cowards! I curse you all! If you leave me now, you will face a fate far worse than death." Velho's words disappeared into the chaos, the air itself sucking his power away. I could feel his shock. His indignation. His anger. But the show was over. He fought back. We battled each other with our eyes, our direct stares an active war. But the power of the universe was too strong. And he knew it.

And then a sharp, piercing siren cut through the chaos. As Velho's henchmen fled and the police car approached, Velho finally broke the stare. I felt the release. The moment our eyes were no longer locked together in our dance of death, I felt all the energy drain out of my body.

"This is not over. This will never be over." He spat the words just as he turned around and fled. And, despite my current feeling of power, I knew he spoke the truth.

I felt Eduardo's arms around me, holding me up. The wind disappeared, and the night became silent once again. I glanced over and saw Lisboa rushing toward Chico, who still lay prone on the ground. In all the chaos, we hadn't been able to reach him yet. I felt myself collapse to the jagged cement. Just as before, my body felt weakened and immobile. I lay there, staring into Eduardo's eyes.

"We did it, Clara," he whispered, stroking my forehead. Then he lifted me and carried me to the car. As he placed me in the back seat, I whispered, "Chico?"

"He's going to be okay. Lisboa is taking him to the hospital. And I'm taking you home."

I nodded, too weary to argue. As long as I knew Chico would be okay, I was satisfied. It was hard to believe what had just happened. I had warred with evil and come out the victor. Perhaps we had changed our destiny this time, but I knew it was a battle that would never end. And, even if we managed to survive the showdown, we'd done nothing to save the Odún.

14

I WOKE THE NEXT MORNING to the sound of birds. I stretched out on the bed, my eyes still closed, enjoying for a moment that delightful sensation of waking from a dreamless and restful sleep. The satin sheets felt cool beneath my skin, and a light breeze blew from the open bedroom window carrying with it a slight hint of bougainvillea.

I reached over to find Eduardo already gone. My feeling of bliss evaporated as all the events of the preceding night crashed through my mind. The initiation, the images, the travels through time, the meeting with my nemesis ... the final showdown. I opened my eyes and sat up straight in bed. It was over. The battle I'd so dreaded had already occurred. Had the terror ended? I'd had no dreams, no transporting visions. Nothing but deep and restful sleep devoid of anything remotely sinister. Was it over? Could it have been that easy? I didn't think so. I needed Eduardo. We had so much to talk about. I needed to feel the strength of his arms around me. I needed to make love to him.

I tossed the sheets aside and got out of bed. I felt a heaviness in my chest, a sensation of uncertainty. Suddenly, nothing seemed to make sense. I wandered into the kitchen, deciding that a cup of strong coffee would set things right and allow me to think more clearly, to figure out what, exactly, had happened last night and if it had changed anything. But in my still half-asleep state, I was startled to find both Lisboa and Eduardo happily sitting at the kitchen table, newspapers spread before them and the television blaring.

"*Boa manhã, linda,*" Eduardo said, a warm smile on his face. He stood up, kissing me on the lips.

"Good morning to you, too."

Eduardo seemed to be in good spirits. Taking my hand, he led me to the kitchen table, where he showed me the newspaper headline. "Mayor turned Macumba Lord," Eduardo translated for me.

I nodded, too shocked to speak. I grabbed the paper and stared in bewilderment. There he was. An enormous photo covering the entire top half of the front-page news. Bento Velho, his mask gone, his expression cold as he held a bloody knife above the prone body of twelve-year-old Chico. The terror on the boy's face was palpable. There was no denying it. There could be no justifying it or hiding it. It was all there. In black and white. And, as I looked around, I realized that the truth was splashed everywhere. Nearly every Brazilian newspaper lay across the kitchen table, and every headline had more or less the same message.

The Politician's Mask Comes Off
The Real Face of Rio's Mayor
Mayor Bento Velho—Macumba Lord?

And every paper featured similar photographs of Velho's face. His maddened eyes, his macabre smile, his evilness. It was out there for everyone to see. His mask had truly come off.

Unable to suppress a small tremor of joy, I looked up at the television. And there he was again. Velho's cold smile and deadened eyes, splashed across the morning news. Brazil had gone mad. This was a scandal of the highest sort. The mayor of Brazil's most famous city, the man who would take Rio de Janeiro to the next level by creating greater economic security and a stronger middle class, the respectable politician had suddenly been unmasked. People were shocked. Appalled. Excited. Velho's real identity as the Macumba Lord of Brazil, and specifically of Rio de Janeiro's largest black magic cult, was simply too shocking. Brazilians loved it—the intrigue, the deception, the malice, and the magic. They were fascinated. The entire country was glued to their television sets that morning.

I sat on a kitchen stool, continuing to listen to the newscaster, watching the scenes flicker before my eyes. The streets of Rio had become a wild arena, people dancing and shouting and clamouring for a new social order. The news had struck something deep within the heart of Brazilian society. A society on the cusp of economic change yet steeped within its aura of sex and spirituality, death and dynamic faith, magic and the macabre. A Catholic society with more gods than saints and more healing witch doctors than physicians. A society enveloped in its own history of slavery and dictatorship yet struggling to embrace democracy. Suddenly all the unspoken things, the ritualistic beliefs and spiritual blessings, the crucifixes placed at the crossroads to fight Exu, and the drums to bring out the power of Oxala ... this deep undercurrent of Brazilian society had been brought to the forefront. Literally splashed across the front-page news. It wasn't supposed to happen. These were secrets, meant to be kept hidden. And the fact that the underworld had suddenly become the real world was both terrifying and dreadfully exciting.

"I ... I don't understand." I finally found my voice, turning to look at both Eduardo and Lisboa. "How did this happen?"

Lisboa smiled, holding up her Instamatic camera. "So simple, *não?*" she quipped, handing me a handful of pictures. And there they all were. Picture after picture of Bento Velho. Some were closer. Some were farther away. In some images you could clearly see Velho's cold smile and dark eyes. In others, Chico's face was more clearly visible, as were the masks of Velho's henchmen. But there were so many pictures of everything that had played out in that alleyway the night before that there could be no denying it.

"How did you do this?" I could only stare at Lisboa, the feeling of underlying excitement starting to spread. "How did you manage to get these pictures, Lisboa?"

Lisboa gave me her usual radiant smile. "I am quick with my feet, hmm?" She winked at Eduardo. I shook my head, a smile starting to spread across my face.

"The gas pedal," Eduardo explained.

"While the two of you appeared to be stuck in the mud..." Lisboa said, giving Eduardo a look, "I was already on the highway. When I got to that nasty alleyway, I was so quiet that nobody knew I was there."

She smiled triumphantly and I could only laugh. I jumped off the stool and rushed over to hug her. "You did it, Lisboa! You're the one who managed to save the Odún."

Lisboa shook her head, hugging me and muttering at the same time. "*Não, não, não, querida.* I merely had the proper tools. I got there before either of you. And I hid behind the garbage." Lisboa wrinkled her nose in distaste. "Not so agreeable. But it had to be done." She sighed dramatically. "And there he was. *Fácil*. Performing his little act. He took off his mask. No doubt preparing for your arrival. His arrogance was his downfall. Poor, poor Chico..." Lisboa looked down for a moment.

"Chico?" I felt my insides shake.

Lisboa glanced up quickly, realizing my sudden panic. "Oh, no. Chico is fine. He is at the hospital. He will be all right. Just superficial cuts. Velho was only using him to get to you."

"I knew that. But still ... he has no soul. He might have killed him anyway."

"Well," Lisboa shook her head, "he didn't have time, did he? He was too busy with your showdown and then with the sirens.... Well, the rest is history, as they say." She smiled.

"So you took all those pictures. But how did they get in the paper?"

"Ahh, Lisboa has friends in high places. As does Eduardo."

I turned to Eduardo, wanting to know the entire story. "And all this happened while I was sleeping?"

Eduardo nodded, touching my cheek gently. "After you went to sleep, I called Lisboa. She met me here after the hospital and showed me all the photos. I couldn't believe it at first. It was the evidence that I had been trying to get for months. But he was always too careful. He was careless that night, Clara. He knew you would arrive. And he was so eager to savour your death that he didn't take his usual precautions. That's how we finally got him."

I could feel the energy emanating from Eduardo as he told the story. "But how did you get it all over the news?"

"A simple phone call. A journalist friend of mine. We've known each other for years. I told him to come over and see something amazing. And he did. And he ran with it. Then we faxed the pictures to every news office we could think of in Brazil. And then Lisboa went to the police station. The police had no choice. They were forced to investigate. They knew it would be all over the news. They went directly to Velho's home and arrested him in bed."

I shook my head, still absorbing all of this information. "So the police actually have Velho in custody?"

"Yes. Along with his financial advisor. It's all coming out now, of course. The fraud, the embezzlement. There's enough there to keep him locked up for a long time. He is finished. He can't hide or ever enter politics again in Brazil. All of his supporters are running away as fast as they can."

"So what does this all mean?" I couldn't sit down. I was too excited. I held on to Eduardo's hand. "Does this mean the Macumba has lost its power?"

Lisboa nodded. "Without their great lord, they'll definitely be struggling. It gives us time, Clara. Lots of time. The Macumba have been exposed. They've lost their clout. The believers will come flocking back to the Odún. The fear will be gone." I could see the joy on Lisboa's face.

"So we did it?" I asked, incredulous. "We really did save the Odún?"

Both Lisboa and Eduardo nodded. "They'll regroup under another leader, I'm sure. But at least we know Velho has no chance now of being our next president, regardless of what happens with our current President Collor de Mello. Without Velho, it will take time for his followers to regroup. And meanwhile, we'll work to open all the closed *terreiros* and make the power of Odún so strong that the Macumba will never be able to take over again." Lisboa's voice was triumphant and powerful. "I might have taken the pictures, but, Clara, you made it all happen." Lisboa looked directly at me, her expression one of gratitude. "You are powerful, Clara. Never forget that."

Standing there, holding Eduardo's hand and feeling his love, and Lisboa's positive energy, I had never felt more at peace. "So it's over then. It's really over," I whispered. I thought of everything I'd been through. Starting with the first time I'd travelled to Brazil and heard the repetitive and beguiling cadence of the drums. The first time I was pulled into the Odún. I thought of those endless hours and sleepless nights studying the rituals and reading the textbooks. And then the beginning of the nightmares. The belief that I'd been possessed. The feeling of utter isolation. Not even being able to communicate with my mother because I didn't want her to witness my slow decline into insanity. This quest for the Odún had taken over my life so completely that it had nearly taken over my soul.

I needed to talk to my parents. My father had been such a demanding presence in my life. My desire to impress a man who could never be impressed had caused me so much angst. But for the first time, I could see my father for who he was—an imperfect human being. And it released me from my insecurity. It also allowed me to be more accepting. I missed them. I would call them today and let them know that I was okay. And I needed to call my advisor.

I was returning to myself. Small pieces of me were coming back, bit by bit. The obsession, the visions, the hallucinations ... they were gone. They'd drifted away in the breeze from the open bedroom window that morning. A bougainvillea-scented breeze that was impossible since Eduardo lived in an air-conditioned condo. We were on the thirtieth floor. Sterile, modern. A view of the glistening sea extended to the horizon, but it was completely urban. There were no birds and no bougainvillea. The birds, the breeze, the aroma of the bougainvillea, had been a gift from Oxala. A final parting gift. A way of saying goodbye. At least for now. And I knew in that moment that it really was over. I could live again. Build up my life. Contact my parents and friends and re-establish relationships that I'd let slip by. I needed to be part of the world again and stop isolating myself. Maybe have a normal life. Looking at Eduardo, I smiled softly. Maybe have a chance at a normal love. Then again, who was I fooling? I'd spent my life so far trying to escape normal. Maybe this crazy and intoxicating life was exactly for me. And I knew Oxala would always be there too.

Both Lisboa and Eduardo sensed my change of mood. "I guess in the end it was reality that defeated evil, not magic."

"We may be surrounded by magic, but people see the reality that they want to see," Eduardo said, his gaze intense.

Lisboa coughed. "Well ... I think it is time for Lisboa to depart." With her usual flourish, she drank the last of her tea, set her cup down with a rattle, and lifted herself off the stool. "It's been a pleasure," she said dramatically, kissing us both on the cheek. "And Eduardo, I never knew you had it in you..." she teased.

Eduardo just shook his head. I was starting to understand that the relationship between Eduardo and Lisboa couldn't be placed in a neat, tidy box. The tension I'd felt earlier was only part of their natural and friendly sparring. Obviously they'd been friends and rivals for years, and would continue to be so.

"And Clara..." She just shook her head. "You are like a

daughter to me," she whispered, her eyes shining. I smiled, but before I could say anything, Lisboa picked up her skirts and swirled around with a flourish. "I will take myself out. *Adeus*!"

With Lisboa's departure, the condo seemed strangely silent. I looked at Eduardo almost shyly. Now that the dramatics were over, what was left? Could we live a life together? What would happen? I needed to finish my dissertation. Although, after everything I'd witnessed, I felt like I had enough material to complete ten dissertations. Maybe I would write a book of fiction instead. But what about Eduardo? I still didn't know how he fit in. My life was in Canada, after all. And his was in Brazil.

"I know what you're thinking." Eduardo's musical voice took me out of my thoughts.

"You're so sure, huh? So what am I thinking?"

"You're wondering what happens next."

I laughed. "Yeah, I guess you do know me. So then tell me. What does happen next?"

"How about this?" Before I could respond, he pulled me close. I inhaled his scent, the lemon aftershave, the strawberries and coffee on his breath. I sank into his embrace, feeling his strong arms around me. I buried my face in his chest, and I didn't want to think about what would happen next. I just wanted to feel. I needed to feel. I felt that familiar desire. I pulled him closer, and I could feel his erection. I smiled, reaching up and kissing him. He responded, running his hands gently over my shorn head, sucking lightly on my lower lip. "Clara, Clara ..." he murmured, his breathing shallow.

I thought of our desperate kiss the night before, when we didn't know if it would be our last. I felt such need, such yearning and desire for this man. I seemed to want him all the time. His hands were exploring my body, running along my breasts, my hips, and firmly cupping my ass while he pressed himself against me. I felt my breath quicken. "I want to make love to you," I whispered into his ear.

He smiled. "Clara, you have no idea." And, with that, he picked me up and carried me over to the couch, laying me down gently. I watched as he swiftly took off his top, revealing his muscular chest, and then pulled off his pants and briefs. I admired his naked body and wanted to feel his cock. I smiled as my eyes drifted back up again to meet his. He was giving me a look of pure heated desire. "Like what you see?"

I nodded. "Oh yes."

He came over and kissed the top of my head, my cheeks, my nose, my throat. I smiled, thinking that this was so different from before, when it had all been so quick and fierce. This time he was going slow, taking his time, savouring the moment. Then he lifted my nightgown above my head, releasing my breasts. He moaned as he climbed on top of me, careful not to rest his body weight. His eyes bore into mine before he bent his head and took one nipple into his mouth, caressing the other breast at the same time. I reached down and touched his penis, moving my hand up and down his shaft. "Yes, Clara, that feels so good," he murmured. He continued to kiss me, moving his kisses down my stomach toward my inner thighs and then to my vagina, where his tongue swirled around my clit. I forced myself to keep still and not push my hips up, even though I was becoming desperate with wanting. I heard my own moans as he continued to lick me, my climax starting to build.

"Come into me," I begged.

In the next moment, I felt him enter me, and my body convulsed around him. My orgasm was quick and fierce and intense. He paused inside me while my legs wrapped around his waist, my hands circling his biceps as I leaned my head back and lost myself in the exquisite contractions. When I opened my eyes, I saw him looking at me deeply. I let him move inside me, slowly at first, sensual and languid. We moved in perfect unison, our gazes locked as our bodies merged. He increased his rhythm, and I felt myself getting excited again, the deep sensation of his increasing rhythm pushing against my G-spot.

I urged him in deeper, wanting to feel him pulsing against me in just the right place. He pulled me up, and I found myself sitting astride him on the couch. I leaned my arms back for leverage and pushed deeper onto him. With each thrust, I felt my climax building again, our gazes locked, our breathing ragged, and our bodies pounding together fiercely. I wanted all of him. I cried out just as he did, and we fell into each other, my body collapsing on the couch while he gently leaned down beside me, holding me close.

The drums and the magic would always be a part of me. And so would Eduardo. Somehow, we would figure things out. I could always finish my dissertation and return to Brazil to seek a professorship or do post-doctoral research at the Universidade. There were so many options. And besides, these were all minor details. After battling the powers of the universe together, surely we could figure out how to battle reality. Because, at least for a little while, that was the world I wished to live in. Not the world of smoke and mirrors and yellow eyes gleaming in the darkness.

I knew my war with evil would never truly be over. But at least we had won one battle. I had gone on such an incredible journey, and I was no longer the same person. I had opened myself up to love and let myself feel the magic and mystery of life. And it was beautiful. All the fear I'd felt for so long. It was still there, lingering in the dark recesses of my mind. But I realized that it was okay to feel fear. Fear can give strength as much as it can take it away. As long as I didn't let the fear consume me. I still didn't believe in fairy-tale romances, but I did believe in what I felt, and I trusted myself enough now to not deny my own emotions. I smiled, lightly kissing Eduardo's cheek and nuzzling my face into the warmth of his neck. The Odún would survive. And so would Eduardo and I. Lying there in Eduardo's arms, embraced within his love, the scent of freshly brewed coffee still in the air, I realized I was just where I wanted to be.

Acknowledgements

The writing of *Clara Awake* has taken me on a long journey that would have never happened without my mom, Maria Vandenbeld, and sister, Anita Vandenbeld, who have always given me so much support and have read every copy of everything I've ever written! And although I started writing this book before my daughter Maya Vandenbeld Giles was born, without her, my life simply wouldn't be what it is. She taught me so much about what it means to love. I also want to thank my dad, Herman Vandenbeld, who has always inspired and supported me. And Luzia Veiga, my childhood neighbour and close family friend from Brazil, who read one of the first versions of this book and who inspired me to travel to Brazil.

The book is very much about love, and also about the incredible strength and energy in female friendships. I want to thank my sister-in-spirit, Romy Tapia Liebowitz, who was one of the first to read this book and whose friendship over more than twenty years means the world to me. I also want to thank my feminist sisters, Linn Baran, Patty Douglas and Renée Knapp for always being there for me.

In particular, I would like to acknowledge Renée Knapp and her work as Publicist and Marketing Manager for Inanna Publications. Thank you to Val Fullard for the beautiful and sensual cover she designed for this book. And a special thank you to

Luciana Ricciutelli, Editor-in-Chief at Inanna Publications for being such a wonderful and compassionate editor, and making all of these incredible and powerful feminist books come to life!

Finally, I would like to share a few of the sources of inspiration for this book. Although it is fiction, it is creatively based upon actual historical events. For more information about Palmares, please read "Palmares: An African State in Brazil" by R. K. Kent published in *The Journal of African History* volume 6, no. 2. The Odún is a fictional interpretation of the Afro-Brazilian religion of Candomblé. For more information about Candomblé, please read *Black Atlantic Religion: Tradition, Transnationalism, and Matriarchy in the Afro-Brazilian Candomblé* by J. Lorand Matory. One of my greatest sources of inspiration for both my anthropological research and the writing of this novel is anthropologist Wade Davis, author of *The Serpent and the Rainbow*, a book about ethnobotany, zombi poison, and Voodoo in Haiti.

Photo: Maya Vandenbeld Giles

Melinda Vandenbeld Giles is a lecturer in Social Anthropology and Women's, Gender and Sexuality Studies and a PhD candidate in Social Anthropology at the University of Toronto. She is the editor of *Mothering in the Age of Neoliberalism* published by Demeter Press in 2014 and co-editor for the forthcoming Routledge *Companion to Motherhood*. *Clara Awake* is her debut novel, based on her graduate research on African-derived religions in Brazil.